PLANTED BONDS

THE HIGH COUNCIL WITCH CHRONICLES

4

JULIE CATHERINE

PLANTED BONDS

THE HIGH COUNCIL WITCH CHRONICLES
BOOK 4

JULIE MEE

Edited by
ALLANA STUART

For Bub and little Bub

ONE
THERE'S NOTHING TO TELL

FERRIS PUT down three letters from her Scrabble rack. We watched her line up the word, her short, pink nails pushing the squares into place. "Part." She announced.

"Alright." I tallied. "Six, plus the double word is twelve."

"And there are no tiles left?" She checked the little box again, although this was clear. The rest of us already had less than seven tiles on our racks.

"We're down to the end," I agreed.

"Took long enough," she squirmed.

Aunt Abeline and Lady Blue Moon both hunched over their letters. Although the game was a blowout for me and Ferris, between the older women the finish would be tight.

"Bonnie, you're up," my aunt prompted.

Ferris and I exchanged a small smile. It was downright weird to hear a lady from the High Council coven called by her non-coven name like a lowly student, but my aunt wasn't part of the witches world. She wasn't a member of the coven and it was illegal to discuss any craft or witchy business with a person from outside our clan. Even our nicknames were off limits. So, at the lake house, Lady Blue Moon was Bonnie Maine. Frankly, it suited her. She looked like a Bonnie.

"What's the score again?" Lady Blue Moon frowned.

"No stalling," Ferris complained.

Before I could answer as official record keeper, my aunt rattled off the tally by heart.

"Mae's at 169, I have 287, you're 253 and Ferris..." She let the sentence trail off. We all looked at Ferris. She sighed and leaned on her hand.

"You can say it."

"Ferris has 89," my aunt told the table.

"Plus the twelve," Ferris added.

I rechecked the numbers. "No, that's, uh, that's with the plus twelve."

"Thanks for inviting me for games night, ladies," Ferris laughed, pushing away from the table. I'd expected her first game of Scrabble at the lake house to be a slaughter, everyone lost against my aunt – first time, thousandth time, it didn't really matter. Aunt Abeline always won, and I had warned her. But, the senior student said she didn't care. It'd be fun to just get out of the castle, she told me. Of course that was before her rock-bottom tally. Luckily, she was a pretty good sport.

We both knew the word-battle wasn't really about us. Everyone at the table knew we would never win. The real contest was between Lady Blue Moon and my aunt.

I grinned at the two women. "Your move." I prompted again.

"Don't rush me." Lady Blue Moon looked down at her letters then back at the board. Her forehead was scrunched into three wavy lines. I felt pretty certain a word had formed in her mind. Now she was doing the arithmetic. If she could use all the letters on her rack and end the game on this go-around she'd get an extra bonus to add to her score. Any left-over letters in our racks would add to her tally, while they also subtracted from her competitor's results. Aunt Abeline's rack still had three letters. If they were high enough value in points, Lady Blue Moon might actually overtake the winning score... the pressure was on.

Lady Blue Moon let out a dramatic sigh. "Alright..." It was now or never. "Particle." She added the four remaining letters to the board. "That's it. That's all my letters." She looked up, watching her competitors for any flicker of acknowledgment.

Ferris, Aunt Abeline and I all sat back.

The game was over.

We turned out the tiles on our racks onto the table below. Time to tally the final score. I went first.

"I had two letter Is." I told the group. "Minus two for me, plus two for Bonnie."

Ferris frowned. "Well, I got a z, an e, and an a."

"Twelve points!" We whistled. "What an addition," I giggled. "Bonnie gets twelve more."

"Wait, so I minus?" Ferris frowned.

"Uh huh." I nodded. "Bonnie, that puts you up to 279."

"This game is the worst," Ferris moaned.

We mostly ignored her, the real drama still to come.

"Aunt Abeline, you're up." I motioned.

We all turned. The scores were unbelievably close. An eight point difference between champion and challenger.

Eight little points.

If Aunt Abeline's three leftover tiles were worth more than four points combined, Lady Blue Moon would win. The first Scrabble victory against Aunt Abeline in the history of forever. Something I had never seen before. No one had ever beaten my aunt.

Aunt Abeline slowly tilted the rack and revealed her tiles. One by one, they fell face up on the table.

T - E - A.

"Oh!" I slapped the table.

"So close," Ferris nodded.

"Come on!" Lady Blue Moon complained. "Three points!"

"Minus three points for Aunt Abeline and add three more for Bonnie. We have a winner. Bonnie 282 points... Aunt Abeline... 284!"

Lady Blue Moon sat back as Aunt Abeline mimed celebratory cheering. She pumped her clasped hands over her left and right shoulders, shaking them in self-congratulations.

"This close," Lady Blue Moon squeezed her fingers together.

Playfully, my aunt shook everyone's hands. "Good game, ladies. Good game."

"Can you guess why I don't play board games?" Ferris slid her chair back from the table.

"Comes with the territory. Somehow my vocabulary is both impressively large and oddly small." I agreed.

Aunt Abeline hopped up to clear the table, pleased as punch. She put our empty glasses in the sink. "Mae, do you remember the spelling contest?" She chuckled.

"Please don't tell that story."

"Have you ever beaten your aunt?" Ferris asked.

I shook my head. "No one has."

"This close," Lady Blue Moon mimed again.

"Close, but no cigar. Mae, tell them the story," Aunt Abeline encouraged. "It was so cute. You did so well."

"Until I didn't," I corrected. "They don't want to hear about that."

"Sure we do," Ferris grinned, sensing schadenfreude teeth in the tale.

"What's she talking about?" Lady Blue Moon asked, finally ready move on from defeat.

I shook my head, but Aunt Abeline was on a roll.

"Well, we've been playing word-type board games since Mae was a little girl," she told the other women.

"So, when the Children's National Spelling Bee came to town, Mae did really well. In the warm-up heats, she was exceptional. She beat the pants off the other local kids in the town."

"I was nine," I added for context.

"And they invited her to the national competition," Aunt Abeline kept on.

"But, I didn't win, end of the tale."

Aunt Abeline ignored me. "In each round, the words get progressively harder, you know, longer, more challenging. So, the regional level was up to seven letters, but the national level was eight letters and more. It was gonna be on television, covered by sports casters and everything..." she let the story flow. "For a nine-year-old, that's a pretty big show. So, Mae told everyone we knew. She organized a huge watch party. Even created posters declaring herself the winner that we hung on the walls... I tried to tell her that was a bit presumptuous, but little Mae was sure. And then we went off to the contest."

"Oh no..." Ferris could see what was coming.

"Uh huh," I frowned.

"Well," Aunt Abeline leaned forward. "Scrabble words are maximum seven letters long, eight if you're building on something else on the board." The others nodded. "So it turned out, that seven-letter words was as high as Mae's vocabulary performed. The second they moved on to the eighth letter, it was over."

"I was toast. Kicked out of the competition on my

very first word." I frowned. "Ricochet. I still remember."

"That's right," Aunt Abeline grinned, her own memories of the event all rose-colored.

"The kids teased me mercilessly," I shook my head. "I was so sure I would win."

"That's a tough word," Lady Blue Moon agreed.

"I crashed and burned."

"Overall though, you actually did very well. It's just that those posters... I think I still have the trophy."

"No you don't." I rolled my eyes.

"Yeah, I do. It's right up here," Aunt Abeline opened the cupboard above the fridge that no one ever used. She dug around. There, at the back of the shelf, was a cheap, gold, plastic bumblebee sitting on a small stand. She dusted it off. "Look at that. I've kept it all these years. You know I'm proud of everything you've accomplished." She patted my shoulder, then read it out loud. "It says... 'Participant, Children's National Spelling Bee Competition'."

"They gave out to trophies to participants? Flashy contest," Ferris grinned.

"Wow," I took the sad little trophy in my hands. "So glad we could all relive that out loud." I passed it along to the others.

Ferris looked at the small plaque closely. "Uh... they spelled your name incorrectly."

"They did not," I grabbed it back.

"Just kidding. It doesn't have your name at all. Just 'participant'."

"I'm not sure if that's better or worse," I groused.

"So what did you do the next day at school?" Lady Blue Moon asked.

"I transferred."

"You did not!"

"We transferred for my work, not for your spelling," Aunt Abeline corrected. "But, yes, for a couple days, she was an awkward little girl."

"That's what I get for telling everyone my business," I shrugged.

"At least your vocabulary's improved," Aunt Abeline smiled.

"You keep telling yourself that," I complained, looking down at my score card. Third place wasn't exactly killing it. The story over, Aunt Abeline tucked the trophy back on its shelf. We shifted slightly in our chairs, a natural stopping point for the night. It was getting late. We should head back to our dorms. Aunt Abeline sensed the changing mood.

"Well, thank you girls for coming by. It's nice to know Mae is well taken care of."

"We do what we can," Lady Blue Moon grinned.

"Listen," Aunt Abeline awkwardly cleared her throat. "Before you head out, I did want to ask," she hedged. "I know you can't say much about what you're *doing*..." she hinted. None of us dared break the rule. "But, I was just wondering... are there any boys at your school?" She tried to keep the tone light and innocuous, but failed miserably.

Ferris, Blue Moon and I burst out laughing.

"Abeline, that is not where I thought you were going," Ferris giggled.

"I just mean... if there *were* any boys at your studies, you'd be welcome to bring them over. Or, at least one... Mae, if you had one special *fellow*, on your mind. In your life. You know... It doesn't always have to be just ladies night." She let the offer hang in the air.

I frowned. "I like ladies nights."

"Oh, don't get me wrong. I like them too," she nodded, graciously. "I love them. Of course. Thank you all for coming, but, I just thought..." she let the baited hook sway in the air. When I didn't bite, she finished the thought. "*If* or *when* there was someone else to invite, I wanted you to know that *that* invitee would be welcomed as well."

Ferris and Lady Blue Moon grinned but kept their eyes on the ground. This was my awkward conversation to have.

"There's no one missing an invite," I shook her off, dropping our dishes into the dishwasher. The others silently gathered their things.

"But you would tell me if there was?"

"You'd be the first on my list," I joked, self-consciously sliding the gold moon charm across the nape of my neck. I hoped she didn't notice how awkward I felt.

"Alright." She let the conversation drop. She had kept so many secrets from me as I grew up, I suppose she felt I was entitled to a few myself. "Fair enough. Good night gals," she waved us off. "Drive safe."

"Bye," Lady Blue Moon waved.

"Nice meeting you." Ferris added.

"Yes, Ferris. We'll play again soon."

We trailed out of the house, through the screened-in porch and out onto the gravel drive.

"Bye," we called again, until we were out of earshot. The door swung closed behind us. In contented silence, we loaded into Lady Blue Moon's car. The station wagon was roomy. I took the front seat, Ferris slouched in the row behind. My aunt waved from the kitchen window. As we pulled out, I watched as the curtain dropped. A build-up of silence flooded the car, as neither woman opted to speak. I tucked my brown hair behind my ear.

"What?" I finally asked.

"Why didn't you tell her about Beck?" Ferris asked.

Lady Blue Moon drove us out.

I frowned. "There's nothing to tell."

The girls exchanged a glance in the rear view mirror. While Lady Blue Moon was now an instructor and no longer a student like myself and Ferris, the difference in our ages didn't really show. Both were equally playing the parts of nosey, pesky gossips. Their smirks said it all. When the silence got too loud, I burst forth once more.

"What?!" I protested. "I can't tell her about my *parabond*."

"No, but your *boyfriend*..."

"Beck's not my boyfriend," I cut Blue Moon off.

"We're friends," I shrugged. They looked doubtful. "Just buddies."

"It's been a long time since I've had a buddy like that," Lady Blue Moon sighed.

I blushed, but maintained composure. "We like hanging out. That's all."

"I think it's a bit more than hanging out," Ferris said. She raised an eyebrow.

"At least I hope it is," Lady Blue Moon agreed. "I'm living vicariously through you, Mae…" she added. Taking note of our expressions, she shrugged. "What? In my room, it's just me and Fluffernickel."

We both turned to her.

"Who is that?" Ferris asked.

"My pet rat." She shrugged.

"Owning a pet rat might have something to do with why you don't have any boyfriends," I suggested.

"Don't change the subject," Lady Blue Moon said.

Ferris nodded from the back. They both waited expectantly.

"I hate to disappoint you, but there's nothing more to add." I shrugged. I should have left it at that. It was a solid, final contention. But I just couldn't control my mouth. "We're friends. Good friends. Nice friends."

The women exchanged a small grin.

"He *just* got out of his relationship with Josie." I shrugged, then frowned at myself for spitting out more. I couldn't stop. "We're friends. And that's it. That's all. Nothing more." If they stayed quiet long enough, I might very well hang myself on my own protestations.

"That's it," Lady Blue Moon nodded.

"That's all," Ferris giggled.

"Nothing more!" They said together.

I glared out the window. "You know, it's bad enough that I've turned into some sort of freak-show celebrity at the coven. I have no intention of letting people talk about my dating life as well. Especially when that life is non-existent. So chill." I refused to make eye contact. The women exchanged a glance.

"Sorry, Mae." Lady Blue Moon appeased me.

"We're sorry," Ferris agreed. They could tell they'd overstepped their bounds. "We get it. No worries. Just a couple of friends, casually hanging out."

Wisely, we all let the subject drop.

I watched the town of Plumpkin go by. Blink and you'd miss it.

I loved the kitschy quality of the individual stores, one-of-a-kind in every way. So quaint and darling. Not that I'd go there for shopping or purchases, the content on their shelves was basically touristy crap. But the feel of the place was enchanting. There was something precious about the small town's little main street. I'd grown to really love it here. There was a feeling of home and precious comfort that I'd missed growing up.

It wasn't just after the spelling bee fiasco that Aunt Abeline and I had relocated. As I kid, we'd moved around a lot. Nowadays, I was happy to stay put.

"Look," Ferris muttered sitting up taller on her bench. "Over there... Damocles coven."

Two blonde women with tightly spun curly hair

and striking red clothing caught our eyes. Lady Blue Moon slowed as we drove by, the pair oblivious to our passing, walked together on the street in the town.

"There's another one," I half-pointed. On the other side of the road, a third blonde, red-clothed guy caught our eye.

"I thought they'd be gone by now," Lady Blue Moon muttered.

"They were supposed to be. That's what the battle was for," Ferris muttered. And yet, here they all were. Where there were three, there were bound to be more.

For the rest of the drive to the castle, nobody spoke. Each of us were lost in our own thoughts.

It didn't seem right. When the rival coven had first arrived in town, Cornelius Child and the other High Council fellows and ladies had challenged their coven to the Battle of Four.

A classic witch battle. Winners take all.

It was the only kind of competition feuding witch tribes could compete in without burning the land, the surroundings, and themselves to the ground. Witches drew their special powers, like harnessing and lie-guards, from unseen energy fields. Unbeknownst to the naked eye, the wellspring of power lay dormant in the atmosphere, accessed here and there, always replenish-able and renewable if enough space and time passed between uses. But, if too many witches tried to use the source at once, trouble arose. With repeated expend-ing, the energy sources grew thin and worn. Until the air itself became combustible. When a location reached that point, even a single spell would cause the universe to spark.

The elders called it extirpation.

Any harnessed plant or animal or item or illusion would burst into flames, surging and igniting the air. And a spell-caster also risked severe burns. While the underlying magic that caused the random flames remained undetectable to society, the forest fires were very real. So large groups of witches had to hold their powers in check, or suffer the consequences, a result that didn't benefit anyone.

Hence, the witch battles.

At the arrival of the Damocles tribe, a Battle of Four was announced. Ferris and I had both been dragged into the competition. That's where we met and grew to be friends. We were two of the four battalion members chosen to fight for the coven. And, as luck would have it, I recovered the winning orb. We beat the Damocles tribe at their own game. The rules said they should have departed... so why were they still hanging around?

As Lady Blue Moon pulled the car into the High Council parking lot, I spotted my other classmates bumping a volleyball in the air. Beck, Greg, and Marcy. When I saw his slim, lanky body in action, I couldn't help but grin.

"Just friends, huh?" Ferris teased, catching my expression.

I blushed, but hid it by rolling my eyes. "Bye, Ferris."

The second Blue Moon parked, I hopped out of the car.

Greg and Marcy set up the ball with expert precision. Marcy spiked it to Beck's waiting receiving position. All three teens were athletic. They could control the padded ball to their whims. When he saw me coming, Beck stepped out of the game.

"Hey, parabond," he grinned, raking his hair out of his face. Something about the way he said that phrase made my knees buckle, so sweet and casual but also intimate. Two words he would offer just to me. His one and only parabond.

Thankfully, I stayed on my feet.

"Hi," I smiled.

"How was your aunt's?"

The girls waved behind us and headed into the castle. "It was good. Blue Moon actually almost beat her. She was so close. It was cool."

"Abeline?" He clarified, as if there was any other option.

I nodded.

"I'd like to play," he offered. "Sometime."

"Yeah, for sure." I said. "Maybe. It's kind of a girl thing."

"Scrabble's a girl thing?" Beck frowned.

"Well, no," I started, but I didn't have a real justification why he wasn't invited. Instead, I just shrugged.

Greg and Marcy came over, ball in hand.

"I'd take a battle of brawn over brain any day," Greg said.

"With your brains we'd be lost," Marcy giggled.

"So what? You're only with me for my body," Greg complained. Then he flashed his physique in several weight-lifter poses. "Who could blame her?"

"Oooh," Marcy swooned. She felt his arms and pecs. "Lookin' good babe. My man has some muscles."

"I know what baby likes." He flexed again.

I stifled a grin. Didn't want to encourage his antics. "Alright. Well, I'm headed for bed." I waved off the collective.

"See you later, Mae." Marcy winked.

"Later, Beck," Greg added.

I looked back surprised. "Oh, he's not coming." I told them. Beck kind of laughed as well. We exchanged a quizzical look. Why would they think he'd be coming?

"I'm headed to bed *myself*," I clarified.

"Oh?" Marcy raised an eyebrow.

"We sleep in separate bedrooms," Beck laughed. "Here," he held his hand out. "I'll take it back out to the sports shed."

Greg tossed him the volleyball.

I shook my head. "No one's doubling up in the bedrooms."

"Oh, Mae-mae..." Marcy shook her head, giving each of us a pitying smile, then she shot Greg a salacious grin. "Speak for yourself."

TWO

THERE HAVE ALWAYS BEEN
WITCHES IN PLUMPKIN

"DID you guys see the way Vince split that rock in half? It's like Nicolette's bonded to a superhero," Marcy gushed the next morning, a little pep in her step as we climbed the tall staircase back to our dorms. She playfully squeezed her hands on Nicolette's shoulders as we scaled. Three floors up, two to go. No one could accuse us of not getting enough cardio.

"He's *so* great," Hilde mooned. The rest of us looked her way, our curiosity piqued. Several of the girls grinned. That was quite a compliment and sigh coming from the younger girl. The kind of puppy-love sigh we all recognized for ourselves. Realizing she'd maybe gushed a bit too much, she flushed bright red. "What? He is."

Nicolette frowned. "What he is, is a jerk."

"He just tells you what he thinks," Hilde defended.

Sloane and I glanced over her head with small grins. But we weren't cruel enough to tease her. Let the preteen have her crush. She'd realize boys were more complicated than they first appeared soon enough.

"Hey, Mae." A lady and a student I'd never met before gave me a wave on their way down the communal stairs.

"Hi, Mae." Two more random witches also chimed in as they passed.

Politely I offered a stiff wave back, but I didn't lose step with my friends.

"I wish *I* had those talents," I told the girls as we climbed. "Water-splitting?"

Vince was an expert water harness. We'd seen him open the seas, hold up water walls, create currents from no wind, and today, he'd used a concentrated blast of water to split a stone in half. While Hilde was impressed, I was jealous. He had concrete skills that were clearly delineated and seen. Nothing like a dreamcast.

"Oh please. You're not still moaning about how you don't have much power?" Marcy frowned.

I shrugged her off, but it was true. I *didn't* have much witch power. There were four types of witches; chemists, lie-guards, empaths and dreamcasts. All the other skill sets were both visceral and concrete. Chemists created physical potions and spells. They understood the chemical or botanical make-up of the world around us. If you pictured an old, wrinkled, warty witch in a black cloak dropping ingredients into a cauldron, spinning the potion with a crooked stick, that was closest to a chemist. They could mix a million elixirs with all kinds of intentions (glues, truth serums, poisons, explosions, you name it). They were a capable, talented breed. After them, the second type of witches were the lie-guards. Lie-guards created illusions right out of thin air. They tricked your brain through manipulation, and, once they did, the illusion was as good as real. They could conjure up anything they wanted, and as long as the details were right, no one would ever know their illusion wasn't real. It was a robust weapon. The term lie-guard applied to both the witch and their creations, and you had to be skeptical of what you saw. They were also extremely powerful. Empaths came next. Like Vince, they were sometimes also called Harnesses. They controlled things: earth, water, air, animals or plants. I'd seen empaths control birds (that was Marcy's specialty), split open the earth, and spin up water with their hands. Beck was also a harness. He could manipulate the weather. Again, a handy, tangible ability to use. All three types of witches were able to mobilize their skills. The last type of the witches were the dreamcasts. And I fell in that group. Dreamcasts encountered visions of the future while they slept. If straightforward in story-telling, the tool of learning while one slept could be a powerful tool and a decisive aid, only, like me, most dreamcasts conceived their ideas in complicated visions that were more like puzzles than straight up guides to follow step-by-step. Sometimes I didn't dream at all. And if I suffered insomnia, my powers were inaccessible. But the others seemed to think I did alright. So far, they were right. I had managed to be successful in some tricky situations. But, it was beginners luck more than anything else.

Some witches were two-fers, having more than one power to call into play, but most of us had only one specialty. So our training also involved learning how to use our own strengths and also combat the other's skills.

"I just think I could do better," I admitted.

"You just won the Battle," Sloane teased me. "Cut yourself some slack."

"Hey, Mae," two fellows waved.

I nodded back.

"The Battle of Four," Nicolette corrected its proper title.

"Now everybody knows you," Sloane added.

"*Every*body," Marcy moaned.

"Believe me, I know." I frowned. "But I had help- a lot of it. Vince can do his whole thing on his own." I tried to point out the difference but the others were unconvinced. I couldn't blame them.

"Mae, what's up?" More students nodded.

I waved them off as well.

Since the completion of the battle, those sort of greetings happened a lot. Everyone on the grounds wanted to claim me as their pal (well, everyone but Brandi, but who cared what she thought). They were constantly seeking social proof that they personally knew the champion. I did my best to meet the demand without actually having to be a new friend. It was exhausting.

"You're like a superhero, too. It's pretty cool for our class to have a champion," Hilde nodded. A bit of her star-struck nature was reserved for me as well.

"Fat good it did," Marcy scoffed. "I see the damn Damocles everywhere. Even buying my iced coffee. I thought they had to leave town."

Sloane agreed. "That's the ruling."

"Actually," Nicolette shrugged. "If they don't practice any magic, they can stay wherever they want. *That's* the ruling. There have always been hundreds of witches around Plumpkin. Most are not practicing."

"My family has four generations," Hilde agreed.

"Mine as well," Sloane added.

I looked ahead on the stairs. That was the common experience. Most coven members came from a long line of witches and wizards. I guess I did too, I just didn't know it until they were already gone. My Mom died when I was six, my grandparents were dead before I was born, and Aunt Abeline raised me, but she was rejected from the coven, so she never spoke of it. I didn't even know it existed as a child. I'd only found out my mother was a coven member at the start of the parabond selections. I'd never even heard that word before.

Parabond.

Your fated partner.

Beck and I had matched. Although the road to get here had been strained and bumpy, now that we'd arrived it was really more than I ever could have hoped for.

And that wasn't the only new truth that I had learned.

On the day of the Battle of Four, I discovered new information about my father. Like Mom, he had also been a member in the coven, but, his presence here before me was mostly unknown. I had plenty of questions. Like, how'd they meet? And were they happy together? What was her witch skill? And his? What was it like to be her parabond? Why did they split up? And then, after all those came the toughest question: why had he killed my mom?

It wasn't the kind of family history I wanted to discuss with the girls in the stairwell. In fact, that last little detail was a truth I'd shared only with Beck. But, luckily, the girls had already moved on.

"Their red robes give me the heebie-jeebies," Marcy shuddered.

"They're not robes." Nicolette rolled her eyes.

The Damocles tribe made a point of wearing a red wardrobe, just like how our ladies and fellows wore white track suits when they were instructing other members of the coven. But the strangers weren't cloaked in red robes. They had dresses and hoodies and long-sleeve tees and t-shirts. Very normal. They just happened to all be in shades of blood red.

"What, are you *trying* to be contrary?" snapped Marcy.

"Just stating the facts," Nicolette backed down.

"Well, I still don't like seeing them," Marcy dismissed the so-called facts without thought.

"There's an easy fix for that. Don't go to town." Sloane shrugged.

"What, and spend all my free time in the library like Mae-mae and Becky?" Marcy asked.

"Hey! Why bring me in to this?" I complained as we arrived on our floor.

"They're not even making use of the stacks." Marcy laughed. "If Beck was my man, I'd make better use of my time."

"We know," Sloane groused.

Marcy frowned.

"He's not *mine*," I couldn't help adding. "We're just friends."

"We know," Nicolette repeated the complaint. Others smirked. I frowned.

"Well, on that note, I'm gonna wash up," Sloane extricated herself.

"See y'all in class." Hilde nodded.

The girls all parted for their separate dorm rooms.

I ducked into my space quickly, careful to close the door right after me so as not to invite in any random stares. The idea that I was a healthy, well-adjusted teenager would be seriously undercut by the interior decor I'd hung in my dorm room. It was like police captain's murder board. One wall had been transformed with clippings and printouts and blurry old photos all stuck on the wall. Bits of masking tape poked out behind old photos. Any clue I had found about the lineage of my mother or father in the High Council coven was pasted up on the wall. It hadn't started there, but posted there, it was easier to see all the information in a clear, living timeline.

Marcy was right.

Since the semester began, I had spent as much time in the archives as logistically possible. But it wasn't for reasons she thought. Since the Battle of Four, my dad's presence was always on my brain. I was obsessed. But, if you discovered your estranged father had killed your mother, you might grow a little focused as well. Especially over a man you'd never met. I had no clue who he was. Some days it felt like there was a killer in my midst.

And his victim was the woman who'd given me life.

Learning Dad's identity was my entire new goal. But finding any details about that time in coven history was a long, slow slog. I had to dig through all the archive books, piece together any possible mention. It's not like they had social media and Google when my parents were around. I had to compile my own list. And it was pain-staking to come together. I had hoped I could rely on Lady Mauve for more information, but ever since the Battle, she hadn't been coming around as our instructor nearly as much. I rarely saw her in the castle walls. I suspected it was because of the on-going presence of the Damocles coven.

There was more trouble brewing than anyone was saying out loud.

For the past few weeks, our first year lessons had gone back to business as usual, but the continued presence of the other coven in town was on everybody's mind. Marcy was right about that too. They were supposed to have left. Without their promised exodus, trouble might restart at any moment. Far as I could tell, the Damocles witches were waiting for something. What it was, there was no way to divine. I was just glad to be out of it.

Safe in my room, I caught a glimpse in the mirror.

Oh boy.

My hair and skin were covered in dust. Magical rock-splitting in the quarry had been exciting, but it was a dirty business. I checked my clock. Twenty minutes until we were expected in the science lab. If I hurried, I could wash up before classes. I stripped off my clothes and locked myself in the bath.

The water felt great rushing over sore muscles. Witch training was surprisingly physical, but lucky for me, the instructions included plenty of rest. It was literally in the curriculum. A necessary requirement. My witch abilities came out while I slept.

Plus, in all the other skill sets, I had a head start on my classmates.

During the Battle of Four, I had already seen and enacted a lot of the techniques we were learning in class. There was no better way to apprentice than to be thrust into the task head first. But thankfully, the battle was over. I was happy to sit back now and let my class-mates try their hands at the skills.

It felt best not to be noticed.

To disappear.

To go silent.

During our lessons, I was just another anonymous student in the crowd. Even if twenty random ladies and fellows said hello to me as soon as I walked out the door.

When my shower was over, I stood at the lip of the tub and squeezed the excess water out of my long, brown hair. It splattered on the porcelain below. I tugged a terrycloth towel under my armpits, dragged it tight across my breasts, and hurried back towards my room. Nicolette and I shared a jack n' jill bathroom, so as I was headed out of the shower, I always had to beware of the two exits and doors. We'd bumped into each other several times at the sinks, but so far, overall we made a pretty good pair. I kept the door to my room locked and closed. I never checked, but I assumed she did the same. Lucky for me she didn't often have visitors over. And I made it a point, if I dropped by to see her, to only do so from the outer hallway door. I kept the boundaries firm. My privacy was essential.

I padded out of the shower back to my room, happy to slip safely back inside my private world. But when I got there, I wasn't alone.

"Ready to go down to the - whoa. Hey, there." Beck had been leaning over, examining my wall of clippings, and only looked up in passing as I entered the room. But at the sight of my bare shoulders and the tiny towel, he straightened. His cheeks blushed. "You're a little wet," he noted.

"That's what happens after a shower," I frowned. "I'm also not dressed."

But I didn't have to tell him. His eyes flickered to various parts of my skin. My neck, my shoulders, the tops of my thighs. He took note of the towel, his lips involuntarily pursing. I flushed from within.

"It suits you," he said, his smile opening into a playful grin. "When I let myself in I didn't know you'd be naked," he said, stepping towards me.

"Almost naked," I corrected, adjusting my grip.

He came towards me and I let him. I raised my face to greet him, a tiny motion. My posture changing to meet his.

"Almost naked," he softly agreed. He moved my wet hair off my shoulder, but didn't touch more. He stood chest to chest with my frame, meeting me and also towering over me. I could practically feel his heart pounding a foot away.

Or maybe it was just mine, beating out of my chest.

"If I had known," his voice was a murmur, "that you'd be *almost* naked, I wouldn't have let myself in."

"No?" I raised an eyebrow.

"No," he agreed. He skimmed his hand through his hair lightly tousling it. "But now that I'm here..." A teasing smile crossed his lips.

My breath caught in my chest.

"Hey, Mae? Are you done in the shower?" Nicolette called through the door. I had locked it, as I did after every exit, but even with the plywood between us, Beck and I both jumped out of our skins. Instinctually, my hand went up to protect my towel wrapping and Beck stepped back a respectful distance away.

"Yeah, hey." I called out, highly uncomfortable. "All done, thanks."

Beck and I looked at each other and stifled our giggles. The moment's sensual energy had fizzled.

"So, I'll just- I'll wait outside," Beck nodded to me and made a beeline for the door.

"Yeah, of course. Great. That'd be good," I sputtered.

He closed himself quickly out in the hallway.

In the bathroom, I heard Nicolette pause. "Was there someone there?" She asked through the door.

"Nope. Nothing. Just a miscommunication," I re-tucked my towel and went about getting ready for science. In the bathroom, I doubted Nicolette's curiosity was satisfied. But I didn't care. "I'll see you downstairs," I told her.

And I didn't offer more.

THREE
YOU REALLY LOVE SCIENCE

AFTER DRESSING, I brushed a comb through my hair and added mascara to the top lashes on my lids. It's not that Beck and I were a secret, exactly. We weren't under wraps. Everyone seemed to know about our interests. I just didn't know what we *were*.

A messy flirtation was the simplest answer.

Nobody's business?

That was true too.

We'd been enjoying some small things together. Since our first kiss in the elevator, we'd made out a little here and there all over the High Council grounds. We'd stolen kisses in various nooks and crannies of the castle, a little touchy-feely and sometimes pretty flirty when no one else was around. But, in public, it was business casual. And in private, it wasn't serious.

I wasn't serious.

We both knew he'd only just broken up with that other girl.

Josie.

Obviously, I knew her name was Josie. And I liked her. She was a cool girl. I just didn't love talking about her in regards to him. They were over. Since our time in limbo, it felt so right for Beck and I to parabond. He was so sweet and so kind. But you didn't just move on from one serious relationship to another overnight. And considering their history, I wanted to take my time. See where things went.

To call him my guy at this point felt naive... and foolish.

Plus, it wasn't even an issue. We didn't talk about it. We didn't *discuss* it. We just... had fun here and there, when no one else was nearby. Plus, there was something a little exciting about sneaking around.

I never knew when a tiny touch from Beck might blow my mind.

I frowned at my mirrored presentation. I would have liked to have straightened my hair out and really looked my best, but I knew he was waiting and there wasn't a whole lot of time between classes as it was. I settled for a wet top knot with tiny wisps of tendrils framing my face and a shiny coat of lip gloss delivered to my mouth. I looked pretty okay in my low mainte-nance style. I topped off my plain t-shirt and khakis with my mother's full moon charm and took a small step back. The gold necklace sparkled just enough to catch the eye.

Not bad. Some might even say presentable.

Beck was leaned against the wall, one leg crooked

up real casual like, when I came out of my room. As I exited, his eyes lit up. I flushed as well, locking the door with a smile.

"All set?"

"Ready."

"You look nice." He smiled.

"Thanks."

"But, I prefer what you were wearing before," he grinned. "In the towel."

I rolled my eyes and gave him a playful push as we headed down the hall. "Go to class."

"I saw you added two new photos." His tone turned serious.

I nodded. "They're from the Solstice Festival."

I'd taken photocopies of the grainy old photos in the archives yesterday morning.

"You think he was there?"

"Maybe. They're from the right season. I'm getting closer," I nodded.

"What will you do when you find him?"

"I don't know," I admitted. "Send him to jail?"

He nodded, a distant look in his eye.

"Thanks for all your help," I added.

"Happy to be along for the ride," he grinned.

My cheeks flushed. When he looked out from under his hair in that cute sideways style, I always felt the butterflies bubbling up inside.

"I'm happy too," I told him. I felt the heat of my attraction grow thick in my chest.

His eyes lit a fire within me, and he bit his bottom

lip. But neither of us said anymore. We looked up to join the others waiting at the elevator. They were just loading into the car as we arrived.

"Mae-mae, Becky! Over here!" Marcy waved.

Greg stuck his big mitt out to stop the doors from closing, so we hurried inside. Once on board, the other couple fell back into the compartment. Casually, they tumbled together, Greg's arms slung loosely around the curves of his girl.

"Can you believe, for once it was here when we called it?" she motioned to the car. "You look nice," she complimented my style, then frowned at her own reflection. "It was so hard to get the dust out of my earlobes." She checked herself out in the mirror. It was an optical trick that elevator companies employed on one wall. The humans in the tiny boxes would be too distracted by looking at themselves to think much about the safety qualms of traveling up and down great heights inside a tiny, metal cage on a wire. I was just glad to give a rest to my calves.

"I told you," Greg smirked. "It saves time to shower together. I could scrub those earlobes." He gave Marcy's waist a little tug, bumping their hips together.

"And I told you," she swatted him lightly, "Sometimes a girl needs a little time to get ready, all by herself. Isn't that right, Mae?" She looked to me for support. "To make all this work," she wiggled for Greg, "a girl has to keep a few secrets." Marcy winked at us all. "Don't we, Mae."

I didn't know what to say. In the same time as me,

she'd managed to fully blow her hair out, sculpt a fresh face of makeup, and dress in a cute set of clothes.

"Marcy, you look fantastic," Beck approved, shooting Greg a grin.

"Don't look her over," Greg complained.

"I wouldn't dream of it," Beck laughed. "Eyes and hands to myself."

But that wasn't true.

Suddenly, I felt a warm touch on the lower part of my back. I straightened. Beck slid his hand in behind me, cupping my body, but he didn't look my way in the mirror. Instead, his fingers did all the work. They laid gently against my T-shirt, his hand so warm, subtly caressing my back. Lighting up my skin. I looked up to his face. He smiled, but didn't glance in my direction. Instead, warmly and serenely, he stood still beside me, eyes straight ahead, pretending nothing was going on between us, his fingers delicately grazing my curves. I drew a shaky breath and looked forward too.

We both pretended it wasn't happening.

This fire between us.

Our quiet interaction. Like a thousand fireworks going off in my brain.

My limbic system soared with desire.

Our private, public secret.

His fingers laid claim to me completely, massaging my body in a sexy slow touch. The other couple didn't have a clue. We played it so cool, while my breath caught ragged in my chest.

"You look good, honey." Greg complimented and they exchanged kissy little pecks.

"Thank you baby, I know," Marcy teased him.

They barely seemed to notice, but while we worked to hide the passion between us, Beck and I had gone stock-still and white hot.

Neither he nor I acknowledged the secret. But his tiny touches sent desire rushing through me, crashing in waves. Desperate. Emboldened. I feared we'd be caught.

Beck felt it too.

His smile grew bigger.

I could sense the energy rising between us.

It was growing harder to contain.

"What do you think we're doing in science today?" Marcy asked us, returning from the lips of her man to include us again.

Beck strummed my back.

"No idea," he grinned. "Just along for the ride."

"Mm hmm," I agreed. Unable to open my mouth.

"Blowin' something up, I hope," Greg enthused.

"Maybe," Beck agreed. Cool as ice.

I wanted to chime in, chill as him, but I could barely stand on my feet. Beck's nimble fingers rotated around. Toyed with my skin.

Pretending I wasn't on fire took all my attention.

So illicit and sensual in front of our friends.

Could they intuit my excitement? Could he?

"I don't want to get messy," Marcy complained. "I just blew out my hair."

But, maintaining my composure wasn't enough. I wanted to play the game as well. Why let Beck have all the fun? Keeping my eyes straight ahead, I swung my fingers by my side, a pendulum, free and loose. Casually, between my legs and Beck's thigh they floated, until they softly brushed against his pants. The impact was tiny. Barely a rustle.

But I felt it explode like a minefield inside.

Beck cleared his throat and shuffled.

I let my fingertips slide there, across his pant leg, the back of my hand resting on the fabric covered skin. Touching, ever so slightly. Claiming him as my own. First on the outer thigh, then grazing my way in.

Beck coughed.

"You alright, Becky?" Marcy worried.

"Fine. Good," he nodded, turning slightly red, then recovering. It was my turn to be stoic and calm.

"Whatever it is, it'll be an adventure," I said with a slow smile. "Cooking up something fun."

"Our own brand of magic," Beck agreed.

We snuck a look at each other. He smiled. I blushed.

The chemistry in our fingers smoldered beneath our clothes.

"Look at you two," Marcy teased.

Our smiles dropped. Protectively, I crossed my arms. We stepped apart.

"What?"

"You really love science," she observed. "You're practically glowing."

The elevator dinged. The doors to the metal box slid smoothly apart.

"Oh. Yeah. Yup, you bet," I agreed. "Chemistry... and science..."

Beck grinned. "Explosions," he added.

"And fire," Greg mooned.

"No fire!" Marcy, Beck and I all said at once. In the Battle of Four we'd seen enough fire to last forever. Extirpation was bad for everyone.

We laughed, all on the same page, and exited the elevator as a group.

"Hey, Mae."

"Hi, Kingsley!" Immediately, a couple of second-year students waved as I stepped out of the lift.

I was already annoyed to lose Beck's sexy touch, and the idea of greeting several teens I'd never met before in my life seemed awfully dumb, but I tried not to let my annoyance show. I offered a small wave and moved on.

When would my champion status wear off?

"Ah, shoot. You know what, I forgot something upstairs-" Beck stopped short and pulled back on my arm. "Hold up, Mae. You guys go on. We'll catch up."

We had to act fast to catch the lift before the heavy doors closed.

Greg and Marcy shrugged as I re-boarded with Beck. "See you there."

"What'd you forget?" I asked as the doors collided, but he didn't press a button, instead, Beck pulled me in.

"Nothing." He grinned. "You just can't tease me like that, then go on to science like nothing happened," he told me, his body enticingly close.

"Me! I was just standing here. What about your fingers?" I complained, smiling.

"That's where they belong."

"Oh really?" I raised an eyebrow. "On my back?"

"Mm hmm, they fit perfectly. That's Anatomy 101."

"I don't know." I frowned, then tilted my head towards him. "You better show me."

Beck obeyed. He slid his hand in behind me and threaded it down on my skin. This time, just above my hips, he applied more pressure to his finger tips and the placement pulled my body towards his.

"See?" He murmured. "Perfect fit."

For a moment, I reveled in the proximity.

"You look nice." Beck looked me over, approving every inch in his view.

I blushed.

"Not as nice as in a towel, but it will definitely do," he teased.

I swatted his chest. But Beck didn't fall back. He just stood willing. Close. Waiting for an invitation. Things slowed down. Grew still. Held in his arms, I accepted him in.

Beck leaned down.

He kissed me softly. Gentle at first. Leading me. Our lips pushing in. He tasted sweet. Soft and juicy.

His mouth moved against mine, slow and tender. Then adding pressure. His fingers massaged my skin.

I kissed him back, the heat between us growing, unhurried in its build.

The connection was slow and sensual. Not white hot or frenzied like it had been with others in my past. We didn't race towards crescendo, just played together in the moment, forever happy, sweetness growing. Like I could kiss him forever. His searching hands on my back.

I floated my hands to his hair.

It felt so good to wrap my hands up soft and smooth. His hair was so sexy. I loved the way it fell over his eyes.

Those eyes.

"We should go." I whisper-warned him, his kisses covering my mouth. "Someone's bound to need the elevator."

"Let 'em wait." He smiled through kisses. "I don't mind," he murmured.

Beck pushed me lightly, walking me backwards. Together, we shuffled until I leaned firmly against the mirrored wall. He slid his tongue into my mouth and the chemistry crescendoed. For a moment he looked in my eyes, and saw how blitzed out on passion I was, then he moved down to my neck. He kissed me gently, his lips nipping quickly, moving nimbly, drawing sighs from deep within my soul. I wanted to object, but who could object to that? Instead, I let out a pleasurable moan.

Suddenly, the room shuddered to life and started to lift.

"Beck, whoa." We realized immediately what was happening: someone had called for the lift. "We're moving."

He stepped back, sensing my mood shift, and I straightened everything in reach. Thinking quickly, Beck pressed the button for the next floor on the route. We fell away from each other, fastidiously organizing our wardrobes. I tried to fix my hair in the mirror.

"How do I look? Okay?" I worried, as if with one glance, someone would know the fires that burned between us.

"You look incredible," he teased.

I rolled my eyes, but couldn't keep my frowning expression in tact. Beck was too sweet. Too sexy. His eyes sparkled, just a tiny bit naughty. I wanted to fling my body on him, but any moment, we'd be caught.

The elevator dinged and we hopped off, one floor up and a million miles above where we'd started. Lucky for us, the second floor hallway was empty. It took an extra beat to calm our beating chests.

"That was too close." I chastised. "Someone might have seen us."

"Would that be so bad?" He pawed towards me again.

But, I didn't give in. We could both see that a continuation wasn't likely to happen out here in the open. For the first time, Beck frowned. "Mae, I'm serious. I like you. I don't care who knows."

"I like you, too."

"And the other?"

"You want to make out in front of everybody?" I purposefully frowned.

"I thought we could start with hand-holding, but I'm open to seeing where it goes," he joked. I could see he was patient, but it was waning. "You and I, boyfriend and girlfriend. Would that be so bad?"

I shrugged. Our bond wasn't exactly a secret. We hadn't been fooling anyone if that was the plan. Every one of our friends knew we were unofficial partners. There was no need to proclaim a title now. "We don't need to hump like Greg and Marcy every day and every minute." I checked in, and he nodded along. "So then we're good. There's no need to announce things to the world."

"It's not an announcement..." he pouted.

How could I help him to see?

"Beck, there's a lot of eyes on me. Everywhere. So much attention. After limbo, and the Battle... is it so bad to keep this just for you and me?" I touched his arm lightly. I could see I was winning this battle. "At least for a while?"

"They're not gonna talk," he complained.

I raised an eyebrow. That was not my experience. "So far, my time at the High Council has been wall-to-wall gossip. Everybody knows my business."

"If they do, then let them talk," he said. "I don't wanna hide what we have."

"It's not forever," I conceded. "Just for the present. We keep the details between us."

He nodded, but I could tell he was disappointed.

Together, we walked down the stairs. Class was starting soon, we didn't want to be late. He was right. It would have been nice to hold his hand as we walked together. Instead, our fingers hung loose by our sides.

"Not forever..." I said again, but that didn't feel like enough, "and don't forget, you can secretly touch me whenever you want."

Beck grinned. "Whenever?"

I nodded.

"Wherever?" He followed up, his one eyebrow cocked.

I swatted him, and didn't answer. Instead, I let my fingers scrape his palm. The graze set electric waves through us both.

"Just make sure you don't get caught."

FOUR
GATHERED AT THE CASTLE

OUR FLIRTY, blissed out faces wouldn't fool anyone, so as we hit the ground floor, we put the previous conversation to bed. But, we didn't have to worry about pulling anyone's focus in the atrium. There was already way too much going on.

"What's all this?" I asked out loud to no one in particular.

"What the-" Beck echoed.

The giant windows in the foyer were obstructed from their usual, beautiful forest view. All around the castle, something was off. A smattering of clothing peppered the familiar scenic vista in a flourish of red.

The Damocles coven.

They stood around the perimeter of the High Council castle, their backs facing our stones. Eight or ten of them, standing stoic. Like the start of some sort of protest. I glanced at Beck, but he looked as perplexed as me. The red-wearing coven members should have been long gone, not coming closer. I knew the foreigners had been spotted around town by myself and others, but standing here in our garden seemed a direct slap in the face. Why were they gathered at our castle? It wasn't a huge mob, there were plenty more of them I'd seen at the Battle of Four, but that didn't matter. I had an uneasy feeling. From the gathered crowd of High Council patrons watching the other council's progress, I wasn't alone in this inkling.

Something was wrong.

The ladies and fellows stood around the glass foyer in little gossipy clumps, watching with uneasy trepidation. As far as I could tell from where I stood at the back of the room, the Damocles witches didn't seem to be trying to *do* anything, but their very presence made everyone uncomfortable.

As I ventured forward with Beck, random coven members waved and called me over, reeling me in as best they could, but I didn't bite. It wasn't until I spotted someone I knew that we worked our way into the crowd. Everyone stood with deep frowns on their faces. The closest person we could reach was Lady Rain.

"Hey," I came along side of her and Beck followed.

"Morning," she nodded in her traditional frown, her eyes never leaving the exterior red-clothed interlopers.

"What's going on?" Beck asked.

Rain's eyes left the foreign contingent to flit both to me and the taller boy. When she didn't see anything of interest from either one of us, she went back to staring outdoors. "Well, random first year I don't know, I think it's pretty clear, they're staging a protest. A stand in."

"Can they do that?" Beck asked, a hand rifling through his hair.

"Does he not have eyes?" She frowned my way. Since I'd brought him with me, my status had lowered as well. "They *can* and they have. And to think, I broke my arm in the battle."

"The Battle of Four," Nicolette piped up from behind us. None of us had heard her approach. We turned to look at her and she bowed her head, embarrassed to be caught eavesdropping. Lady Rain raised a vicious eyebrow and frowned. If I didn't know Rain so well from fighting through our coven battle, I would have cowered on the spot under such a sharp rebuke. Through multiple exposures, I'd learned not to take her icy demeanor so personally. But Nicolette dropped her head again and scurried away from our group. Rain turned back to face the exterior, perturbed.

"How is your arm?" I looked down at her injury. Her forearm was still wrapped in a cast, but it wasn't slung to her shoulder any longer. That was progress. The bone was healing. She'd dressed up the plaster sleeve in a sleek black, fabric sheath.

"It hurts. A lot. I soldier through the pain." She raised her head, proud of her own resilience. "But, I didn't do it so they could break all the rules."

"You think that's bad," Ferris joined our huddle. "Ethan's still out in the field." She nodded a greeting.

"Still?" At this I was surprised.

"Without a shower?" Rain looked aghast.

"Without anything," Ferris nodded grimly. Her eyes also never left the waiting red clothed witches.

"But it's been weeks!" I blurted.

Ferris nodded towards the other coven. "He's tasked with protecting the council's most precious plants. He and the others can't return to the castle. Not until Damocles vacates."

"Like they were *supposed* to," Rain agreed.

"That's terrible," I told her.

We all stared at the backs of the blonde, curly heads. It was clear, the Damocles coven wasn't going anywhere soon.

"Can't the elders at least call them back or send someone else to replace him?" Beck wondered.

"At least for bathing?" Rain nodded, finally letting Beck into the group.

"I don't know. It's - this wasn't the plan. It's a mess." Ferris looked around to make sure no one was watching us. Of course they were, we were three of the four battalion members. There were as many eyes on our backs as on the Damocles clan. But the redhead played it cool. Her voice dropped so only we could hear. "Just... be prepared. Things are bound to get worse."

We nodded. We had that feeling as well.

Out of the corner of my eye I saw our other class-mates peel themselves away from the spectacle and head down the castle halls to our class. It was time for our science lesson.

"We should go," I told Beck, nodding in their direction. He nodded. Before we left, I checked in once more with the others. "If you need anything, let me know."

"Likewise," Ferris nodded.

"Leave me out of it," Rain shrugged. "I've done enough for the witch world."

As we departed, neither woman budged. They just kept on staring out the doors, like so many others as well. It felt strange to leave to focus on something as mundane as a science lesson, but Beck and I did as we were told. We followed the schedule, last to arrive at the lab.

Tej, Sloane's parabond, shook his head as we entered. "Here they are," he noted, as if the room was waiting for our arrival. His five o'clock shadow made his expression even darker.

"See, they're just fine," Hilde noted, as if that had been up for discussion.

"I don't like this," he said, pacing. He peered out the science lab doors. There wasn't anything of note to see in the hallway.

"Nobody likes it," Vince rolled his eyes.

Marcy frowned. "Mae won the Battle."

"The Battle of Four," Nicolette interjected, almost automatically. Again, her clarification wasn't exactly welcome, but she didn't care. "They won fair and square."

"Who said life was fair?" Vince turned his bad attitude on his partner. Although fate had bonded them together, it hadn't made them like each other, and Nicolette knew better than to continue to argue if he was in a fighting mood.

We all knew better than to pick a fight with Vince.

Especially a sour Vince.

I looked around our little collective. The grim lines on their faces were all the same. The carefree attitudes of the morning had disappeared. While by any honest metric you could argue that our five couples had only just arrived at the Judicial Studies of the High Council, at this point all of us had been around long enough to know that the uninvited trespass of the Damocles coven meant things were about to get weird. There could be serious trouble. How wasn't clear, but the feeling was palpable.

"What's gonna happen?" Hilde wondered, bringing back my attention.

Everyone in the room looked around. Finally, a couple people offered shrugs.

"No one knows," Sloane said the words out loud.

"Cornelius should just go out and blast 'em." Greg pretended to shoot imaginary guns full of witchcraft. "You know he could do it."

"And start another magical fire?" Sloane shook her head.

"Well, they've got to do *something*. I don't want to be held captive in the castle," Marcy pouted, tossing her hair over her shoulder.

"Like some fairy tale princess?" Hilde asked, her eyes growing wide.

"More like a prisoner," Vince disagreed.

"Oh, right. Of course." Her little cheeks burned.

"In my eyes, you're a princess, babe," Greg assured the young girl. He winked.

Rick, Hilde's parabond, shifted, clearly uncomfortable at Greg showing the young girl too much attention. But it was all in good fun. Little Hilde glowed.

"Ah... sorry to interrupt." We all spun to see Lady Blue Moon in the entrance. She nodded to me, then head-counted everyone. Awkwardly, she cleared her throat. "Ah, hi. Good. You're all here. Hello, everybody." She gave a little wave. "Everybody, yes. I know you were expecting Fellow Stone to carry on with your science lessons, but... there's been a change of plans." Lady Blue Moon shuffled into the science lab with a folder full of papers. It was no surprise to see her carting around contracts. Her official title was the Paper Master for the school. Although we'd grown to be friends and often hung out with my aunt outside of the coven, in the castle, she spent most of her time organizing, filing, and signing all the coven's necessary paperwork. Even though I loved her social calls, it wasn't great to see her coming in an official capacity. It always meant new rules.

Every contract that we signed took away a little more of our freedom.

"What kind of change?" Tej asked.

"What's going on?" Hilde worried.

"Where's Fellow Science?" Marcy wondered.

"Fellow Stone," I corrected.

"Whatever."

A room full of questions greeted Lady Blue Moon at once. She held her hand up, nodding. "Fellow Stone is busy downstairs with the elders. As I said, or I tried to, your lessons have been put on hold until the situation with the Damocles coven has been resolved. It's nothing to worry about, but I have been told to give you strict instructions that no one from this room is to be involved with the forming protest. In any manner. In any circumstance."

All eyes floated in my direction.

I nodded stiffly.

Fine.

Accidentally, I had inserted myself into the coven-to-coven, head-to-head battle in the past few weeks by stupidly being in the wrong place at the wrong time. But falling into the middle of one fight was plenty. I would be sure to steer clear of this fray. I had no contact with the Damocles coven. Since the Battle of Four ended, I hadn't said a word to a single person from their group. And I didn't want to. We did not part on the greatest of terms.

"In fact," Lady Blue Moon opened her paperwork. "There's nothing to worry about," she repeated. "But, Cornelius Child and the elders have gone to the trouble of drawing up a little contract stating your guidelines." She passed out a sheet of paperwork to each of us. We quickly read it down.

. . .

As a student in the first year of education at the Judicial Studies of the High Council coven, I do not have the training or skills necessary to help with a siege undertaken by another coven on the castle grounds. I have full faith in the abilities and capabilities of the Elders of the Council. I will not interfere, leave the castle walls, nor speak to any council members without permission at large, until these unprecedented events are over.

"You just need to sign and date below," Blue Moon pointed to the clearly labelled requirements.

"You're serious? We're stuck like prisoners?" Vince asked.

"You called it!" Hilde was impressed.

"Yes, you're trapped... in a magnificent castle," Lady Blue Moon tried to spin around the terms. "With delicious food and snacks."

No one bought this version.

She sighed. "Until the end of the protest, yes. You're to stay here." She nodded. Sales pitch over. "The elders don't want any... events... like last time." She lowered her gaze.

"She's talking to you, Mae-mae," Marcy told me.

"Yes, I know."

"Breaking the rules. Making us look bad," Greg added, shaking his head.

"We were all there," Beck defended.

"I have no idea what you're talking about," Tej countered. "When the fires first started, I stayed right where I was asked. Safe and warm in the castle." He eyed Lady Blue Moon.

She wasn't buying. She knew very well that everyone of us had broken the rules but for Rick. *I* was the only one that got caught.

I frowned. I hated the feel of everyone's judging looks.

"I would argue that in the last occurrence, things turned out fairly well," Rick's slow, thick cadence caused us all to turn. He spoke so infrequently, with a voice so formal and stern it made us all sit up and take notice. "After all, it was Mae's ingenuity that won the Battle of Four for the coven."

"The Battle of Four," Nicolette said.

"He said it correctly," Vince snapped. But Nicolette just shrugged.

Heads turned back to Lady Blue Moon.

"They should be thanking Mae," Marcy quickly changed her tune. "Not locking her up in some tower."

"It's not a tower," Nicolette corrected. "It's a giant, magnificent castle." She echoed Lady Blue Moon's sales pitch.

"Where we're forced to eat and sleep and drink," Marcy listed.

"It's practically a jail!" Greg fumed. "I'm not signing!"

Lady Blue Moon's posture shrunk. "Hold up, there's no need to worry."

"You keep saying that!" Marcy frowned.

"And *that* makes me worry!" Greg added.

"No need to shoot the messenger," I defended her. "She didn't write the thing."

"Well, I don't care." Greg pushed it away. "I have a little thing I like to call freedom."

Others followed. Pushing the paperwork back as well.

Lady Blue Moon shifted. Her face became even more uncomfortable. "Ah, you should know, if you don't sign, the High Council can arrest you for breaking coven protocol. Then you really *will* be a prisoner," she admitted.

Our jaws dropped open.

"But guys, not to worry! This is no sweat. It's a really good contract. Mae's correct in that I didn't write it, but I did deliver it to all the students. They're just looking for written proof that you'll do what is reasonable and sensible and safe. After... last... time..." In the room, she didn't win a single friend.

I looked around at all the crossed arms and stubborn faces. "Give me a pen."

"I just have a pencil on me, will that be okay?" She asked.

I frowned, this was killing my momentum.

She realized and hurried. "Yeah, of course it is. Here you go." Lady Blue Moon passed me the writing utensil and I scribbled and dated my name. I handed the thing off to Beck. He signed next. I stared my friends down, but no one further objected. If *we* were in, the others begrudgingly followed.

Rick and Hilde next.

Then, Nicolette.

Tej and Sloane took their own turns, then handed the instrument to Marcy and Greg.

She frowned but they both added their signatures.

Vince was the last to add ink.

When all ten sign-offs were complete, Lady Blue Moon gathered the papers back into her hands.

"Well, alright." She nodded. "That wasn't so bad." She would have been more convincing if she hadn't been shaking while she spoke.

"What now?" Hilde wondered, her voice sounded small and meek.

"Class is dismissed," Blue Moon said.

"We can do what we want?" Greg asked.

"Within reason. Do you need to see the document again?"

"Free time!" Greg immediately forgot the stir he'd been making. "Who wants to play volleyball?" He whooped his hands in the air.

"I do!" Marcy cheered.

"I'll try," Hilde agreed.

Others nodded as well. Soon they'd gathered a whole team.

Lady Blue Moon smiled. Whatever indignation the students had felt about the paperwork and the contract, the issues had already fallen by the wayside.

We were being let out of class early and all was right with the world.

"What do you want to do?" Beck asked me. "A little ball could be fun."

Determined, I shook my head. "You go ahead." I told him.

I would take this little break as an invitation to learn all that I could about my dad.

FIVE
THE LIBRARY ARCHIVES

WHILE MY CLASSMATES headed off to catch up on sleep, or relax with a game, or whatever, I made a bee-line for the library archives. Based on my mom's age, the four year enrollment period and other guidelines, I felt pretty sure about a five year window when my parents might have met. Every class size had up to ten patrons and only half of those members were guys, so I was starting to narrow it down. What I really needed to find were some class lists or even a coven lineup. There was a discrepancy between the students in the school, who were referenced by their real names, and their color names they earned once they graduated and stayed on in various roles. When they became color-coded as ladies and fellows the men and women mostly lost their family names like flimsy alter egos. And the cross-over wasn't one-to-one. Not every kid in the Judicial Studies chose to stay and work at the coven. It appeared that if you wanted a higher education, or a family of your own, or even a specialty occupation, those were all reasons to leave the coven. Plus, there was travel and/or a disinterest in magic (once you learned the skills, maybe they were like any other, boring or simple tools in your arsenal), or, there could be a million other reasons a fully-trained witch might decide not to stick around. Plus, the paperwork was not consistent. Some notations used initials, while others referenced coven members by grades or years. It was a mess. Nothing was organized. The whole collection of archives was just a hodgepodge of articles about events and actions the Council underwent. Not every newsletter was kept. Nor were the articles particularly timely in manner. To say it was an incomplete history of the coven was a drastic understatement.

But still, I dug in. I'd started my search with my mom. If I could find records of her time in the coven, I would know exactly when she entered and finished her four years. After that, I could find her parabond. There was a chance that might be my father.

Not every paranormal partnership had a romantic underpinning, but a lot of them did.

If I could figure out who the fates had paired her with at the start of her Judicial Studies, then perhaps the rest her experience would also become clear.

It was strange no one had ever prepared a straightforward timeline or succinct lists of enrollment. I thought about suggesting it to Lady Blue Moon. That kind of data collection would be right up her alley. But for now, the newsletters, photos and clippings were where I would have to begin.

Mom's name was prolific in the documents.

She entered most of the contests and challenges, and won quite a few. But her parabond was not as easy to find.

"Look at this," Beck leaned over the book he'd been wading through. His wavy hair fell in front of his eyes. At close proximity, I caught a delicious whiff of his essence, woodsy and warm. I'd tried to encourage him to join the others playing volleyball, but he'd just shrugged me off. "I'd rather be with you," he'd said. Which was sweet. And in this field of messy bits and pieces, I could definitely use the extra set of eyes. I'd have to remember to make it worth his while.

"This guy," he pointed. "I've seen him before. I think." It was a grainy photo of someone winning the Spellbinder Award, whatever that was, but Beck wasn't looking at the winner. In the side of the frame was a guy standing in portrait, only half of his face caught in the square. On the other side of the winner was an older girl. We looked at the headline. *"Fellow Shadowcast celebrates landslide win."* The caption read: *"Fellow Shadowcast hoists his arms. Fellow Tangerine, Lady Fire look on."*

"Fellow Tangerine..." Beck drew a line off his text through the air back to the tentative list we'd been making. His index finger rested on another name. "Is Ben Xavier... maybe." His voice trailed off. He'd been so confident at first. I leaned over his arm.

"No, I think you're right... maybe," I agreed. It was definitely possible. "Put him in red."

Red for maybe... maybe not.

Most of our information was coded in that color.

There were still a lot of holes to fill.

"They amused themselves with an awful lot of contests," I sat back from the books.

Beck grinned. "Guess it's either that, or take over the world," he said. "What else can you do with a bunch of secret witch powers?"

We both sat back. We'd been piecing old lineages together for several hours and all we had to show for it was another maybe to add to the pile of unknowns. It was a bit disheartening.

"So many witches leave," I frowned. "If my dad left the Council too quick, I might never learn who he was." I closed the top folder.

"They want to travel, see the world, I get that. We should too, before having a family."

"What?"

"No, I-" Beck flushed bright red. "I didn't mean *we*, us. I meant like *we*, the royal version. Like *we all should*. Like the whole world." He raced us forward. "I'm not talking *our* future. God. You won't even commit to the present."

I frowned. He frowned. This wasn't headed where he wanted to go.

"Which is fine. We talked about it, I get it. I just..." he regrouped. "I wanna see the world, and I won't be full of regrets and ditch my kids when I'm old."

Ah.

He didn't finish with '*like my mom*', but he could have.

Beck had some family issues of his own. It was something we had in common. An unhealthy relationship with an absentee parent, only, Beck's Mom had taken off when he and his sister were mostly grown. My dad did it before I was born.

But I considered the possibility. "You think he's out in the world, playing tourist? Is that a reason to go?"

"He left his kid. A helpless baby. Could there be a worthwhile reason for that?"

"I guess not."

But deep down, I knew I was hoping to find one. A reason. That my dad left because he had to, not because he chose to. Was that too much to ask? That once I had all the pieces, the answer would make sense. That maybe the evidence against him was faulty, that he didn't kill my mom, and that he'd be here by my side if he could. I ignored this niggling sensation.

"Whatever his motive... he was stupid." Beck reached out and took my hand.

"Same for your mom."

I let our fingers interplay. For a moment, we were quiet. Beck ran his thumb back and forth on my skin. Slowly, I tented my fingers, he matched my movement. His hands were larger, rougher than mine. I lined up our palms and extended the digits. We looked at the disparity between them.

"Your fingers are bigger."

"Longer," he nodded.

Our hands folded down, entwined.

"We fit nicely together," I noted.

"I think so," he said softly.

"Here, let me see," I offered. I put up my other hand, and he matched it, both palms side by side. We examined the discrepancies, mostly finding any excuse to keep touching. The energy flowed hand to hand. I felt goosebumps on my arms with a rush of pleasure. "Yeah," I softly noted. "Definitely longer." The fingers of our other hands folded together as well.

"They fit nicely too," he said.

For a moment, we sat like Cheshire cats, smiling at each other.

"Come here," Beck pulled our hands towards him, standing up.

"Beck," I objected, but let him lead me anyway. He dragged me off my chair until we were standing together, our entwined fingers shoulder height.

"You only come up to my chest."

"You're too tall," I teased.

He led our entwined hands in half circles, away from our bodies, pulling the palms out, then tucking them down at our sides. He held me there. The action left my head and chest exposed in dangerous proximity, but I didn't try to get out of his control. Instead, I looked up, almost leaning in, our upper bodies very close. I watched him. He watched me back.

This was far too intimate for such a public setting. But that's what made it so delicious.

The energy pulsed.

The way he held my grasp, it felt like I was giving in to his body. To his desires. To his whims.

He had full control.

And I didn't want to let go.

"I think I'm just right," he said softly, his glance flitting between my eyes and my mouth.

"Not too short, not too tall," I nodded.

Beck bit his bottom lip, watching me. "We should probably let go," he murmured. "Someone might see us, get the wrong impression."

He was teasing me. Waiting. Wondering if I would fold. But the library wasn't a super populated area, we could probably enjoy this whole space to ourselves. The risk of discovery was almost non-existent. None of our friends ever ventured around. I liked the tension.

I was certainly enjoying him.

I sighed. He smelled so good. With my hands folded in his, down below, our faces so close together, I was powerless to stop his approach.

"We wouldn't want that," I agreed. I shuffled forward. Beck followed, til there were only inches between us.

"I really want to kiss you," he murmured.

"I really want to let you," I told him.

He learned towards me.

Slowly.

Our breath catching.

Our lips opening.

Slam!

I stripped apart from him, my head jerking at the sound.

The second floor library entrance door smacked against the wall and ricocheted back to its frame. A boy came marching through.

"You have got to be kidding me," Beck rolled his eyes as I slipped out of his hands. "You're timing is evil," he sputtered.

"What's that?" The spikey-haired guy who caused the commotion laughed as he passed us by. "Talkin' about your sister?" He clearly wasn't in full control of his faculties. "I just heard '*evil*'," he grinned. "Thought, that sounds like my girl. My ex-girl." In response to my surprise, he grinned and phony whispered behind his hand. "It's okay, he's her brother and I'm her parabond boyfriend. I say out loud what others don't dare."

"Clint is Brandi's ex-boyfriend," Beck explained by way of introduction.

He offered a little bow.

"And they're not on great terms," Beck added.

"Yet, my yoke is forever tied. She'll get in your mind if you let her," he confided. "A true evil. You were right." As he spoke, Clint swayed a little back and forth.

"Dude, you know she's my sister."

"Yeah, well, truth hurts."

I couldn't agree more. To my mind, although they were only separated by two years, Beck's sibling Brandi, was the human personification of a hissing, coiling viper, always ready to attack. You never knew when she'd strike next. Only guarantee was it was coming. Not because you deserved it, simply because you were there.

The girl was a loose cannon.

But I wouldn't have said that to Beck. She was, after all, his darling sister. Clint might not have said it either, if he hadn't been slurring his words.

"Are you drunk?" I asked.

"Shhh. No!" He looked around, as if someone might have been watching. "My secret stash." He put a hand up to whisper once more.

"At three in the afternoon," I raised an eyebrow. "Aren't you special."

"You're just mad 'cuz I won't share." He lurched a bit to the right.

"Clint," Beck said, patting his back, trying to lead him away from our table. "My sister lost out big." But the older boy wasn't going. Instead, he lunged for a book.

"What's you got here?" Disdainful, Clint flipped over the manual Beck was reading. "Isn't there a better use of your hours and minutes?"

"Like day-drinking?" I asked.

He gave an exaggerated wink. "I gots me some beer."

"They put our schooling on hold," Beck shrugged, reclaiming the book. He didn't bother to explain what he and I were researching. Either he was protecting the privacy of my family's history or he simply knew already that his sister's drunk ex-boyfriend wouldn't care.

"Did you sign the contract? I was like, no way man, I'm not signing." Clint huffed.

"So you didn't?" At this I was surprised.

"I mean, I *signed*. But I let Blue Moon know who's boss." He puffed out his chest. Beck snuck a small look in my direction. We stifled our smiles. But Clint barely noticed. He was on a roll. "Nobody pushes old Vox-y around." That, I caught on pretty quick, was a third-party reference to himself.

"Clint Vox," Beck added.

"No, I got it," I nodded.

From the floor below, someone burst into the library and shouted. "The Damocles chick and Cornelius Child are meeting. Right now! It's going down."

"Holy crap, man! Come on." Clint took off running.

Beck and I looked at each other, and dropped all we'd been doing. The Damocles leaders were meeting with the elders of the coven? Across the first floor, everyone else raced to see what was happening as well. We ran down the stairs out of the library and into the atrium, but there were two burly Fellows standing guard at the door. Over their shoulders, we could see, the rumors were true. Cornelius and the elders were outside, discussing something with the woman I recognized as the Damocles leader. But from this vantage point inside, it was impossible to hear.

"Uh-uh." The large fellows turned us away with the other students. "Ladies and fellows only. Students aren't permitted off the castle grounds."

"But that's not fair!" Clint objected. "We don't wanna *leave*, we just wanna hear."

Other students also bartered. "Technically the gardens are still part of High Council," Tej tried to reason at the front of the group.

"Mae!" Behind me, a random student called me over. I looked in their direction, set to wave hello and blow them off, but when they caught my eye, they gestured towards the stairwell.

"Hey, come on," I whispered to Beck. Together, we followed, headed towards our new beckoning friend. She was smart. There were balconies all over the grounds. We could hear what everyone was saying if we watched from another spot, higher up. We left Clint and Tej and the others to fight their own battle in the atrium and quickly followed the girl up the stairs.

"Out here," she directed. We ran behind her and made a quick turn out through the first balcony door. It was totally unguarded and offered a great view. Other students were already crouching, careful to see and hear all they could without being told to go back in. We also ducked down.

"Thanks," I whispered, kneeling in beside her. Beck flanked my other side.

The balcony was already brimming. Lots of students had come out to hear the details of the meeting they weren't permitted to attend.

"You're in no place to make demands." An elder told the Damocles tribe. I quickly noted their numbers in red clothing had gone from ten to more than twenty. Their protest was escalating. The fact that our elders were even entertaining their presence seemed to me a very bad sign.

"Even so, here we are," the blonde didn't back down. The woman leading their group stood ramrod straight in defiance. "We won't go home unhanded."

"Natalia, you're wasting your time. The castle can't be breached," Cornelius scoffed.

"Then we'll begin in more accessible locations." She threatened. But, almost immediately, she softened. "You know what we want. Child, make me a deal and bring this all to an end."

"We already did, the Battle of Four. You broke it," Lady Mauve crossed her arms and frowned.

"Watch out, shhhh, move it, hey, coming through." Greg and Marcy pushed their way through the upstairs crowd. They shoved in beside me, pushing aside the girl who'd brought me along this far.

"What'd we miss?" Greg half-whispered.

I shook my head. "Shhh. I don't know. We only just got here ourselves."

We looked down at the garden below.

"I wasn't speaking with you," Natalia snapped at Mauve. The women glared back and forth.

"You can't hold us captive, then act like it's a barter," Cornelius scoffed.

"Thus far we've restrained, but I can't promise they'll hold course."

"*Restrained,*" Marcy scoffed. "Please."

Our second floor hideout shushed her.

"We are running out of time," Natalia told the High Council leaders. "We need to act now."

"I told you, it's not happening."

"Then difficult times will rain down. We have our strengths."

The threat hung in the air.

"If you breach these walls, you'll come against the full force of the High Council," our leader countered. A few students in our second floor crowd let out a small cheer. It drew the elder's eyes.

"Get back inside," barked Lady Mauve.

Our group, now discovered, stood and started to follow instructions. But me and some of the others stayed to listen more.

"The battle won't start on your doorstep. There are other, weaker locations. Non-coven members," Natalia said. "We can start with their homes. Work our way up. Remind you what's at stake."

The elders didn't flinch. But my heart sunk in my chest.

"What non-coven members are they even talking about?" Marcy wondered.

But Beck and I knew right away.

There were two, high profile, non-coven members who'd directly helped in the Battle of Four against the Damocles coven. Marcy might not have known it, but I did. Because I'd called them for help. They had joined the battle at my bidding.

Beck and I locked eyes. At the same time, we spoke.

"Josie!"

"My aunt!"

SIX

PICK UP… PICK UP!

"WE SAID *GET INSIDE*," the elders ordered, waving up to our floor.

"Lock that down," Lady Mauve instructed other fellows on the concourse. "Get them out of there." The men she was speaking to took off inside. I ducked out of her view, but I didn't head for the halls.

"Mae-" across the group of students who were begrudgingly heading back inside the castle, Ferris came straight for me. She'd clearly had the same perilous thought. Josie and Aunt Abeline were in great danger. Her arched eyebrow said it all. Both Beck and I understood. We had already frantically grabbed our cell phones and called our loved ones, me, Aunt Abeline, he his ex-girlfriend.

Instead of moving back inside, we walked further down the balcony concourse. My aunt's number rang three times.

Pick up. Pick up.

No answer.

"Straight to voicemail," I told the others. "No answer."

"Josie didn't either," Beck told me, lowering his phone.

"Come on," I said. We were already leaving. I wasn't sure if they would object after the contracts that we signed, but Beck and Ferris were already coming. "Will you drive?" I asked. Ferris nodded.

"Stop right there!" A man's voice shouted somewhere behind us, still in the distance.

"Come on," I totally ignored him, taking control. Beck and Ferris hurried after.

"Where are you going?" Greg asked as we departed, but we just ran along the terrace floor, away from the front entrance meeting spot of the High Council elders, towards the gardens and the parking lots at the back of the grounds. The wrap-around balcony extended the whole second floor.

"You up for adventure?" He asked Marcy.

"Babe, I'm up for anything." So they followed at the rear of our pack.

We picked up speed, until we were full on running, turning the first corner out of sight before any fellows breeched the balcony's second floor.

"There." I pointed to the ivy.

"Up and over," Ferris agreed, taking her turn at leading the team.

I glanced at Beck, but neither of us hesitated. If the Damocles witches were threatening Abeline and Josie, we had to go protect our clan. Whatever some paper said. When everyone was safe, we could deal with those consequences.

As we lowered ourselves over the ledge onto the green ladder, Greg and Marcy climbed out above our heads. We spider-climbed our way down the trellis and vines 'til we landed on the grass.

"What are you doing?" I stopped them.

"We're coming with you," Greg panted. Marcy nodded.

"What? No. You can't. That's too many missing. The Council will notice."

"Uh-uh. You don't get to have all the fun while we sit on our butts at home," Greg snapped.

"Not again," Marcy nodded.

"My aunt is in trouble," I spat back. "The Damocles just threatened her life. Weren't you listening? This isn't some joke."

"So we'll help."

"To do precisely what?" Ferris stood by my side ready to back up my play, whichever way that I chose.

"He has a car, Mae." Beck interrupted. "We'll split up. I gotta check on Jo."

For a moment, I was surprised. He wasn't coming to help with Aunt Abeline? But of course, we had to keep both of them safe. That meant splitting up. So, I had to do my part alone.

No. Not alone.

Ferris was helping. And Greg and Marcy would help Beck. I would have liked to have him stay by my side. But, he was right. Josie might also need help. He had to go there.

"Fine." I spit. "You go with Beck. But, wherever he goes, he's the boss. You do what he says."

"Yes, ma'am'." Greg gave a fake salute, but I didn't stick around to play his game. Ferris and I were already off and running. We piled into her car at full speed. I dialed the number for my aunt again.

"Pick up," I told her, but the real Aunt Abeline didn't co-operate. All I got was her machine.

You've reached the freelance office of Abeline Kingsley. Leave a message and I'll return soon as I can.

"Aunt Abeline, if you get this, do not go back to the lake house. Leave Plumpkin. Get out of town. Go somewhere safe. There are..." I stumbled, "bad people coming." That was generic. But I still had to warn her. "They're dangerous. Very dangerous. Stay far away. I'll tell you more when I can."

As Ferris drove, I followed up with a text.

Lake house not safe. Get out now. Leave Plumpkin. Don't trust anyone. Call me ASAP.

. . .

The messages sent. I lowered my phone to my lap. That was all I could do. But still, it felt like nothing. What if I was already too late? Who knew where Aunt Abeline was, or what dangers she'd face? I stared straight ahead. The ride felt like it took forever. Ferris looked over in my direction, to check on me, but she didn't say a word and her foot never let up on the gas. Numbly, I watched the scenery fly by. What sort of trouble had I brought to the door of my aunt?

"We'll get there soon," she finally told me.

I nodded, dumbly.

The farmlands raced by in a blur. I didn't have proof something was happening. It was possible the Damocles were just building on empty threats. I hadn't even heard their entire conversation. Aunt Abeline could be out gardening, or down by the water. She just might not have heard her phone and all might be perfectly good when we arrived. But the pit in my stomach didn't dissipate. There was a much more likely possibility that even now, as we drove across the county lines, the Damocles coven might be descending on my sweet, unsuspecting family member in the safety of her home.

This was totally my fault.

Because of me, she was at in trouble. At least that seemed to be the way the Damocles thought. I was the one who had asked her for help in the Battle. At the time, I'd thought it was clever. She and Josie were never High Council members, but they had some witchy skills. Coven members could not interfere in the battle, but, outsiders weren't as restricted. When I contacted Josie and my aunt, I had never considered I might have put a target on their backs. Or a price on their heads.

I texted Beck.

Any luck over there?

Still no answer. He wrote back. *Almost at her house.*

I fidgeted with the phone, willing the highway trip to shorten. But like Beck said, we were almost there.

"It's the next left," I told Ferris, even though she likely knew that. As we crested the final, familiar hill before the cottage laneway, we could already see that we were right to fear. There were emergency vehicles parked all the way out to the highway. While their sirens were off, their cherry lights still lit up the forest with red and blue waves. A police officer stood guard at the laneway, blocking traffic from entering the rural road.

"No," I murmured. This was what we'd feared, but it seemed like a dream. "No, they can't be stopping things." My eyes took in everything at once.

Ferris pulled off on the side of the road as close as she could to the lane. Before she had the car in park, I was already out of my seat, running for home.

"Mae, wait!" Ferris followed.

I didn't bother with the road. Instead, I headed to the forest. The police officers couldn't stop me there. I ran down the path through the woods that I'd known since I was a kid. Today I couldn't care less about the wild growing raspberries, or the other thorny plants. It was a path that would end two houses from my home. I must have walked it a thousand times. Today, I raced through the trees, my feet flying over roots and exposed rocks that threatened to trip me, but it didn't matter. I didn't slow. As I broke through the foliage by our house, I could see, it was worse than I imagined.

"Oh my god."

Down our street there were more emergency vehicles, but they couldn't get too close to my family's plot of land. Or what was left of it. The whole tract had collapsed into a hole. The earth was swallowing the cabin. The building's walls were topsy turvy, collapsed and fallen, broken, tumbling, clinging to the surface, their innards falling into a giant crevice in the ground.

"What the hell?" Ferris caught me. Her eyes widened in surprise.

It was like a crater had opened under the footings of my house. The earth had split and ravaged the cottage foundation. Rescue crews were examining the hole, poking and prodding from all directions. But it was clearly to unstable and unsafe to go inside. Half of the screened in porch and the kitchen were gone. The back half of our home, Aunt Abeline's bedroom, tottered dangerously above another fault line. The blonde hair and red robes of the rival coven were missing, but I knew immediately it was their harness who had opened this hole. An empath of the earth. I'd seen him do it before. Cause craters and earthquakes. But today, he had crushed my whole world. Every item my family held dear was scattered throughout the holes.

But where was Aunt Abeline?

"Aunt Abeline!" I shouted, crashing through the remains of the final plants, careful not to stumble. "Where is she?!" My eyes searched wildly around. I drew as close as I could to the crater.

"Whoa. Hey now. Who are you looking for?" A bearded officer, looking far too formal in head-to-toe uniform slowed me. He held his arms up with a frown.

"My aunt. This is her house. Where's Aunt Abeline?" I didn't stop moving.

"Abeline Kingsley," Ferris offered behind me.

The officer didn't lower his hands, as if he thought his overly calm demeanor could rub off on me as well. It didn't. "No one was harmed in the tremor," he told me.

I tried to move on, but he kept ground.

"Abeline!" I shouted up and over his shoulders. I tried to push by.

"Whoa. Please be careful," he followed, trying to reign me in. "You cannot get close."

But I just kept on moving. "Abeline!"

Around us, behind us, a crowd was starting to form.

"She wasn't inside," he repeated.

But the feeling of dread built even taller inside me. They'd over-looked a simple truth. "If she's not in there, she'd be out here!" I told him.

"Where is she?" Ferris tried to bridge our communication. "Have you seen the woman who lives here?"

"I told you, the woman wasn't here." He shrugged. "She's probably running errands. What a horror show to come home to. Did you try her on her phone? For these parts, tectonic plate movements are incredibly rare." He let out a low whistle. "Just wait 'til she gets home."

But Ferris and I were not fooled by this classification. We both knew a freak earthquake didn't cause this disaster. It was the work of the Damocles clan.

Helpless, I checked my phone again.

Still nothing from Abeline.

I knew that wasn't like my aunt.

Presenting as more calm, I moved away from the officer, trying to get a better sightline into the wreckage.

"I can't let you go in there. It's for your protection," he grew more gruff. Like he knew what I was thinking.

The only message I had was from Beck.

Josie's safe. She's with us.

I breathed a small sigh of relief, but I couldn't shake the feeling about my aunt. It was simple. If my aunt was alright, she would have called or texted me back. She would be here, by my side.

None of the emergency personnel had tried to enter the house. They hadn't explored to be sure. Didn't even know where to look.

"I'm going in," I told Ferris.

"She's not inside," she shook me off. "The officers looked."

"There's a stairwell. To a bunker. Deep underground. My mom's old hideout. If Aunt Abeline sensed coming danger, she would have gone there. They," I gestured to the emergency crews, "don't even know it exists. She would have hid, Ferris. Deep underground. There's no way she could have known they'd attack with an earthquake."

"It's too dangerous. Tell the firemen about the hideout."

"No. I'm going. With or without your help."

She nodded. We both knew, it's what she would have done as well. "I'll help."

When the cop wasn't looking our way, I hurried forward to a broken window.

"Hey, no. You can't go in there!" The officer spun around, but Ferris balled her hand into a fist. She held it by her side and created an alternate lie-guard vision.

"You mean my friend?" She called him back. Confused, the officer looked up. "She's headed out to our car. In case she gets better reception" Ferris gestured to a shadowy figure that looked a lot like me disappearing into the depths of field. A lie-guard illusion she had built. The mirage walked away from the scene, a smart idea, since it meant the ruse wouldn't need maintaining.

The officer pushed his cap up on his head, certain he'd seen me go in. But there I went, or there went my fancy new illusion, through the forest and out of his sight range. "She went to her car," he reconfirmed the story she'd told him.

Ferris smiled sweetly. "I'll wait here," she told him.

The officer nodded.

In the opposite direction, I lowered myself down through a broken living room window, onto a collapsed shelf. We'd spent so many nights casually curled up around the fire, reading marvelous books, playing in-depth games of Scrabble, but now, I barely recognized the room. Everything comfortable and secure about our family home felt like it had been stuffed into a plastic bottle and shaken by a three-year-old's hands. Nothing still stood where it used to, dangerous wiring and smashed lighting hung down off the walls. The floors were littered with debris and broken glass. The ceilings creaked with unease as I passed. The fire crews were correct. It seemed, with even the slightest of breeze, the whole room might come crashing down, or worse, disappear forever into the ground.

"Aunt Abeline? Are you in here?" I tentatively called.

I inched my way forward. An array of sparks sputtered out of an outlet to my right. I ducked, but the fire didn't catch hold. The large black fireplace in the center of the room groaned on its side. The whole room had sunk and was tilted on a steep angle down. The black stove leaned forward, out of its walled home, the ash from the floor gate fluttering out. "Aunt Abeline? It's Mae. Where are you? Call if you can hear me. I'll move towards your voice." I was greeted by nothing but silence. Still, I moved forward.

I looked towards the kitchen, but the front of the house had been crushed.

"I'm coming back," I told her, crossing the trembling threshold. I kept my body lowered to the subfloor. The safety and assurance of the earlier foundation was totally destroyed. Every step seemed to groan under my weight. There was no way to be sure where to stand. I tested each floorboard before making my way. Progress was slow. When the boards didn't creak with too much urgency, I crept across the living room, picking my way back to the guest bedroom and the secret tunnel deep into the basement.

Crack!

Suddenly, the whole building lurched. The wood framing around me bounced. I braced myself in the hallway, and watched as the ceiling swayed. A cloud of dust and drywall filtered down. There was no way to tell how long the cabin's framework would hold out. The cabin's origin story was showing, decades ago, log-by-log built by hand. I was only halfway across.

"Mae, hurry!" Ferris called through the broken window.

"Almost there," I replied, although that was a lie.

I fought my way back through the house, but the hallway wasn't passable. A gash had ripped apart the floor. Splintered wood jutted up, razor sharp, dividing the house apart. Through the crevice I could see the ground had split deep into the earth. I couldn't see how subterranean it went, but I could ascertain the width. There was some good news there. As luck would have it, the fault line hit the lower bunker as well as the upper levels, and part of the secret shelter's guts spilled out in the same hole. My mother's hideout had suffered a fairly large quake. One side now hung open, with nothing to stop it from dropping off into the earth.

I could see, the bookshelf, usually so upright, neat, and orderly had tumbled into the gash in the ground, smashed into pieces, and was collapsing like a bridge. Books and contents were strewn inside the hole. Papers and debris were everywhere, mixed with broken, jagged shelves and detritus that covered the rocky ground. It was a mess. A decorative moon and star pillow, lovingly stitched by Grandma Mim teetered, precarious, on the far edge of a dangling couch.

Crack, crack!

Everything around me shifted. The whole structure shuddered, and the floor under my feet dropped four inches down. I grabbed at the walls for safety, but the sheetrock cracked. A tear raced across the dry-wall boards.

It was definitely time to go.

"Aunt Abeline, are you in there?"

The house heaved once more. I held on to the bathroom doorframe, not that it could save me if the entire house were suddenly sucked deep into the earth. But I didn't care. I would get what I came for.

"Abeline! Abeline Kingsley!"

The walls moaned, but no one replied.

The officer had been right. My aunt wasn't inside.

I'd gone as far as I could.

"I'm coming out," I called to Ferris. Being just as careful to pick my spots on the way back, I began to move in reverse. The house felt even more precarious, like even one out-of-place step could send the whole thing crumbling into the void.

Ohhhh.

At first, I thought the timber was letting out another sigh, no longer able to carry the load it was built to hold.

Ohhhh.

But it didn't come from above. The moan was deep underground.

A woman's moan.

"She's here!" I shouted. I wasn't sure, but also I felt certain. Deep in my bones. "Aunt Abeline, I'm coming for you! Hold on. I'm on my way down!"

The moans petered off, but I knew what I heard. I raced back to the chasm entrance. As I hurried, one foot crunched through a weak spot in the floor. I slammed through the boards, up to a knee, but pulled my appendage free.

"Abeline, where are you? Talk to me, make more noise."

I moved forward more slowly, with renewed respect for the chaos around me, but still, I headed back down the hall. The wall on my left let out a shuddering sigh. The doorway, which moments before I had used to brace myself, was now dramatically bowed. The whole house was seizing inwards. There was no time to wait for more signs.

Ohhhh.

The moan was definitely below ground. I felt pretty sure of what happened. My instinct was right. When the Damocles witches came, Aunt Abeline had indeed hid in the bunker below the cottage. But, if you were trying to escape an earth harness, underground was the worst place you could go.

"Hold on Aunt Abeline, I'm coming."

There was no way to get to the guest bedroom. The space held the secret stairs, but I doubted that they still offered a clear passage to take me down. Too many other things around me were unrecognizable and mangled. It would be impossible to cross the hallway and get to the bunker from that direction, but I could go straight underground. I could climb out of the moaning, groaning structure and traverse across the dirt below the foundation and go down to bunker level. Then enter through the gash in the wall.

"I got this," I whispered to pump myself up, bending low on the edge of the splintered subfloor to pick out my new path. "Aunt Abeline, I'm on my way."

Crack!

Something heavy shifted. Two walls tumbled. The ceiling lurched.

There wasn't time to pick a perfect route. I dropped my feet over the sawdust and swung my legs into the hole. It wasn't like wall-climbing, exactly, more like traversing peaks and valleys on a precarious, crumbling road, but I ducked and moved forward, keeping close to the wall as I descended underground.

Clumps of the earth above me tumbled into the crevice. Pieces of our former home bounced and scattered off the dirt walls. Their ricochets echoed a great distance below. It was a long drop to the bottom.

Crack, crack!

Suddenly, the entire living room smashed above me, the wall of hallway disintegrated, raining large chunks of sheetrock and projectiles into the hole. I hugged the ledge and shielded my face. When I looked back, through the jagged opening, I could see the entire contents of the room were now sliding towards me. The floor was giving way. In moments, the furniture and other items would rain down where I clung to the ground.

The largest, and heaviest among them was the iron fireplace.

It heaved uneasily in my direction.

The fire proof doors swung back and forth, taunting me. The only thing stopping it from smashing right through the room was its bending, twisting chimney stack still affixed to the ceiling above. It creaked and groaned but held.

I had to go on.

More in the living room above me shuddered, but this time I didn't pause to take in the scene. Above me, I heard it.

*Jig-jig-*The stove pipe was stretching, the weight of its body dragging it down, unmoored. The pipe stretched taut. The weight niggling at its joint.

Ohhh.

Aunt Abeline's voice floated more clearly. I was almost on par with her floor.

I reached out toward the couch, half dangling in the entry, but it couldn't hold me, with my added weight the thing teetered out. The embroidered pillow I'd seen earlier tumbled into darkness. This was it. The hole in the bunker where it met the gash in the floor.

Almost met.

There was a three-foot drop between where I stood and the exposed floor. There weren't any more hand holds or pathways, I would have to make the jump from there.

"Here goes nothing." I murmured, steeling my nerve. I steadied myself and leapt across the hole. My fingers scrambled on the other side, looking for some-thing to hold. I landed, but the momentum bounced me. I slipped backwards, dragging the couch out with me, unable to stop my own fall.

"No, no!"

Luckily, the sofa got lodged in the hole. I smashed down on top of it, but the cushiony chair held. Wedged between the crevice walls, I shoved off its bolstered back and scrambled into the bunker. In my hurry, I smushed my thumb against my Mom's old photo album, skittering it across the room. "Ow!" I yelped pulling back. But it wasn't the only important thing on the floor.

"Aunt Abeline!" I cried. As soon as I was safely in the bunker, I saw the crumpled body of my aunt. She was trapped, pinned helpless under the weight of a heavy table whose legs had snapped in the tremor. "I've got you," I told her, pushing the table top with all my strength. It barely moved an inch. I couldn't free her. The furniture was made of solid wood. I wasn't strong enough alone to lift it, but Aunt Abeline was in no condition to help. She wasn't aware of her surroundings, only semi-conscious of what was happening, her breathing was very shallow.

Quietly, she moaned.

Her chest looked crushed. I didn't like the sight of her leg bones. Even if I shoved the table off, there was no way she could walk her way out. She couldn't even acknowledge I was there.

"Aunt Abeline, can you hear me?"

Her silence scared me most of all. Her breath was narrow and scraggly. In her chest, something rattled along. She needed serious medical attention. I had to get her out.

"Ferris! I found her!" I shouted, although I could no longer see up to the window where I'd entered.

"Mae, the whole place is gonna go!"

"We're both down here in the bunker. But I can't lift her. And a table has got her pinned."

"Where is she?!" Tears sprung to my eyes at the sound of a new panicked, joining voice. Beck! "Mae, I'm coming."

"You can't go in there!" Ferris fought him off.

"Yes, I can."

"No, you can't!" She held strong. Maybe used her powers against him. "The weight will crash the whole building down. Mae's underneath in a bunker. We don't want the top floor to land on their heads. Mae," she shouted out to me. "I've been holding them off, but I'm gonna let it go, unleash the emergency crews. Tell them where you are. Can they find you and pull you out?"

"I don't know." I looked around helpless. "I don't know!" I shouted once more. I picked up Aunt Abeline's limp hand. There was barely a pulse. "Aunt Abeline, do you hear me? You have to hold on. We're gonna get you outta here," I told her. "I don't know!" I shouted out loud.

"Mae, it's Josie! You're in the bunker you showed me?"

That was right, in what felt like another lifetime, I'd invited Josie in to see the lower level of this home.

"Yes!"

"How badly damaged?"

I looked around. "One side is collapsed. The wall has crumbled. Most is still good." Amazingly, in the underground structure the infrastructure had protected the bunker from most of the tremors made by the harnessing witch. I ran to check the stairwell, but my initial impressions were dead on.

The stairs were untenable.

Debris had clouded the hallway and most of the treads were unsafe now or gone.

It didn't matter anyway, Aunt Abeline couldn't walk herself out.

"The stairs are shot to hell!"

"Most hideouts have a second exit. One that leads outwards, in case the owners need a quick escape," Josie told me.

I spun around.

I had spent hours and hours hanging in Mom's hideout and never spotted a second trap door. But she did have a knack for thinking ahead. And she loved all things secret.

"I don't know," I worried, checking around.

"I didn't see it when you showed me, so if it's there, it's going to be hidden."

The building shuddered.

From the cottage, the entry to this bunker was camouflaged in deceptive floorboards, covered with a rug. Maybe the second exit out was hidden in the same manner as well? I hurried room to room checking all the floor coverings, tossing them aside, but no flooring held a secret door.

"I don't know!" I called up. "I don't see any..."

"Mae, you have to get out of there," Beck pleaded.

"I can't find the-"

Phoom!

The whole building exploded.

No. Not exploded. Collapsed.

A giant cloud of dust kicked up in the air as the room fell pitch black. I dove to protect my aunt, covering her face and chest as best I could, waiting for the impact to hit, but the bunker held firm. After the deafening crash came several layers of wood, brick, drywall, shingles and a smattering of other items piling up in the hole, filling it in.

Then, there was nothing.

Slowly, the dust cleared. But no light entered the bunker.

Instead, an eerie quiet set in.

Aunt Abeline and I were trapped below ground.

SEVEN

READ A BOOK

I RAISED up off my aunt's limp frame and sat back on my heels to take in the damage.

She barely moaned.

"It's okay," I told her. "I'm gonna get you out." But the belief had drained from my voice.

The room was pitch black.

"Beck!... Ferris!... Josie!..." I shouted each of their names one by one, but the earth and debris stopped the words from carrying to my friends above. Quickly, I pulled out my phone. The screen shone bright, but there wasn't a signal. We were too deep in the ground.

I couldn't call them.

They couldn't hear me.

They had no way of knowing we'd survived the collapse.

How long could we last, alone in the bunker? If the filled hole had sealed us underground, soon the oxygen would run out.

I spun my phone's glow around to take in the damage. Even with the light, I couldn't see more than three feet in front of my face in any direction. A cloud of dust had made the atmosphere thick. Dirt covered all the objects in the room in a filthy new coating, but the space hadn't sustained much more damage itself.

Why hadn't I dreamed of any of this? I wondered.

As a dreamcast, I was supposed to see the future in clues and abstract images while I slept. I'd gotten into the habit of recording my dreams' phrases and images in a notebook on my nightstand the minute I woke up. But last night, my only vision was of someone peacefully reading a book. Not a relevant image. But I guess I shouldn't have been shocked. My witch powers had always seemed... well... unreliable might be an accurate word choice.

Aunt Abeline was a wind harness, though her empathic skills had never been formally named or trained. Still, she was naturally talented and in the Battle of Four, she had proven it. Even untrained and untested, the women in our family were naturally witches. Magic ran in my bloodline. Not that her powers could help us now. I wouldn't even be able to get her to ball up her palm. She needed serious medical treatment.

Beck and Josie's powers also couldn't help me. As a weather harness and a chemist, neither could dig in the ground. Ferris' skills were more open-ended, but it would take ingenious vision on her part to come up with an illusion that would help save us. Still, I held on to hope.

Aunt Abeline and I would get out.

I felt it in my bones.

Just before the collapse, Josie had suggested there might be a secret passage. That made sense. In times of fear, the initial instinct would be to hide, but if a siege was held for any length of time, the ability to sneak out undercover would become a real asset. It seemed like something my family, the very people who went through the trouble of building the lake house and the hideout, might have added to their plans.

"Don't fail us now," I murmured to the previous Kingsley generations.

I'd checked all the floors before the house came crashing down. Now, I felt along the walls. Any weird lump, nook or cranny I thoroughly explored. At first I used the light to guide me, but I couldn't see much of anything to help. I decided to pocket the phone and save the battery while I could. Instead, I felt around the rooms.

Since I couldn't trust my eyes. I had to rely on my other senses, running my hands over the walls I'd seen so many times before. In movies, people tapped on plumbing pipes to let people above ground know they were still alive, but here all the plumbing was self-contained inside the hole. The toilet was compostable, so was the sink. No pipes and no plumbing ran up to the surface. There was no way to get the word out to the rescue crews above. Still, I felt confident my friends would be working hard, doing everything they could from the ground level.

I would see those beautiful faces again, I told myself, doing my best to keep my own spirits up. There was no way I'd seen the last of Beck.

I ran my hands blindly along the paneling.

Maybe I should do what my dreaming told me, I mused, and read a book. I had a light. If I could find the right book to read, maybe there'd be instructions. Fate could guide me to the page I'd need. I'd just open it up and poof! All our problems would be solved.

I must have been starting to get loopy because the thought of that almost made me laugh. Maybe we really were running out of fresh air.

But, why discount any idea?

I often misinterpreted what my dreams were about. If I'd seen a novel in my dreams, what harm could it do to find one now? I didn't have a better idea. I went to pull a book off the shelf. Only... the bookshelf wasn't there. The original quake had knocked it out of the room and the large pieces had broken apart.

I had seen it shattered in the hole.

But now I remembered smacking into Mom's old photo album as I entered the bunker.

It had fallen off the shelf and landed somewhere on the floor. I couldn't see it. It wasn't a novel, but it did had book dimensions. Was I supposed to look through those photos? I'd seen them so many times before. I flipped on my phone light and quickly found the album. I cracked it open. Sierra and Abeline smiled hello from the familiar photos of the early days of their family. The pictures looked eerie now, in the low light and harsh phone glow. Mom and her sister. I quickly flipped through each of the pages, but nothing helpful jumped out. I slammed it shut in frustration. Using the light, I stared around. There weren't any other texts. All the other books had split open on the rocky ledges in the hole. I remembered the flutter of papers.

It was strange that the bookshelf fell, actually.

Usually, a structure as large as that would have been fastened onto the wall. It was dangerous to leave such a heavy piece of furniture unmoored. Unless, you often intended to move it... like when you wanted to use it to hide a door.

The bookshelf was definitely large enough to hide a secret passage behind!

Excitedly, I hurried back to Aunt Abeline and I brushed the hair from her face. "I'm gonna get you out," I told her.

Thin, wheezy breath was her only reply.

I shone the light over where the books had once stood and laid my hands on the bare wall behind the missing shelf. My fingers slid left and right. The surface was flat but there was a break in the wall. I pushed on the seam and part of the facade hissed and opened. It popped backwards, revealing a secret latch.

Josie was right!

There was a hidden passage out of the bunker. Back up to the woods.

I shoved the door open and blindly rushed ahead

into the corridor behind it. Thankfully, the tunnel was built in a direction leading away from the earthquake's impact, and the secret exit to and from the hideout was still solidly intact.

I didn't bother with the light. I just ran. Fast as I could, holding protective arms out in front of myself. But there was nothing to stumble over. A vertical strip of light at the end of the shaft beckoned me forward. I raced towards it. At the mouth of the exit were two large metal doors. Through the crack in between, I could see sunlight peeking through the forest, shining into the tunnel.

Freedom!

I tried to shove the door open but it was too heavy to move on my own. Untouched for so long in the forest, a heavy growth of brambles had grown over-top. I could see their gnarled branches as I forced it open a crack. The weight of the brush was too strong to push open. But all I needed was a crack.

"Help! Over here!" I shouted, pushing at the door with all my might. "Beck!" I called him. Banging on the metal. "Josie! Ferris! Help!" I smashed my shoulder into the door. "Anybody! Aunt Abeline needs help!" I didn't know where I was exactly, but I felt confident the tunnel had brought me up beside the laneway in the forest nearby. There were enough people milling about the disaster that as long as I kept yelling, I was sure to be found. "Over here!"

"This way!" I heard Ferris running.

"Hey!!!" I banged some more.

Other voices and heavy footsteps crashed through the woods. I collapsed in the doorway, still trapped below ground. I watched as the rescue team arrived to save us, all through the crack in the metal doors.

Beck yanked off the brambles. "Mae, we're here! We're coming."

His voice brought a lump to my throat.

I stifled a cry, but relief overcame me.

Someone else threw open the doors. Mid-afternoon sun flooded the tunnel. Immediately, I was embraced in Beck's arms.

"Paramedics," I cried. "Someone. Hurry. My aunt. She's down there. You need a light. She's too weak to get up off the floor. It's bad. I couldn't lift her. I don't know what's wrong." What felt like a thousand arms reached in and helped me to safety while still others ran back down the tunnel ramp I'd just climbed. Official crews headed in with their gurneys and supplies. In all, there were dozens of people trying to help. Rescue teams, nosy onlookers, and friends surrounded us. They pulled me clear and breached the tunnel, trained for the chaos they'd find. I wanted to stay and help, do something, be more productive, but my body was so exhausted they easily led me out. Beck carried me out of the fray to a waiting ambulance. I tried to wave them off, but a paramedic checked my vitals.

My head was swimming, my body was shaking, but I tried to tell them I was coming around. "I'm fine, help my aunt."

"Don't you worry. We're helping her as well." The

paramedic gave me oxygen and wrapped a blanket around my shoulders. He tried to get me to lie down, but I wasn't willing to bend. I insisted on watching as they retrieved her. Aunt Abeline came out of the tunnel on a stretcher.

"No." I tried to get up. "I should be with her."

Paramedics worked furiously, as they carted her to another waiting ambulance van.

I felt a huge shiver. All the hair on my arms stood on end.

Someone was watching.

A lot of someones.

My aunt and I were the centre of the world. The disaster's victims and survivors. Of course we were the macabre show on the street. But it was more than that. I had a creepy, awful feeling that someone who shouldn't be there was there. Watching. Waiting.

"Aunt Abeline," I murmured.

I tried to look around but Beck and the paramedic slipped from sight. A darkness took over.

"Where's she going?" I wondered. "Where are we?"

I slipped in and out of consciousness.

I reached out and felt Beck's large, rough palm.

"Wait, wha- where are we going?"

"They're taking her to the hospital," the paramedic told me, packing me into the back of the car. Beck held my hand. "We're headed there now."

EIGHT

THE SECONDS TICKED OFF

IN MY DREAM, faceless men and women marched in orchestrated patterns. Row upon row, with clear places to go.

Destinations in mind.

They swung their arms in quick motions, propelling themselves forward. Marching in rhythmic sequence. Holding their heads high.

Large clock faces adorned their backs and ticked the seconds off, round and round the little hands went. Shoulder to shoulder, the timepieces pulsed forward, counting the minutes, seconds, and hours although none showed the same exact time. Although the people all marched in tandem, every timepiece was different.

I observed their never-ending movements and walked in between them, although no one seemed to note I was there.

On and on, they marched forward.

The clocks on their backs.
Suddenly, I sat up where I lay.

NINE

I WANNA SEE AUNT ABELINE

"HEY, PARABOND," Beck's kind eyes came into focus. "There you are."

I was laying in a hospital bed, the white sheets tucked up to my chin. An IV bag hung beside me, the tube in my arm. Computers around me whirred in repetitive patterns, tracking my vital signs.

"You passed out," he told me, shuffling a hand through his hair. "That was quite a rescue. How do you feel?"

"How's Aunt Abeline?" I wondered.

Beck smiled. "I'll take that as a good sign."

I tried to sit up, but things still felt woozy. "Is she alright?"

"It's complicated. The doctor said she's stable, for now, but he said something about the chest compression, and the weight against her ribs. I'm not sure. You both gave us quite a scare." He tried to take my hand.

"I wanna see her," I said, pulling back. He looked a

bit hurt, but not surprised. I fought with the tubes and wires fed into my arms. "Ow."

"Hold on. Don't do that yourself. I'll get a nurse."

I flopped my head back on the pillow. What was happening? We'd gotten out. Beck's words were quite uncertain, but Aunt Abeline had to be alright. I got her out. That couldn't be our last Scrabble game. She wasn't allowed to go.

Especially not like that.

Another coven purposefully attacking my family? And for what? To send a message to my coven's elders? The Council elders didn't care about me. But the Damocles couldn't hurt them, so instead they hurt my aunt. What a bunch of cowards.

At least Josie was alright.

I remembered hearing her voice. She was above ground with Ferris and Beck, above me in the hideout. She must have escaped from the Damocles' grasp. I hoped they hadn't torn apart her home. These women didn't deserve what had happened to them. They only became involved in the head-to-head battle because I'd asked them for help. They did it for me as a favor. They had no idea what the battle was about. Any injury to either of them, any destruction, would be directly my fault.

I will make this up to you, I promised.

"Hello, Mae. Welcome back," a chipper woman in her late forties with pink, cheery scrubs and tight black curls blew into the room. Beck trailed her.

"I want to see my aunt."

"Uh huh. I know. Well, soon enough." She checked several readings then glanced at my chart. "Any pain? Lasting nausea?"

"I'm fine."

"Well, that's good to hear." Satisfied with my healing development, she slid the IV out of my arm. "Have you been seen by Dr. Barth?"

I shook my head, pensively rubbing my newly free arm.

"Okay, well, you'll have to stay until he can officially release you. But not to worry, I don't think they'll need to observe you overnight. Everything looks good. We just need to wait on the all clear. In the meantime, I don't see why you couldn't visit her. Abeline's lucky to be alive. Your quick thinking may have saved her life."

I got her into and out of the trouble, I acknowledged to myself. To the well-meaning nurse, I merely nodded. "So, she's alright."

"Well, no. But she's better than she was," the nurse acknowledged. "You can show her where she's at?" The woman checked with Beck.

He nodded, shoving his hands into his pockets.

"Alright. A quick hello, then you're back here to get signed out." She tapped my blanketed leg, gave us both a warm smile then continued to work on her rounds.

I pulled the sheets back.

"I'll let you change," Beck noted.

I realized someone had stripped me and tucked me

into a hospital gown. My clothes were folded neatly on an empty chair. I shook my head. "I need to see her now."

Beck understood. "This way."

The hospital gown wrapped tightly around me and didn't leave any gaps, but the material was light and airy. It felt odd to walk so openly through the halls. As we left the privacy of the room, I again felt a strange sensation of being watched. My hair stood on end.

"Do you feel that?" I wondered.

"What?"

"I don't know. Something... off."

"You're still in shock," he warned.

We looked around, but Beck was right. There was nothing strange or out of the ordinary where we stood.

"I just want to see her. See for myself."

"Mae, you should prepare," he told me. But he didn't stop my path. "In here." Beck pushed open the door just as a blond doctor with red scrubs and a stethoscope was coming out. He was so busy making chart notations he barely noticed us. I was surprised by the piercing blue eyes in his face. But the second I saw my aunt, I forgot all about the handsome doctor and rushed to her side.

"Aunt Abeline!"

She was unconscious. Her eyes didn't flicker. The nurse was right, she looked rough. A tube was lodged in her throat. Other machines whirred all around her. It was pretty clear, she wasn't stable on her own.

Gently, I took her hand in mine. It was warm to the touch. At least that was a good sign.

"I'll give you a minute," Beck said. He backed out and closed us in by ourselves. As he departed I shot him a grateful smile.

"I'm here," I told her, brushing the tendrils from her temples, looking down at her closed eyes. She looked almost gray. "You gave me such a scare. I'm so sorry, about all of this. I never should have gotten you involved. It's all my fault. I'm so glad you're alright."

My unconscious aunt didn't respond. Just lay there, still and small, her fragile body unmoving on the bed. I looked at the needles in her arm. The stiff sheets of the bed. The never-ending beeps of the dials.

Suddenly, I retched.

Once, twice in my throat.

The sensations were all too much to bear.

I ran to the bathroom and threw up in the toilet. It took three violent hurls to empty my stomach, and several more dry heaves before my nervous system calmed. I gripped the porcelain basin and tried to stop my arms from shaking.

Waves of familiarity crashed down.

I had been here before.

For days at a time. I'd already lived this life.

Clutching the warm hand of the most important woman in my life.

I'd already played this all out. With Sierra in the bed. Now it was happening again.

The unknown illness.

The sick hospital plight.

The sights and sounds and the emotions.

I was much younger then, but everything else repeated the same.

I spit in the sink and rinsed out my mouth. I caught sight of myself in the over-the-sink mirror. In the white, cotton robe, I was totally washed out. I cupped my brown hair behind my ear and went back out to my aunt. I sat by her side.

"Sorry about that," I jokingly told her.

'That's alright,' I wanted her to chuckle. *'Your body is just reacting to unpleasant stimuli. Oh, that's a good seven-letter word. I should remember that for the board. Don't worry, Mae. It's been a tough day for us all.'* Instead, she lay silent in bed, unresponsive.

The same raven-haired nurse popped her head in the room.

"How's our patient doing?" she asked, carrying a sippy cup of juice. She passed it to me, going straight to my aunt. She checked her vitals.

"Will she wake up?" I looked down at the liquid. Hopeful.

"That's for you, dear, not her. Gotta get your strength up." The woman had an efficiency to her hands, but a kind tone in her voice. She had comforted a lot of families, I could tell.

"Can you explain to me what's wrong?" Obediently, I drank the juice. It tasted better than vomit.

"Typically, we let the doctor fill you in. But you should know, it's a complicated case. We might have to wait and see how it goes." She fluffed the pillow behind Aunt Abeline's head and repositioned her to be sitting up more. "Dr. Barth will be here soon. I'm just gonna check the catheter here, and, yup, just as I thought. Don't worry Ms. Abeline," she told my aunt, "we'll get you all set up." She clipped out the full catheter, sliding the bed pan under, just in case, then she gave me a little wink. "Be back in a jiffy."

Alone again, I settled at the bedside of my aunt.

"This all reminds me so much of... well, you know." I mused. It was an unspoken topic between us for most of my childhood. But here and now, it couldn't hurt to give voice to the truth. "You look so alike in the bed. Maybe it's all the tubes. I hadn't been in a hospital since..." I trailed off. *Since she'd been murdered,* I added to myself.

Aunt Abeline didn't know that truth.

To her knowledge, Sierra died of undetermined factors, not magical poison. It wouldn't help her condition to break that news now.

"We'll get you home quick," I told Aunt Abeline. But the word caught in my throat.

Home. What home would we return to? Not the lake house. That whole property had been destroyed. I shook my head. The building wasn't important. Aunt Abeline and I had always felt home was where you made it. It was true, the cottage held more memories than any other building we'd been in, and we'd have to deal with the aftermath of the earthquake, but we'd cross that bridge as we came to it. For now, just opening her eyes would be a big step. It was the first hill to climb.

The nurse breezed back in with an empty catheter bag. I sat back on the bed.

"All done? Alright." She took the sippy cup from me and placed it aside. "Maybe we should give our patient a rest. You can get dressed. Dr. Barth is coming." Those same, efficient hands clicked the new bag onto its stand.

"Alright." I looked down at myself. I did look quite a mess.

"Your young man is still waiting," the nurse warned me.

"He's just a friend," I answered by rote.

She tapped my shoulders and left me there in the room.

"Okay. I'm gonna go. You rest up," I told Aunt Abeline. "I'll be back before you know it." I kissed her head, and gently squeezed her hand. Then, as the nurse had instructed, I let her rest. Outside, Beck rose to attention the second I exited her room.

"How is she?"

"I don't know. I guess we're still waiting. She isn't conscious." I nodded. There wasn't much else to report. He looked so worried and sweet. I'd been through a lot on my own, but after checking Josie was safe, he'd come running right back to my side. I didn't tell him about the vomit or the similarities to my mom's final days. "They said I should change back to my normal clothes. No one wants to see me in this." I gestured to my flimsy wardrobe.

"I like it. I'd like you in anything." He told me.

"You have to say that."

"No, I don't. We're just friends, remember?" Was I mistaken, or did the hurt creep back into his throat? Had he heard me declare him as such to the nurse? I decided to ignore that little jab.

Once back in my room, I grabbed my wardrobe off the chair. "Be right back."

"Don't come out in just a towel," he joked, trying to smooth things back over.

I quickly re-dressed in my dusty, earth-shaken wardrobe. The clothes were dirt-covered and grubby, but that was fine. Even in grimy clothes, it felt good to get out of the flimsy robe. Beck was being such a terrific partner, doing everything for my benefit, I decided to thank him and maybe lighten the mood.

I opened the bathroom door, hiding myself behind the doorframe, and held out just my hand with the hospital's limp gray hand towel dangling down.

"How's that for a towel?" I asked. It was a terrible, stupid striptease. Not even a striptease, but still I held the towel out.

"Mae..." Beck's voice sounded strange.

Immediately, I felt dumb and silly. My aunt was still seriously recovering. What a gross time to be flirty with a guy.

"What is it?" I dropped my arm and turned out of the stall. "Is Dr. Barth here to release me?"

"Not exactly," Beck's tone was off.

A shiver ran down my spine.

As soon as I crossed the threshold, I saw why.

We were no longer alone.

In my hospital room there were six members of the Damocles coven.

TEN

YOU DESTROYED MY WHOLE LIFE
FOR A FLOWER?

"YOU!"

I lunged at the closest blond haired guy. I didn't know his name, but I recognized that face. That ugly frown. Kristoff maybe? He had been at the battle. No, Kristoff was the one with the spiders, an insect harness. This boy was an earthquake empath. Immediately I knew he had caused the tremor at my home. He caused all the damage. Put my aunt in the hospital. How dare he show up face to face with me now.

Without thinking, without any idea where this was going or what my plan was, I dove at him. Intent to put hands on him. To attack him. I wanted to hurt him like he'd hurt me. Like he'd hurt Aunt Abeline. But I didn't get close.

Immediately, another witch flashed her palm into a ball and bounced me back across the floor. She'd created some kind of bubble. In my fury, I bounced off the jelly surface and fell at the base of the bed.

Beck dove into action too, balling his fist, blinding the whole crowd with a refraction of sun. The light blazed at full glory across the room, shining straight in their eyes. They shielded their faces and recovered from the glare. I took full advantage of the blind spot and swung a bed pan out at the earth-empath's ankles. I made solid contact with his shin, buckling his legs to the ground. He let out a terrible howl. At this slight, another witch in their group immediately started to respond.

"Enough!" The woman I recognized as their leader held up her palm. Her voice was sharp enough to grab everyone's attention, but immediately, she dropped her tone. She was mindful of the world going on around us on the small town hospital floor. She didn't want any more attention than was necessary, considering they were a group of six striking blonde people all dressed in head-to-toe red clothes. "Guard the door," she intoned to two of her followers. "Keep out anyone unwanted."

They nodded and stepped outside to guard the door. The earth empath boy rubbed his shin. He glared in my direction. The rest of her waiting coven members glared out from behind their leader as well. One of them, I realized, was the good looking doctor. Why hadn't I paid attention to his red scrubs before?

"Have we got your attention?" she asked.

Beck helped me back to my feet. My anger simmered beneath the surface but I was done lashing out for now. Six against two was not a fair fight.

"You have a lot of nerve." I glared. "We already won the Battle. Get the hell out of town."

"We can't," she admitted. "Not 'til we get what we came for. I don't like how we've had to go about obtaining it, but here we are. We need your help."

"Are you joking? After you destroyed every good thing in my planet? You think I'd help *you*?!"

Beck shifted but stayed stoic by my side.

"Earth can be shattered. Earth can be repaired," she said.

The earth-harness boy cracked his knuckles and sneered. I'd like to crack him upside of the head, I thought.

Petregaard. I suddenly remembered his name.

"We have bigger problems," she told me.

"My aunt almost died."

"Actually, she's dying now," the boy sneered.

"Shut up." I hurled the bedpan at him. He easily swatted it away. "What is he talking about?"

"I must admit, I do not like these tactics." The woman shook her head. Members of her coven shifted uncomfortably as well. The doctor looked down. "But we're desperate."

"You lost the Battle, fair and square," I reiterated.

I tried to stop my voice from breaking. They didn't deserve my anger or fear. But I couldn't hold the emotion for long.

"You're right. And you should know, we never meant to hurt her. Your aunt was a horrible casualty. It was supposed to be a display of power on an empty building. I never considered she might hide underground."

"That empty building was my world."

They shifted, uncomfortable.

"No, it wasn't," the woman said. She stared at me, until I was forced to break eye contact. "It was just your home. And homes can be rebuilt. We will help how we can with your aunt." She nodded. "Mae, may I call you Mae? I'm Natalia."

Inspite of myself, I nodded. Good manners kicked in, even when I was enraged.

"Mae, there's a plant."

"A plant." I spit the word right back.

"It's a very rare species. The High Council has it. We need a clipping as well."

"You destroyed my whole life for a flower?"

"Your Aunt's life, actually." Petregaard jeered. "It was her home. It's her body."

I wanted to slap that ugly face.

Beck put a hand on my shoulder as if he could feel this fresh wave of anger taking control. My hands balled into fists, but I didn't lash out.

"What is he talking about? Aunt Abeline is recovering."

"No." Their coven leader shook her head. "She isn't."

"But the doctor... Dr. Barth. He's coming."

"He *is* coming, but the news will not be good." Natalia looked over her shoulder. The blonde doctor stepped up.

"Mae, my name is Dr. Winters. Do you remember me? I looked in on your aunt, at her chart, at her situation. There's a lot of internal bleeding. The table crushed several important organs. Her heart isn't beating on its own. The structural damage-"

"What? No. What-" I cut him off.

His matter-of-fact information was over-taken by my swell of emotions. He switched gears. "Machines can keep her alive, but her body can't fully regenerate on its own. Without our help, I'm afraid she's dying."

"No. Why? How could you-? What needs to be done?" I melted onto the bed. Beck tried to catch me. The realization was too much, all too fast.

"How dare you come in here," Beck snarled at the group. "You did this. You kill her then ask for favors?"

"She's not dead," I wailed. "She can't be."

"I can keep her going. Three days, maybe longer." Dr. Winters nodded. "I'll do what I can with the supplies that I have. But modern medicine cannot save her."

I wept into Beck's chest. How could they come in here, knowing they caused this disaster and act like nothing had happened? Tell me the news so matter of factly? Like if they said it straight forward enough it'd be fine that they'd killed my aunt.

"No one was meant to get hurt," Natalia reiterated. "But, for us, this is better."

"It's *better*?" Spittle shot from my mouth.

"I'm sorry. That was cold," she agreed. She thought about how to phrase what came next. "Now you want what we want. Mae, you alone can save your aunt. We've seen what you can do in battle. Ingenious, really. You can do that again. The Valdeez leaves we search for will stimulate her recovery and rebuild her organ system. It's a revolutionary plant. Stronger magic than you've ever seen. It's healing properties are potent. They'll save her life. As Dr. Winters said, we'll keep her safe until then. But first you have to get the branch. All our attempts have failed. Retrieve the Valdeez. We'll use the first leaf to save your aunt and the rest will come back with us."

"And that will bring her back?" I asked, wiping the tears from my eye. "You can save her?"

"If you can bring it back in thirty-six hours, yes. I believe that it can," their doctor nodded.

"Mae, your coven has the branch required. Get them to give it to you. Give the remainder to us. Everybody wins. Then we will leave. And never come back." All around her, the Damocles coven members nodded.

I'd heard such promises before.

I'd won the whole damn battle, and yet still, here they were.

But that didn't matter. The Damocles exodus wasn't my problem. All I cared about was my aunt.

I frowned. "How can I trust a word you say?"

"You can't." Natalia let her brisk honesty hang in the air. "But it's your only option. We'll stay with her here, nearby, watching over. Make sure she feels no pain. Dr. Winters will do whatever he can to prolong her. But, the window is short. At most, you have three days. After that, the supplies will run out. Mae, get the Valdeez plant, quick as you can."

The hair on my arms stood on end.

So the High Council was correct.

The Valdeez plant *did* need protecting. It was one of the special plants the High Council had sent an emissary into the forest to guard. Ethan was out there, protecting it. But he wouldn't stop me from doing what needed to be done. If it meant saving Aunt Abeline, nothing would stand in my way.

"You give us the plant, we can give you back your aunt."

ELEVEN

THREE DAYS

I SPENT the next ninety minutes with Dr. Barth and various nurses hearing the medical details of my unconscious relative. It was no use, what Natalia and Dr. Winters had said was true. Aunt Abeline had been crushed, almost to death. Her injuries were vast. Modern medicine didn't hold much hope. Pain mitigation was their only viable option. The doctors said it would be wait and see at best. If I wanted to save her life, to really bring her back to her health and vitality, a magic potion was my only chance. I had to return with the Valdeez plant, very soon.

As Beck and I entered the waiting room, a smattering of people all started talking at once.

"How is she?" Ferris asked.

"What's going on?" Greg demanded.

"How are you?" Marcy asked, concerned. "What's been happening?"

Josie looked up, silently, watching.

I stared around in shock. It had been hours since we'd left the castle. I'd been to hell and back and yet here they all were, waiting for me, wondering how it went.

"You're all here," I stuttered.

"Of course, Mae-mae! We're here for you." Marcy jumped up and hugged me.

"And it hasn't been fun," Greg added, slouching in his chair. The others frowned his direction. "Well it hasn't. I hate hospitals."

"What did the doctor say?" Ferris frowned at him. "Are you alright? Is your aunt?"

"I'm okay." I told them. I hugged an arm across my chest and shifted my weight. "Aunt Abeline's..." I faltered.

"She's stable for now," Beck helped me. "She made it to the hospital. They've got her on a ventilator. And Mae's been signed out."

"Well, that's great," Marcy cheered, but Ferris and Josie sensed there was something more.

"What's actually happening?" Josie asked.

Her look could always cut through to the core.

Beck glanced at me. He raised an eyebrow. The others had been here all day, but it was up to me how much more I wanted to share. I didn't *want* any of it. I sighed and sat down. Involuntarily, every one of them leaned forward. My voice dropped to a whisper. "The Damocles coven followed us here. They claim they only destroyed my home to put on a show to threaten the High Council. They didn't know anyone was inside. Their doctor says he can restore Aunt Abeline to perfect health, *if* I do what they ask."

"What are they asking?" Josie's eyes narrowed.

"Absolutely not," Greg shook his head. "We don't negotiate with terrorists."

"Greg, if I don't, my aunt will die."

"Oh. I hadn't thought of that. In that case, do whatever they said."

"Do you think you can trust them?" Ferris asked.

"I'm not sure I have a choice."

"She doesn't trust anyone as far as she can throw them," Marcy added.

"Well, that wouldn't be far. Have a look at her arms," Greg said.

"What do they want?" Josie asked again. Right to the point.

"The leaves of a Valdeez branch."

The black-haired girl sat back. Ferris also stiffened. She recognized the plant.

"Oh good!" Marcy sat back. "The way you were talking I thought this little adventure might be difficult, but the High Council has a garden and a greenhouse. You can just go in and snip whatever you want," she smiled.

"The Valdeez isn't planted. It's grown. Propagated from a single seed. It's incredibly rare," Josie informed her.

"Well, fine. Then you can *grow* it," Marcy shrugged.

"You'd need... god, I don't remember exactly, but

lowland leaves... hold on, I recently saw it in my book." Josie pulled a botany text book out of her book bag.

"You carry a textbook with you?" Greg laughed. "Read much?"

"You know I work in a book store, right?" She frowned.

"You can sell books without reading them," Greg laughed.

"I heard about it too..." Ferris remembered. "Fresh water soil, aerated seeds from the mountains... there's something else. I think it involved a volcano." She frowned. "Mae, if you had a lifetime, you might not gather all the ingredients for that."

"I have three days..." I checked my watch. "No, two and a half. Tell me again, what's the exact recipe. Lowland leaves, underwater fertilizer..."

Josie's fingers danced across the index. "It might have been this," she flipped open her text. "Yeah, this one, or maybe it was in Henderson's Clippings, Biology and Plants." She read down the page. "I can find you the recipe."

"I'm telling you, it isn't doable or every coven would be growing heaps of the stuff," Ferris shrugged.

"We don't need a heap, all we need is one sprig."

Josie found the right page and we leaned in together. There it was. Classified in print.

"Read it out loud!" Marcy exclaimed.

We hunkered over the book, our eyes quickly moving down the page. Josie started reading.

· · ·

"*The Valdeez plant is heavily endangered and increasingly rare in our community. It is a species with several threats to its survival. Plants are put at risk for multiple reasons, including: climate change and the loss of natural habitat to cities, agriculture and industry, over-farming, and naturally slow cycle rates of reproduction. The germination process of the Valdeez plant (Eleiochadray Hixenuate) is especially uncommon as the unfertilized seeds for the native species must first aerate in a disparate climate, separate to the natural growing habitat of the fertilized plant. Traditionally, this migratory path of seeds was accomplished by filamentary bird migration, which has through evolution and time run a continually shorter and shorter natural course. The Valdeez aeration of seeds is facing two different threats to its survival in both localized locations, one atop the Gentureapan Mountain range, and its sister city of hills, the Lorry Range. While migratory paths between these mountains and the lowland trees of the Aboritorum Forest were once common, such flight paths are now increasingly rare. In addition to these plants, several shrubs and climbers are also at risk.*

Once an aerated seed is returned to the forest floor, it must grow in damp-to-wet conditions, preferably with nutrients from an algae rich soil, such as that found under the underwater Cucumber Coffee Tree (Gymnoclada Klischatrop) in fresh water lagoons. There are numerous studies that hypothesize that the Valdeez plant cannot blossom without the additional influence of nutrient rich sap from the nearby Pokna volcano (dor-

mant for two-hundred and fifty-eight years at time of printing) but this claim has never been proven to scientific certainty. Further tests would be necessary to explore the efficacy of such postulation. While the Valdeez once grew throughout the deciduous trees of Eastern and Central Great Forests, it is now highly endangered. Its roots, leaves and bark have been excessively harvested for their reputed medicinal properties to the point that any natural Valdeez plants are not found in the wild. Any remaining plant should be considered highly valuable.

"Oh, that was long," Marcy was lost.

"And boring," Greg snorted. "You read that book for fun? Dodged a bullet mate," he patted Beck on the leg. To his credit, Beck rolled his eyes. He didn't need a compliment from Greg.

Ferris' memory was correct, it was a three step germination process that the book warned was notoriously difficult. "Where are you going to get an aerated seed? It can't be done," she told me.

Josie nodded and frowned.

"It could if..." I tried to see the bright side but I didn't find one. "I don't have a seed," I admitted.

"No one does," Josie added.

We all sat back. This news washed over my friends.

"So we ask for the Council's help," Beck offered.

"They won't help," Josie snapped. "*Any remaining*

plant should be considered highly valuable." She re-read. "The witch leaders won't go around just handing it out."

"How would you know? You've never even been in the tower." Greg frowned. "Are we allowed to discuss this stuff with a person not in the coven?"

I'd been so wrapped up and fearful about my aunt I'd totally forgotten that Josie wasn't an actual fellow witch. I looked, stricken, between them.

"She can read a book," Beck snapped. "She brought it with her."

"I don't know," Greg tilted his head. As if he was analyzing the facts.

"Sorry Jo," Marcy shrugged.

"I say she stays," Beck crossed his arms and stood up.

"I say she goes," Greg countered. He also got to his feet.

"Mae? What do you think?" Ferris wondered.

They all looked to me.

"Well…"

The Damocles visit was my business, as was my aunt, but the talk of the plants and Council were gray areas. There was no way I'd choose to send Josie away. She was the one who'd got me out of the bunker. She was smart and reliable, unlike Greg. But, I also had enough on my plate without worrying about the conse-quences of revealing council secrets to an outsider.

In my hesitancy, Josie took the hint.

"Right." She sat back. "Right, of course. I'll keep

reading up on my own. If you need me, Mae, you tell me. I'll help. However I can." She stood and nodded at the others. "Bye, guys. Bye, Beck."

"Bye, Jo."

Greg and Marcy shot a look my way to see how I would take all this in, but I didn't flinch. Inside, I felt a jealous twinge at Josie singling Beck out, even though their goodbye seemed straight-backed and stiff.

She waved and departed.

"Josie," I stopped her before she'd gone five steps. She turned. I reached for something to tell her how I was grateful. How over and over she had done the right thing for me. How I knew she would always be there. How leaving, both here and the High Council itself, was the hardest and therefore the strongest character choice. How I knew she was a great witch and I would always choose her on my team. "Thanks."

It wasn't much, but I offered it anyway. She nodded and left.

"Your friend is right." Ferris pulled us immediately back on track. "Far as I know, our coven has only two of the Valdeez branches in our possession. They *are* highly valued. The chemical make-up of the plant is super powerful. Almost legendary. Rumored to be like a fountain of youth."

Marcy's interest was piqued. "Like Botox?"

"No." Ferris cut her off. "Basically, it's a medical miracle. Regenerative. All-powerful."

"Oh, like a superhero comic." Greg nodded.

"Kind of. I guess," she said. "Both plants are locked

under heavy guard, one in the castle, one out in the forest."

We both knew what that meant. Ethan, *her* Ethan, was one of those guards.

"Well, if you explain to the elders what you need, they can give it to the other coven and this whole thing will be over." Marcy shrugged. "Can't hurt to ask."

Greg nodded.

"I agree. I say we go to the Council," Beck said. "You can't keep this secret, Mae. It's too big."

There was subtext.

Don't keep it secret Mae, like you keep all the other secrets.

He still didn't understand.

This secret is too big.

"That's precisely why I should keep it hush hush," I implored him. "If they say no, what would I do then? Aunt Abeline's life hangs in the balance. If they refuse, we're totally screwed." I explained. "It *can* hurt to ask. It could be deadly. I have to get the plant on my own."

Ferris and I exchanged glances. She understood me completely.

Marcy and Greg's and even Beck's entry into the High Council coven had been a far less bumpy road than either of ours had been. I silently wished to myself that I'd left the other couple at home, or turned them away and not Josie. But, this whole thing was happening so fast. It was too late to walk them out now.

"But how?" Marcy asked.

"You can't steal it from the castle and you can't steal it from the forest," Beck said.

"I know," I feared.

"You won't have to steal from the forest," Ferris told me. Her eyes narrowed. "With me by your side, Ethan will hand the Valdeez plant over."

TWELVE

A FIFTY-FIFTY PARTNERSHIP

"ARE YOU SURE? Ferris, this isn't your problem."

"And it shouldn't be yours. The High Council should have banished the Damocles coven right out of Plumpkin. It's what I would have done. Mae, that attack could have been on any one of our houses. And the sooner those red-heads leave, the sooner Ethan can come home."

"Heh, red-heads. They're blonde actually. You're the red-head," Greg noted with a grin.

"And yet, you know what I mean," Ferris rolled her eyes.

"She's got you there," Marcy shrugged. Greg pouted.

"I don't know-" I frowned. I needed to think. Ethan and two other Fellows had been sent out into the forest as a precautionary emissary with plants and other chemicals of exemplary value when the Battle of Four had begun. Only, no one had let them come home.

They were still out there, still guarding, while the Damocles coven stuck around. While Ethan was safe with the others in the forest, Ferris was bound to feel better when her boyfriend returned.

"I want to come," Ferris confirmed. "It'll be nice to see him."

"We'll come too," Marcy said. Greg nodded.

"We all will," Beck assured me.

I looked at all the sweet faces willing to go out on a limb for me and my family. In the midst of this awful ordeal also came an outpouring of kindness. The kind of faith and comfort from others that before we'd arrived in the town of Plumpkin, Aunt Abeline and I had never known.

"Thank you," I nodded, standing. "So much."

The others followed my lead.

"In and out and home for dinner," Greg laughed.

"Well," Ferris and I exchanged a glance. "There's a little more involved than that," she said. "We'll have to pose as the Damocles witches, or maybe robbers. Remember, we can't just ask Ethan for the branch. He's guarding it. So are two others. He can't just hand it over. I'll create a lie guard disguise, and get him a message. But don't worry. He'll go along with the plan."

"Ooh, dress up. I love a cute costume," Marcy giggled.

"Give the old Greg a brand new Marcy," her man grossly wiggled his eyebrows. She slapped his arm but looked intrigued at the thought of a new-Greg as well.

"You understand that if you get caught you'll be in a serious lot of trouble," Beck warned them.

"I don't plan to get caught. Anybody else?" Greg asked. The couple grinned.

"Honestly," Marcy yawned. "So far, the High Council has been a bit of a snore."

Beck and I exchanged glances.

Again, *not my experience.*

Beck seemed to be holding onto a similar sentiment, but neither of us said any more. I checked with Ferris. Was she alright with all of the risks that this held?

"Don't look at me," she said. "It's been weeks since I've seen my parabond. Whatever we can do to end the standoff, I'm in."

Both she and Beck nodded, determined.

"Actually, can I speak to you for a second?" I asked Beck. "In private?"

Beck scrunched up his face, but nodded and followed. We stepped down the hall.

"What is it?" he asked. The second we were alone, his arms naturally reached out to cover me, protect me with his embrace. I wanted to cuddle in, but the others were still watching. I swerved my body to slip away from any pose that might be perceived as too intimate. Beck noted my discomfort and also pulled himself back.

"I, uh, don't want you to come," I told him.

"What?"

"I need someone to stay here. With my aunt. Keep an eye on the Damocles coven."

"Is this because I wanted to tell the High Council?"

"No!"

"'Cuz I went to help Josie?"

"No, I- Beck, I just need someone I can trust."

"Mae, if you won't ask for help, you're gonna need me in the forest."

"I have help. I'm covered. Where I need you, is here."

"Mae-"

"Beck, please. I can't do this if I don't have somebody watching. I need your eyes on them. On my aunt. To tell me what's going on."

"She'll be fine. She's unconscious." He tried to fight more, but seeing the hurt in my eyes, he gave in. "Okay. Yeah. Alright. I'll stay. It's alright. Whatever you need."

Impulsively, I crashed into his chest. "Thank you." I nuzzled my head into him. With Beck taking care of things here, I could do what needed to be done in the field. For a moment, he hesitated, knowing full well the same eyes I'd worried about only moments before were still watching our every move, but I just didn't care anymore. I wanted him to hold me. To tell me I could do this. To tell me it was possible. His warm arms engulfed me. He tucked me into his chest.

"You got this," he quietly told me. "You can do this,

no problem. Ferris will help and Greg and Marcy... will be there."

In spite of myself, I laughed.

"I'll watch over Aunt Abeline. Maybe we'll play our first game of Scrabble," he kept things light. "I hear she's pretty good."

I stifled a small smile. He was being so great.

"You can trust me." Beck swooped the hair out of my face. "In and out and home for dinner." He repeated Greg's far too casual claim.

I offered a sad smile. He stared deep into my eyes, holding my gaze. I looked into those deep pools of kindness, blue and cool. Beck was the sweetest, kindest boy I had ever known. How had I ever grown so lucky? And he wanted me. He wanted to be my boyfriend. Beck leaned in, closing in on my mouth with those soft, pink lips.

Embarrassed, I tilted my head down. "People might see," I demurred.

"Let 'em stare," he murmured. But he didn't close that final gap. He waited. For me to come his way. If we were in this, it was a fifty-fifty partnership.

I looked back, unsure.

So much inside of me wanted him completely.

Needed him.

Desired him.

I just wasn't ready to share our attraction with the world.

It was too fast. Too much. Too messy.

I didn't want to deal with the whispers about being his girl.

I already had too much on my plate simply being Mae.

How could I make him understand? It wasn't him. It wasn't about how much I liked him. I'd tried to tell him in the elevator already. Clearly, I'd hopelessly failed.

I could just kiss him here and now and live with the consequences.

Awash in warm, soft, goodness. All the world would fall away.

It was tempting.

I bit my bottom lip in anticipation.

"Sorry to break up the party," Ferris informed me. "But if we want to arrive after dark but make headway in the sunlight we should probably go now."

THIRTEEN

FORTY MINUTES INTO THE FOREST

ABOUT FORTY MINUTES into the forest, the fun and adventure wore off for Marcy and Greg.

"Are we there yet?" He moaned.

"Who knew such a daring adventure would require so much hiking?" Marcy complained.

"Quiet. You'll tip off the emissary," Ferris told them.

"There's nobody here. We're lost in the forest," she said.

It did feel like we were walking in circles.

"We are totally, totally alone." Greg said. "*A-roo!*" He let out a howl.

"What are you doing?!" Ferris and I both jumped on him at once.

"Ease up, I was just kidding."

"If we don't make this hand off clean, Ethan could end up in jail." Ferris snapped.

"So could both of you," I added.

"And Mae's aunt will be dead." Ferris finished the threat.

The final truth hit with a thud.

"Okay, geez. Sorry. But when you said rescue, we didn't think it would take this long to complete," Greg frowned.

"I was thinking, like twenty minutes," Marcy agreed. "I guess that was pretty dumb."

"All my blisters have blisters," he said.

But Marcy caught sight of my worried expression. "We'll suck it up. Don't worry Mae-mae, we're good. We're here to help."

"Well, you can start by not talking," Ferris sniped.

"You got it. Mum's the word." Greg and Marcy mimed zippers closing over each of their mouths.

I sighed. I'd hoped there would be safety in numbers. But I might have been better off to have rejected their offer when it had arrived. Still, you never knew what you might find on the forest floor.

Crack, crack.

"What was that?" Marcy wondered, turning around.

The rest of us had reflex enough to duck down in the shrubs.

Greg pulled Marcy lower as well.

Shhh.

I held a finger to my lips to keep her silent. We watched and waited. But no one appeared or made any more noise. When we'd held still for what felt like forever, Ferris slowly stood.

"Just the forest settling," she decided.

Greg and I nodded. But an eerie feeling had set in.

"I don't like this," Marcy admitted.

I don't like it either, I thought to myself, but, we had no choice but to go on.

The goosebumps were long-lasting.

We travelled forward, far more somber. The others felt it too. Truth was, on and off, I'd had an unsettled feeling since we'd first left the hospital, but I assumed that was just part of how it felt to work outside of the rules. Risking that any moment we might be caught red-handed. And we didn't have a back-up idea. I knew in my heart that Lady Mauve and Cornelius Child would never help my aunt. Not if it meant anything less for their coven. Even if it had no cost to them directly, I still felt sure that they'd say no. And what we were doing tonight, was essentially stealing. Even if we did have an inside man and a framework. If we were caught, there would be serious repercussions.

As Ferris forged ahead, I fell back and checked my phone.

No new messages from Beck.

No news is good news, I supposed. I thought about writing to him as well. It would be nice just to touch base. But there was nothing new to report.

Marcy fell into step.

"No news is good news," she said, reading my thoughts. She weaved her arm into mine in that overly familiar way that she had. I smiled, sad and silent, but tucked my device in my pocket. "You like him a lot," she noted.

"Who, Beck?"

"No... Cornelius Child," she rolled her eyes.

"We're just good friends," I fell back on my company line.

"You and Corny?"

"Me and Beck."

"Greg wouldn't like it if my friends looked at me like *that*," she said. "I'm just saying."

"It's complicated. He and Josie are barely over," I shook my head.

"That just means it's time to strike." She squeezed my arm. "Make your *move*. For god's sake, have a little fun while you're young!"

I looked up, surprised and grateful for the bold girl. She was so supportive and free. How I wished I could live my life out loud like her. She never seemed to care what anybody thought.

"Look," Ferris pointed. She'd knelt close to the ground. We hurried up to her side. There was ash strewn about and the earth was disturbed in half circles. "This is where they made camp."

"Hoof prints," Greg noted, pointing out the most obvious disturbance.

"We're getting close," I agreed.

"Oh my god. We're like real life trackers, this is so cool!" Marcy giggled. We other three shushed her. "Sorry, I know. Sorry." She zippered her lips.

We travelled another hour in total silence. The sun

had long since lowered, but above us, the moon shone bright. The forest was silver and sparkled. A small wind picked up through the trees. The branches around us started to lightly moan. We picked our way across in the silvery glow.

We marched for so long I thought we might have lost track of the emissary completely, when suddenly, in the distance, we noticed an orange glow. Ferris held a hand up to her lips, then pointed. Someone had lit a small fire. Whether it was to cook food, keep warm or just pass the time, we didn't know. Just like that, I could no longer feel the cold. My adrenaline kept me warm.

We crouched together.

We'd found the High Council envoy.

Ethan and the other two guards were hanging out around the fire. Undisturbed, their horses mulled nearby.

"Does he know we're coming?" Greg whispered.

"I hope so." Ferris nodded.

"What do you mean you hope?"

"He would have seen it in his dream."

"Did you dream about this?" Marcy asked me.

"No," I admitted. It wasn't a question I had wanted to be asked. My visions were frustrating. I hadn't imagined the earth quake, or a warning about my aunt, and I didn't see the Damocles threat growing. From when I was unconscious until now, I could only remember one stupid dream. "In my vision, everyone marched around with big clocks on their backs.

Stomping in rows. This way and that, only, none of the clocks ever matched."

"They should have synchronized their watches." Marcy was so serious, I almost laughed.

"I do not understand your powers," Greg shook his head.

"You and me both," I told him. "But, at some point, it will probably make sense."

It always did.

The biggest trick was to figure out the meaning before it was too late. Hind sight wasn't very helpful. But, dream or not, I had figured out a way to help the plan. We needed to make sure Ethan knew we were coming.

"Marcy, can you get a bird to deliver a message? Or do something to get Ethan's attention?" I remembered I'd once seen her get a hawk to deliver a beer to someone's hands.

"Yeah, that should be possible."

"If we can signal we're here and get him to separate from the others, Ferris can tell him the plan," I said.

"What is the plan?" Greg wondered.

"He tells us where the Valdeez is, maybe makes it easy access. We dress up as the Damocles coven and snatch it. Ideally, never seen by his friends," Ferris said. "Then Ethan tells High Council it was the Damocles that stole it."

"Which it kind of was," Marcy nodded.

"Then it's back to the hospital to save my aunt."

"Well, what about us? Did we march all this way for moral support?" Greg asked.

"I'll be sending the bird," Marcy offered.

Greg frowned. So it was just him with no task.

"What were you hoping for?" I wondered.

"I dunno. Maybe perform a little magic."

"What's your power?" Ferris asked, skeptical.

"We're both harnesses," Marcy said proudly.

"Animal?" I wondered. I realized I'd never actually seen Greg in action.

"Rocks," he said.

"Like you can throw them?"

"Or turn them over," he shrugged.

"He's really great on a hill," Marcy boasted.

We looked around. The forest was flat.

"You're our safety net," I offered. "In case there's trouble."

"Like a super hero," he nodded. "If you need me, boom, I'll swoop in."

"Exactly," I nodded.

"Here," Ferris slipped a gold ring off her finger. It had five small stones in the shape of a daisy. "If you can get this to Ethan, he'll know who it's from and come looking. That and the dream, should be clear. Just don't lose it."

Marcy took it. "Ooh, pretty." She slipped it on her finger and admired it on her own hand. Noting the frowns on our faces, she pulled it back off. "This will work, I can do this." She changed her tone to a more professional one.

"We'll wait 'til you get close," I told the older girl. She nodded.

Ferris moved stealthily through the forest. We watched her slip between the leaves without so much as a rustle at her feet. The realization of how cleanly someone could move through the trees without being noticed was a little un-nerving. Greg and Marcy clomped around like a herd of elephants, but others, you might never see coming.

Again, I felt another chill.

I shook it off. We'd be headed for home soon.

When Ferris had settled several feet from their camp, she gave a small signal in our direction.

"Now, Marc," I said.

Greg's girlfriend readied herself. She grew still, holding her hand at her side, her other palm lifted up the special ring in her hand. Her lower fist balled. I could feel the energy buzz in the air.

Suddenly, through the trees, we heard a great flapping of wings. A majestic owl swooped through the trees and glided down. In a smooth motion, it snatched the ring off Marcy's outstretched palm. She didn't flinch at its talons but Greg and I both dropped to the ground. The bird was huge. Its wingspan beat Marcy's hair like a fan. But still, she didn't falter. After picking up the ring, the nocturnal bird carried on. It swooped through the trees into the High Council camp.

Swoosh.

It cut through their campfire area, swooping through the space. The boys all jumped up. The bird was far bigger than any of their heads. I didn't see the package drop, but from the way he responded, Ethan clearly did. While his campmates jumped out of their chairs in awe at the owl, trying to map out the continued route of the impressive bird, Ethan picked something up off the ground. He looked around, but tucked it in his pocket. Her task complete, Marcy released the owl back into the night. The giant bird was free to hunt and pillage the forest floor once more.

Ethan and his friends stared out from the other side of the forest.

"Not bad for a first year harness," Marcy praised herself with a wink.

"That's my babe," Greg whisper-exclaimed.

"Shhh." I hushed the couple.

Whether she'd planned it or not, Marcy's bird's trajectory kept them all facing away from the spot where we were hiding. Ethan stuck with his mates for a few minutes, *oohing* and *ahhing* about the impressive bird they'd discovered, but when he felt it was clear to do so, he motioned to the others and ambled into the forest, presumably under the guise of taking a pee. His peers were too concerned with watching for the return of the owl to really care where he went. Ethan stepped into the trees, quite close to where Ferris was waiting for him.

Back at our camp, the three of us silently cheered. The plan worked!

"Think he really drains the lizard?" Greg whispered. "Gotta make the visit authentic."

"Ew, no. Gross," Marcy swatted his arm, then couldn't help but grin. "Actually, at this point, it's been so long since she was with him, she'd probably appreciate a little dangle."

"Can you two not be gross for just a minute?" I complained. "If Ethan can do this for us, he'll basically save my aunt's life."

"Everybody pees, Mae," Greg was not deterred.

I rolled my eyes.

And in the forest, they were right, Ethan gave a little shake.

"Yup," Greg nodded, satisfied. "The urination wiggle."

"Do you wiggle?" Marcy asked.

"It's like a shimmy and a shake."

"I want to go home," I complained.

But we shut up immediately because Ferris was on her way back to our group.

"It's all set," she told us, ducking back into our stead. "When his team goes to sleep, he'll leave the plant that we want in a sachet inside the tent."

"When will that be?" Marcy frowned.

"Maybe an hour? Two at most," I suggested.

She sighed. "What do we do until then?"

FOURTEEN
GET WHEEL SOON

IT TOOK four hours for their little group to wind down. The owl sighting had excited the boys so much they were wide awake. With nothing to do but hang out by the fire, for the three guys the days and nights must have all looked the same. The idea of a curfew or bedtime meant nothing. All they really had was time. The three kicked back and hung out.

Time marched much slower for the four of us.

Without the benefit of a chair or a fire, our bones grew cold and stiff on the ground. Still, we waited it out. Each time a member of their crew added more wood to their fire, one of us let out a sigh. At some point, Greg and Marcy simply entwined, curled up in the branches, and fell asleep. Gently, they started to snore. For what felt like the millionth time, I envied the simple, happy couple.

"Let 'em sleep," I told Ferris.

She nodded.

We sat with our backs against a fallen trunk, watching Ethan and his buddies' fire glow. "Thanks again. For doing this. You're both taking a pretty big risk."

"I cover my own," she said. "You'd do the same."

"Anytime," I agreed. And I meant it. For Ferris, I'd go to the ends of the earth.

"Besides, the High Council should never have let this situation happen. They should have given the Damocles the plant right then when they asked for it, or insisted they depart the day after you returned with their orb. We already won the battle. You shouldn't be fighting the war. Especially not alone."

I'm not alone, thank god for that, I thought.

I had Ferris and Ethan.

Greg and Marcy.

I had Beck.

My fingers found the phone in my pocket. I fingered the smooth sides but fought the urge to pull it out. Ferris noticed. She glanced at Ethan's fire. Still burning bright.

"Call him, or text. Whatever. He's probably dying for an update."

"I can't risk the glow of the screen. Unless-" I pulled off my jacket and hugged it around the device. I put my body between my phone and the fire. I turned on the screen and nimbly flicked the brightness down to its lowest capacity. The light was barely noticeable. "I'll be right back."

Ferris nodded and kept her attention on her man.

Or what we could see of him. At this distance he was a shadowy lump of a head. A head she loved very much.

I stepped thirty or forty feet from our camp, deeper into the forest. Swiftly, I hit the contact icon for Beck. I turned way down the volume.

"Hey parabond," his thick voice answered. He sounded sleepy. I could almost envision his heavy eyes opening, dragging his fingers through his hair as he roused. This imagined picture of him was so detailed and special it warmed my heart in the dark forest night.

"Did I wake you?" I whispered.

"No, I... what time is it?" He lowered his voice to match mine.

Time.

A flash of my dream flickered in my head. People marching. Clocks behind them.

"I'm not really sure," I admitted. "Late."

"1:07 in the morning," he read having spotted a watch or clock somewhere. "How's it going?"

"We found Ethan's camp. Ferris spoke to him. Now we're waiting for the others to head off to bed. Then, we should be able to grab the Valdeez plant." I relayed. "How's Aunt Ableline?"

"No change," he admitted. "Dr. Winter comes by a lot. He's doing what he can."

But...

The disappointing truth didn't need to be said.

There was a lot hanging on the success of this trip.

Beck cleared his throat. "I, uh, went to the gift shop. I found this hamster in a T-shirt. Says '*get wheel soon.*' With a picture of a hamster wheel, you know? It reminded me of you. And your aunt. Your whole vibe. You know? Something in its little face," he mused. "I gave it to your aunt. So Abeline knows you're with her."

I sighed.

Beck was right. I should have been with her. Not traipsing in the forest with Marcy and Greg. A silence grew between us.

"Are you still there?"

"I'm here." I agreed. "I - it's perfect. Aunt Abeline loves a good pun. Or a *bad* pun. Maybe a bad pun even more," I tried to joke, but the words stuck in my throat. Emotion overwhelmed me. Would Aunt Abeline shower me with bad jokes again?

It all depended on this little adventure.

I sucked back the tears, careful to keep as quiet as I could.

"Hey, it's okay." He whispered.

I tried to stop the flow.

"It'll all be over soon," he assured me. "I-"

Crack, crack.

I spun around and looked out into the silvery forest. Dropping the phone from my ear.

What was that?!

The silence of the trees was ominous.

I stood stock still.

Nothing moved.

Nothing was there.

Over my other shoulder, Ferris signaled. She was

trying to get my attention. The encampment fire had died out. Ethan and the other guards had gone to their tents.

I raised the phone back to my ear. "Beck, I gotta go. Wish us luck."

"You don't need it. You're gonna do great," he said. He always knew just what to say. "Good luck, Mae."

"Thanks."

I tucked the device back into my pocket, grateful for the well-wishing, suddenly overwhelmed with the feeling we'd need all the luck we could get. When I got back to our camp, Ferris had already roused Greg and Marcy and all three were ready to leave.

"Let's do this," I nodded.

The quicker we got the Valdeez plant, the sooner we could all go home.

"Come on." Ferris crept us closer to the camp. We did our best to move as stealth-like as she did in the backwoods. Was silent forest-walking an official part of the Judicial Studies curriculum? If it wasn't, it should be. On the far side of the camp, some of the horses snuffled. Our presence did not go unannounced. The fire in their camp had almost died out, still vital in a heap of glowing embers. We picked across the small clearing to Ethan's tent. Ferris bent low and slid the zipper open.

On the other side of the canvas, Ethan was waiting.

He looked out at all three of us. He seemed scruffier than I remembered, with wrinkled clothes and shaggy bedhead, but still, the same goofy grin.

"Hi," he whispered. His eyes were only for Ferris, but he handed out the small sachet my way.

"Hi," Ferris whispered back. She leaned in to greet him with a long, slow kiss.

"Awww, forest nookie," Marcy giggled.

Amorously, Greg gave his girlfriend's body a little hump.

"Shhh." She shushed him, but I ignored both couples.

All my focus was on the sachet. I opened the package. Inside was an unremarkable twig and six short green leaves attached. This branch was worth the life of my aunt. The trade seemed sad. Just some lousy tree limb. At least we had the thing in our hands. And no one was the wiser.

"We should go." I tapped Ferris' shoulder. She looked up from her guy's embrace. "Thank you," I added to him. "This means more than I can say."

"Just... keep my girl safe," he told me. "I'll be home soon." He added.

"Yeah, you will." She kissed him passionately, sneaking in one final embrace.

I led the charge to take us out of their space.

"We did it," Marcy quietly giggled as we left the camp. "Holy smokes. We actually did it."

"And without my superpowers," Greg noted.

"Keep quiet 'til we're clear." I tried to sound stern, but a warm rush had also come over me. They were right. We succeeded for my aunt. It felt pretty great!

For a while, we trudged ahead.

"I was thinking about your dream." Greg suddenly broke the reverie at full volume.

"Shhh." Instinctively, I looked over my shoulder. We weren't far enough from their camp to be speaking like that.

"Fine," he dropped his voice. "I was thinking about your dream," he whispered.

"What about it?"

"What if all the clocks behind the people just means '*watch your back*'?"

Crack, crack.

Two twigs snapped directly in our wake. We all spun to face the direction they came from.

"That's pretty good advice," a shadowed figure agreed. "You should take it."

FIFTEEN

WE'RE ON THE SAME SIDE

I IMMEDIATELY RECOGNIZED EVERYTHING. His voice, his frame, his cadence from the hospital. Even the sneer was the same. Petregaard.

"Damocles..." Marcy sputtered.

Because he wasn't alone. There were three of them.

"What are you doing here?" Ferris demanded.

"They're Mae's friends," Greg frowned.

"They're not my-" I started to object, but the other coven didn't wait around.

Petregaard signaled his friends.

The back-up guy closed his fist. A huge bubble appeared, trapping us inside it. A lie-guard. The illusion of weird jelly was a Damocles special. I'd seen something similar at the hospital. Inside the sphere, we readied ourselves to do battle. Ferris, Marcy and Greg all balled their hands into fists, one set of warriors to another. I would use my hands to fight, or to stop the other coven from casting... if possible. Ferris tried to command an illusion of her own, but nothing happened.

"They're blocking it," she realized. "Damn it."

"What?"

The boy signaled again, and the jelly around us changed. The large bubble popped and several smaller ones appeared in its place. Instead of being grouped together, they trapped us as individuals.

On this mission, I was in effect working for the Damocles coven, why were they doing this?

"Let us out!" I shouted, but the viscous substance ate my words. I could tell the others were trying similar things, but all our sounds were muffled. "We're on the same side!"

Pop.

Suddenly, my bubble disappeared. I gasped in shock, feeling the freedom.

"Battle girl," Petregaard's eyes narrowed. "I'm not playing around."

My friends continued to ball their fists and call on their powers, but Ferris was right. Something in the jelly boundary stopped their energy right where it was. Inside their bubble concoctions, they were helpless.

"What are you doing? I was sent to get the plant for your coven. I got it. We're coming home."

"And I trust you?" He laughed. Over his shoulder, he nodded to his friend. They shrunk the magical bubbles around my friends. The other Damocles girl balled her hand into a fist and suddenly tree branches and roots slithered like ropes to catch my arms and legs, then tightened like a natural set of shackles on my wrists and ankles. A tree harness. The vines were too powerful for me to struggle against. "Give me the sachet," Petregaard said.

I might have told him where to find it, might have just handed it over, but trust was a two-way street. Ambushing us, and imprisoning us in the jungle didn't make me feel like part of his team. There was no way I was giving up the leaves until I could guarantee my aunt's safety. This Damocles brat couldn't give me that.

"I don't have it. It's with them. You'll have to pop the bubbles."

"Please." He frowned. "Give it now, or I will take it."

"No." I murmured. Then, I had an idea. "No." I repeated, getting louder. "Get back. Back! Get out of here! Leave me alone!" I shouted. "Don't touch us!" I struggled against the imprisoning trees. "Help!"

A sick smile pushed up on Petregaard's cheeks. "Don't you get it? They can't hear a thing in their bubbles. And even if they could, they couldn't stop us." The Damocles trio looked awfully smug.

"We're on the same team," I pleaded.

"Then hand it over."

"It's not just yours. My aunt-"

"Your aunt will get what's coming."

"Natalia said she'd give her a leaf."

"Do you see Natalia here? Dr. Winters?" The others leered.

Petregaard waved a hand and the lie-guard witch came close. "Hold still, girl." He slipped a hand into my pocket. I wanted to wretch as his fingers searched the fabric next to my skin.

"Let them go, Petregaard," I used the earth-harness' name. "You can't have it." He seemed surprised that I knew it, but didn't call off his friend.

The boy dug into another fold of fabric. This time in the breast pocket. I doubted he really thought the sachet was there, but I couldn't stop him from rubbing against my body. I winced in disgust. "Please. At least release my friends, they have nothing to do with this." I kept my focus on Petregaard.

"Little girl," the boy who's hands had touched me sneered, as if it was a point of pride that he didn't know who I was. He grabbed my face and twisted it to the side to face him. "You are not in control."

"Please," I whimpered. I looked out at my friends in their bubbles. They had stopped trying to create any magic. Instead, they were just trying to breathe. The bubbles did two things, stopped their magic *and* the flow of oxygen.

"Come on, Daton. We didn't come for this." Petregaard stepped forward, pushing the lie-guard to the side. His lackey released my cheeks and backed off. Instead, Petregaard patted my pockets. His hands were straight forward, actually searching for the hidden item.

"You of all people should know, there will be collateral damage." The lie-guard hissed.

"No... please stop. Help! Stop! Anybody!" I shouted.

Marcy fell first. Greg followed. Even Ferris collapsed where she stood.

In one motion, Petregaard pulled back his hand, the sachet successfully found. He opened the string and peeked inside. "Good." He nodded at his henchman and woman.

"You got what you want." I spit. "Please, let them out."

"The second I do, those fools will attack," the lie-guard said.

Petregaard nodded. "The bubbles must stand. At least til we're long gone. I don't see another way." The others were smug, but it was my turn to grin.

"I can see another way," I told them. I looked behind their group. Pleased all my shouting had worked. "You remember my dream? Watch your back. The warning was for you."

Crack!

SIXTEEN
EAT THAT! DAMOCLES!

FROM HIS CAMPSITE, Ethan had heard my screams and came running to help. In one swoop, he cracked Petregaard and the Bubble Master with a thick tree branch, knocking them both to the ground.

Pop!

The bubbles that had trapped the others burst. Greg, Marcy and Ferris gulped the fresh air supply. The tree harness girl ran into the forest. I struggled against her vines.

"Stop him!" I yelled, motioning towards the bigger boy. "He's a lie-guard!"

Ethan lunged on top of Daton, stopping him from building another illusion in his palm, but Petregaard, recognizing the plant was already in their possession, didn't turn to fight or even help his compatriot. Instead, he ran. There was no need to stand their ground. The Valdeez plant was running away into the forest.

"Greg - stop that Damocles!" I yelled. I desperately

yanked at the limbs, but the more I struggled, the tighter the plants seemed to become. "He's got that Valdeez branch!"

"I got him," Greg announced.

"Marc, see if you can find the Damocles harness," I told her.

"I'll get her," Marcy nodded. She summoned her birds. "Girl-on-girl violence is not something I go for, but today, I can make an exception."

As Petregaard raced away, Greg pulsed his fist in his hand. A small stone rolled in front of the Damocles coven members. Petregaard easily jumped over the inconvenience. He didn't even slow his stride.

"*That's* your witch power?" I snapped one arm free of my living shackles.

Greg tossed and turned over several more rocks on the route, but Petregaard never slowed.

"I told you, I'm better on a hill," Greg complained. In the trees, a girl screamed, and the vines holding me in place dropped away. The plant harness had to protect her face from attacking bird talons and I was freed once more.

"Gotcha," Marcy grinned.

"I'm still learning." Greg defended.

"Come on!"

We ran ahead to catch the Damocles pack leader. Marcy turned her birds on them both. On our way, we picked up Ferris, who was only just clearing her head. Already, the harnesses had quite a lead. Greg flipped rock after rock. But other than being a small annoyance, the skill was underwhelming at best. To put some distance between us and their group, their lie-guard, who'd broken free of Ethan, suddenly built an eight-foot wall in the forest.

"Hurry!" I shouted.

"Up and over!" Ethan put his hands out and launched me. I scrambled over the wall.

"I got 'em." Ferris balled her hand behind me and imagined the runaway Damocles coven members trapped on a giant treadmill. The faster they ran, the more it spun in place. The two remaining coven members ran futilely, trying to keep themselves upright. The tree harness called vines and plants to their aid. They held on to the ropes and climbed them like swings to try and swing off of the lie-guard tread-mill, but Ferris just slid it over further in her mind.

"We've got to get back that sachet," I told the others. "It's in Petregaard's hands."

"What's his power?"

"Earth harness!" I shouted.

"Oh, like Greg," Marcy realized.

"No, not like Greg."

Petregaard jogged in place, turned and faced us, and balled his hand into a first.

The earth from his feet ripped apart in a vicious, jagged tear. The ground split wide open. The crack came right for us. Marcy and I smashed to the ground on opposite sides. The crevice dug twenty feet into the ground, and rocks and debris tumbled into the unknown.

"Not like Greg," Marcy nodded. We picked ourselves up off the ground.

"Hey, I got this," Greg pouted. To knock down the wall-maker, Greg flipped a rock behind the Damocles lie-guard. The boy was backing away from Ethan, so for once, the rolling stone was a direct hit. He tripped over the rock and fell back on the ground, smacking his head.

"Yes!" Greg cheered. "Gotcha! Eat that Damocles!"

But, the boy didn't stand back up. The brick wall he'd created disintegrated from sight.

"Is he alright?" Marcy feared.

Ethan checked his wrist for vitals.

"Seems fine, just knocked out."

"I am a superpower!" Greg cheered.

"Ethan! What's happening!" Two voices called through the darkness as two new bodies joined in the fray. The High Council guards from the camp had been awakened in all the chaos and now they crashed through the forest to Ethan's side.

"Damn it." Ferris dropped her treadmill illusion and focused on the disguises for all our friends. Win or lose on this mission, it was imperative none of us get caught by the guards. The High Council couldn't know we were here.

"It's the Damocles. They've got the Valdeez plant!" Ethan quickly covered for us. His story wasn't even a lie anymore. We were now literally trying to stop three members of the Damocles coven from stealing the High Council's Valdeez branch. But we still couldn't get caught in this fray.

"Quick, they're running!" I shouted, pointing forward. The second Ferris let go of her lie-guard, the harnesses from the rival coven took off again. Even with the addition of the High Council guards in the forest, we couldn't afford to let them escape. "Go for their hands!" I shouted to Marcy in a voice that sounded nothing like my own.

Ferris' disguises had changed our appearances down to the bone. The blonde-haired group member who I assumed was Marcy nodded and redrew a fist of her own.

Caw!

A massive hawk swooped overhead and searched forward. It cast a huge shadow over the trees as it flew. Even in moonlight, its wingspan blackened out parts of the forest.

Caw. Caw!

Other birds followed. Marcy's orders were clear, while the real Damocles witches dipped out of our view, the birds knew right where they went. Petregaard and the tree harness ducked, protecting their head with their hands. I raced forward and lunged at the boy's legs, tackling him, intent to keep him off his feet until reinforcements arrived.

"Greg, see if you can hold them!" The blonde version of Ferris motioned to the High Council coven members now approaching. "Be sure to attack Ethan, too."

Greg nodded. "Rock power!" He started turning stones.

"I knocked this one out!" Ethan shouted to his council friends. "Give me something to capture the others."

"Here's a sleeping powder," the shorter of the two High Council guards gave a bag of chemicals to our partner.

"Thanks!" Ethan grabbed it.

"I've got a quicksand," his partner held out his arm. They were coming on quickly.

"Let me go! Let me go!" Petregaard tried to kick me off.

"Give me back my sachet."

He split the earth below us, and dramatically, we fell. He caught himself on a precipice, but I smashed into the crumbling crack. I had to claw my way out of the crevice but from the top, he easily climbed out. He turned to run, but tripped over a surprisingly tiny rock.

"Yeah!" Damocles-Greg celebrated, but the victory was short-lived. Petregaard was immediately on his feet again. I dug myself out of the hole and raced after him, Ferris and Ethan closing in from the left and right sides.

"Stop!" Ethan ordered.

But Petregaard ignored him. He was faster and stronger than us all.

Suddenly, a huge wind blew up in the forest. Tornado force gales. The air gusted round and round in a cyclone formation. Anything not tied down in the forest spun up into the sky. Including the people.

The taller of Ethan's peers was a wind harness.

Myself, Petregaard, Marcy, Ferris, Greg, the other Damocles harness whipped up into the air with the detritus, spinning in a giant, empath-made turbine. It was impossible to keep upright as the High Council harness spun us round and round.

"What fresh hell is this!" Marcy shouted.

"A wind harness!" I told her. "Attack his fingers," I pointed to the emissary on the ground.

She tried, but frowned. "The birds won't fly in this."

"Leave me out of your battle!" Petregaard sputtered. But just like us, he couldn't get free of the wind.

"You're the one who cut in!" I shouted. "Give me back my branch."

"It's not yours." He laughed. "It never was. Don't you get it? It was just a lure."

"No!"

"I can't hold the disguises much longer," Ferris warned. In the sky, we tumbled like clothes in the spin cycle of a dryer. It was hard to tell which way was up. Impossible to delicately land. Some of the trees in the forest were starting to bend and split.

"Guys, I got this." Greg motioned. He balled up his hand.

The High Council harness had been slowly walking forward towards where the other Council member was pouring out potion, preparing a trap on the ground. Greg turned over a small stone directly in his path. The witch stubbed his toe.

"Direct hit!" Greg shouted, pumping his fist.

"Damn it," the emissary frowned at the mild inconvenience, but it wasn't enough to break the spell.

"Look out!" Ethan shouted, but the warning wasn't for us. At the feet of his partners, he smashed the knock-out sachet of chemicals and made a big show of trying to protect his peers from some supposed attack, but the swirl of chemicals overcame them. It took them all out. The three High Council members collapsed to the ground.

"Uh oh," Marcy realized.

"Oh crap," Greg added.

"Hold on!" I shouted.

The moment the wind empath's hand released, the cyclone deteriorated. Everyone trapped in the storm came down with a crash. Gravity wasn't something to trifle with. Our bodies smashed into the ground. But, the earth we collapsed on was sloppy and slimy. Luckily it absorbed most of our fall.

And then it just kept absorbing.

"Quicksand!" Marcy wailed.

"I'm sinking," Greg complained.

"That's how it works," the plant harness Damocles member sneered.

I quickly realized that was the powder the other High Council member had dashed across the ground.

"It's right in the name, babe," Marcy said, almost embarrassed for her partner.

"Nuh-uh. It's *quick* sand. Not sink sand," he defended.

"Huh." She thought it over. "What do you know, you're right!"

"Let's just focus on getting out," I said. We were already stuck up to our legs.

"Well, that's easy." Marcy recalled the great owl to pull her out of the muddy trap. It scooped up the back of her t-shirt in giant talons and deposited her on the dry ground.

"Got that right," Petregaard agreed. He shook open the earth, creating a crevice where he had been suctioned into the ground.

"Stop him!" I shouted.

"I got him," Ferris countered. Since the High Council three were unconscious, Ferris could resume use of her lie-guard skills for something more productive than disguises. We all returned to our usual selves and she visualized heavy metal shackles tied to Petregaard's wrists and ankles, holding him down.

The Damocles plant harness called vines to help her out. She used the thick branches like a rope.

"Rock ladder!" Greg commanded. He balled his fist and tried to flip some stones into the quagmire. Several rocks did as he commanded, but they rolled over once and immediately started to sink into the ground. "Damn it! The sand is eating them." He noticed the Damocles girl watching over her shoulder as she climbed.

"Nice harness," she laughed.

"I swear, going downhill, rock rolling is super effective." He shot his hand out like he was shooting Spiderman casting spiderwebs to harness more and more rocks among us. "Rock power!" He shouted. This time, he yelped as a spark shot out of his hand. "Ow!" He looked down. "What the hell was that?"

"Oh no," Ferris realized it first.

"Extirpation." My eyes widened.

"Ah!" The plant harness dropped hold of her vine. It singed to the touch.

"They're burning!" Petregaard clattered the shackles that Ferris used to hold him. Like the other magic being used in the area, the handcuffs were starting to spark. "Let me out of here!"

"Fat chance," Ferris snapped, but I could see she wouldn't have control for long. Her hand was starting to generate fire as well.

"Give us back the Valdeez plants." I demanded. "Then you'll get out." I tried to climb out of the sludge, but couldn't budge.

"These things are on fire!" He shouted.

"And we almost died," Ferris wasn't about to just give him up. "Give Mae back her branch."

"Eat rocks!"

One of Marcy's birds swooped down and snatched the back of Greg's shirt. It dragged him out of the quicksand, but a trail of fire lit through the sky, the majestic beast's tail feathers sparking as well. Embers dropped along its flight path.

"Marcy. Stop. Don't spread it with the birds, it'll only get worse," I warned her.

I had seen this before. In the corn field.

When Spade refused to drop a lie-guard.

The whole field caught on fire because of his spell, but once it was burning, we couldn't use magic to put it out. A forest fire was real. And it could be savage. We couldn't start a blaze tonight. Their spells showered hot embers into the atmosphere. Sparks and small flames kissed the forest floor. Marcy did as she was told and released her harness. The great owl released its talons and Greg fell ungracefully back across the ground. His torso smothered a few newer fires, but the hotter tinder of the forest now threatened aglow. The air itself seemed flammable. The whole place was ready to go.

"No more magic," I shouted.

"You heard the girl!" Petregaard yelled. On contact, his shackles were sparking red hot.

"Let him out!" Shouted the other Damocles girl. "You'll burn him!"

"If I release him, he'll escape!" Ferris warned us as Marcy grabbed my arm from the shore and manually pulled me aground.

"Close the earth." I bargained with the Damocles boy. "Then she'll release you."

"I thought you said no more magic," he frowned.

The fiery nature of the extirpation had spread too hot in Ferris' hands. "Oh my god!" Before we could finalize the deal, she stumbled, her hand flaming bright hot.

"Catch him!" I shouted.

The second the shackles released, Petregaard raced across his open crevice, but it wasn't the path to freedom that he'd hoped. In the time between him opening the hole and being released to freedom, the quicksand had seeped over the walls. The sticky suction had formed around the chasm's walls. The boy's feet slurped him back and he fell forward into the hole. His hands, arms, legs and everything he'd used to catch his momentum sucked deep in the quagmire of sand.

"Argh!" The more he struggled, the deeper he sunk. "Uvie, help! I'm sinking."

We could all see he was worse off than before. And here, the quicksand moved quickly, the gravity of the hole pulling him deeper into the ground. The other Damocles girl considered her options.

"If you use any magic, you'll burn," I warned.

Greg and Marcy were closing in on her.

"Sorry, Pet. You're on your own!" She turned and fled.

"Stop!" Marcy shouted, giving chase.

"Let her go!" I called her off. The Valdeez branch was what mattered. It was Petregaard who had to be captured. "Give us the plant, and we'll help you," I offered.

"I can't reach it," he admitted, but he wasn't overstating his flaws. His arms and legs were all trapped in the mud. He could barely wrench his shoulder forward, let alone free his palm. His fingers were hopelessly stuck in the mud. "I can't move." He admitted.

"Well, I can."

Now was our chance. I nodded to the others. We held hands like a human chain and I waded back out to the crevice where Petregaard was stuck in the sand. On contact, my legs started sinking once more.

"Hurry," he complained.

"Just stop struggling."

"Pull me out."

"Not until I have the plant." I visually searched his pockets like he had done to mine. "Quit struggling." From looks alone, it was impossible to tell which fold of fabric hid the plants. I wanted to dig in to discover, but up this close, I realized how invasive that would be. If I went for the plant, I would touch his muscles, his body, his ribcage as well. Somewhere under all that skin and tissue was his heart. The strength of his upper torso reminded me this was a real human person with hopes and needs, not just some evil archetype. I had hated it when his lie-guard friend had invaded my body. Was I okay with doing the same thing to this boy?

"Petregaard, you can trust us. I'll save my aunt, then give the rest of the leaves to your coven as I promised," I told him. "Just tell me where it is."

He refused to look in my eyes. For a moment, he was silent, but, we both knew he could ascertain his current odds. Without our help, he wasn't getting out. He sighed. "Upper chest pocket."

I dug into his the fabric, searching with diligence until I found what was mine.

"Take your time," he said. "Have a nice feel in the forest."

I ignored him. "I got it," I told the others.

"The second I'm free, I'll take it right back," he warned. I was about to put it in my pocket, but he was right, so I thought better of it. Why keep the branch in his grasp? I tried to pass the sachet off to Greg or Marcy but they both waved me off.

"We're good," they said, aware of the responsibility, or the dangers it might bring. Maybe both.

"You got your branch, get me out of here!" Petre-gaard bellowed. The mud had seeped up to his face.

"Doesn't feel good, does it," Greg taunted. "Should have left the earth alone."

I looked to Ferris. I motioned with the sachet, would she take it? The older girl nodded.

"Catch!" I reengineered my posture, to hurl it her way.

"Got it!" She claimed, but my toss didn't have the best aim. The leather bound package soared through the air. Ferris lunged to the right. She made an excep-tional diving catch.

"Whoa! Ferris with the grab!" Marcy cheered.

The older girl reeled the package in, her body crashing across the mud.

Slurp.

The quicksand immediately sucked her down.

"Ferris!" I shouted. My instinct was to help her.

"What about me!" Petregaard panicked. If we left him now, he'd be helpless. Drowned, face first in the mud.

"I'm okay," Ferris assured us. "I got it."

I couldn't leave him, not after I'd just sworn he could trust me with his life. "Hold on," I told him, wrapping my arms around his chest. "I got you."

"And I got you," Marcy echoed, taking hold of my waist.

"And I got this," Greg finished our chain. "Ready? Heave..."

We all pulled at once. The suction pulling on Petregaard's body let off a terrible slurp as the ground released its dramatic hold.

Schhhh-lock!

In a heap, we tumbled back on the shore. The mud once holding him back ricocheted across the ground like a wave.

"We did it," I gasped.

As we untangled, Petregaard shot to his feet. "You better be good for your word," he said scrambling away from us.

"Where do you think you're going?" Greg tried to get in his way, puffing his chest. But my eyes went back to the quicksand.

"Ferris!" The girl's body had been overwhelmed by the overflow of mud in the sinkhole and her muscled frame was sinking fast.

"Mae!"

Without the rest of us in the sand to equalize the

trap, the earth now pulled her down like a draining sink. I knew at once we didn't have the resources to stop Petregaard from leaving *and* to pull Ferris free. We'd have to pick one and act quickly.

The Damocles boy could see the same thing.

"It's me or your girl," he sneered.

"I like those odds," Greg countered.

But I pulled him away. "Forget him, come on!" I dragged him and Marcy over to make a second human ladder. Petregaard laughed and disappeared into the shelter of the trees. The mud was already up to Ferris' chest.

"It's not enough," I realized. Stretching as far as we could, one body after another, we still couldn't reach Ferris' hand. "Petregaard, come back!" I shouted. "We need help!"

But he was gone.

"What should we do?" Marcy worried.

"It's no use!" Greg wailed.

"Here, take back the branch." Ferris tried to hand back the sachet.

"Put that away, we're coming to get you," I told her. "Should we try to wake the others? Maybe Ethan?"

"I can't run another lie guard," Ferris warned. "No magic, remember? It's just too painful to build. If you wake him up, and he disturbs one of the others, they're gonna know who came here to rob them." Her body sunk lower in the sand. "We don't even have the others as proof."

"There's the one boy unconscious," Marcy offered.

"It's not enough," Ferris said. "What could we say to explain why we're here?"

"So what do we do?" Greg frowned.

"Marc," I turned to the girl. "Send in your birds."

"How many?"

"All of them."

We could see Ferris was down in the thick of the mud. It would take a lot of power to free her.

"What about the extirpation?" Greg worried.

"I can handle it," Marcy narrowed her focus.

"But can the forest?"

We looked around us. There was only one way to know.

Ferris was up to her shoulders. She held the sachet above her head. Marcy balled up her fingers and concentrated all her endurance.

"Here we go... *argh!*" she yelled as she started to harness.

All around us we felt the energy whirl. The air crackled as the birds flew to her aid, showers of sparks shedding from their tail feathers.

Caw, caw.

The mud dragged up to Ferris' chin.

"I can't do it," Marcy cried. "The pain's too much to handle."

"Here, release what you can to my hand." I hugged my palm around hers, trying to help share the tension. "I'll take it," I told her. I could feel what she was worried about. Her palm was blazing hot, with her fingers practically on fire. But with my help, Marcy could hold on just a tiny bit more. She didn't let go and I didn't either. Our hands blazed in agony but we both knew we were Ferris' only hope. I held on for dear life.

The birds swooped down in the mirth.

Caw, caw.

Their feathered bodies nipped and snatched at the sleeves of Ferris' shirt. The fabric arms were all that was left for them to hold onto on the teen girl.

"Just a little more..." I coached.

"*Arghhhh!*" Marcy pushed the harness forward.

"Ferris!" Greg yelled.

The birds beat their wings and pulled the girl out of the ground.

"Hold on!" I shouted.

The birds swarmed Ferris. Sparks rained down on us all. The birds' feathers trailed orange and red rainbows. Marcy sleeves lit on fire. Next came mine. Still, we held on.

"Almost!"

"Oh my god." Greg beat out the flames on mine and his girlfriend's arms.

But, the birds did what they were told. They dragged Ferris forward, lurched her across the mud puddle and dragged her onto the non-sinking shore.

Marcy and I collapsed to the ground.

Spent.

Depleted.

Totally exhausted.

Some of her soaked, muddy clothing had charred

black in the transfer, but Ferris was out of the pit. Like us, she had been rescued.

Marcy released her harness the second that Ferris was safe. We both opened our fingers. Bone-weary. Unable to even gasp for breath. Fighting through the magical fires had taken more strength and stamina than I'd thought either Marcy or I possessed.

Greg looked between our three mud-covered, fire-eaten, prostrated bodies and shrugged.

"I take it back," he said to no one in particular. "Going on missions is actually pretty fun."

SEVENTEEN
NO BACK-UP PLAN

WHILE FERRIS, Marcy and I struggled to regain our composure, Greg ran around and tamped out every blossoming ember he could find.

"Are you okay?" I checked with the others. "We need to move when you're ready. Wouldn't want the High Council threesome to wake up."

Ferris and Marcy nodded.

"How are your hands?"

"A little crispy. I'm gonna need a serious manicure," Marcy admitted. "Oh no!" She gasped.

"What?!"

"I broke a nail."

"I'm covered head to toe in mud," Ferris countered.

"Yeah, but mud washes off. *This* is the absolute worst."

Ferris and I exchanged a glance, a broken nail was the *worst?* But neither of us said anything. The girl had just put herself through hell and back to have our backs, so we could let this little exchange go.

We cleaned up as best we could as Greg smothered the final potential fire. Luckily, the whole forest didn't ignite in the blaze.

"Thanks for the rescue." Ferris nodded.

"No biggie," Marcy flushed, pleased as punch for her role.

"I think I got 'em," Greg told us. We looked at the black little patches of singed twigs and grass.

"That was close." I shook my head.

"Too close," Marcy nodded.

"As long as no one uses more magic, we should be good," Ferris nodded. "The energy field will equalize back to normal over time."

"Don't worry," Greg chuckled. "I'll keep my harness in my pants."

"What does that even mean?" I frowned.

He laughed. "Mae, not everything has to make sense."

Ferris went around the quicksand pit to check on the others. Ethan and the two High Council battalion members lay collapsed in a huddle. Still unconscious. She also checked the Damocles coven member. "They're all still totally knocked out," she told us. "But everyone's breathing. I think the best thing for Ethan's cover is to leave them alone. Let them wake up on their own."

"And earth-man and vine-girl?" Greg looked out into the surrounding forest.

"They're long gone." Marcy sighed.

"Just as well." I noted. "What were we gonna do? Hold them captive in the forest?"

"At least we got what we came for." Marcy dusted off her clothes. "I can't wait to get home. Have a hot bath."

"Ooh, I'll join you." Greg raised an eyebrow. The couple giggled.

Ferris sighed. "I can't wait 'til Ethan comes home."

"Oh yeah," Marcy nodded. "Three weeks in the forest and he will definitely need a shower."

"I didn't think he smelled that bad," Greg shrugged. "Good for him."

"Here." Ferris handed over the sachet. "The sooner you give this to the Damocles coven, the sooner my man will come home."

"And High Council will be free of the red-heads forever," Marcy nodded.

"And Aunt Abeline will be saved," I rounded out the goals.

That was a lot of responsibilities to put on a small little branch.

But we did it.

Our team was successful.

I opened the leather pocket and jumped back, surprised, as its contents sparked a small flame.

"What was that?" Marcy asked.

I quickly blew out the fire, and tapped the contents of the sachet out into my hand. "No." As soon as I did, my mouth twisted in horror. "You have got to be kidding!"

The Valdeez branch and leaves had turned to black char.

They crumbled to ash in my hands.

"What have we done?" I looked up, the despair plain on my face.

The others couldn't hide their shock as well.

"Totally destroyed," Marcy voiced our sorrow.

"What do we do now?" Greg asked. "Do they have any more?" We looked back through the forest in the direction of the High Council encampment.

Ferris shook her head. "This was the whole thing."

"And now it's destroyed," Marcy said.

"What do we do now?" Greg wondered again. He was used to one of us girls having a plan. But I had no clue. The others were also at a loss. I was counting on this branch to restore my family unit, bring order to our universe, save our coven and revive my aunt.

I didn't have a back-up plan.

The world around me dimmed from view. For a moment, I couldn't hear anyone. Or see. Or talk. In shock, I went deaf, dumb and mute. Gently, Ferris took my hand. She tilted the black cinders back into the leather bag. She put the sachet in my pocket and steered me to start to move.

"Well, we can't stay here," she said, obviously thinking of Ethan and the others. "Come on."

EIGHTEEN

A BRAND NEW SCRABBLE BOARD

WE HAD FAILED in our mission.

Ferris, Greg, Marcy and Ethan. They'd all risked their lives and their High Council standings. And for what? A few charred offerings in a lumpy leather bag. The cinders. I should have dashed them on the forest floor. We had nothing to give the rival coven. Nothing to show for our efforts but a little ashy sachet.

The Valdeez plant was destroyed.

As the teens dropped me off at the ward, the others planned to go home.

"We'll sneak back into the castle," Ferris assured me. "No one will ever know we were gone."

"We'll pick up a volleyball at the store," Greg agreed.

"How will that help?" Ferris frowned.

"We went into the parking lot, wandering around cuz it got lost. We were just looking for the ball and now we're taking it back home," he shrugged.

"Greg's a genius at this stuff," Marcy nodded.

Of course she also thought her man was a spectacular rock harness, so her opinion of Greg didn't quite hold.

"That would never work," Ferris frowned.

I said nothing. Just let the group chatter. They'd pulled up to the emergency room entrance, but I didn't open the door.

"You may be the boss lady in battle, but I've had plenty of experience in sneaking around. To get out of school, to get out of the house. Trust me. A stray volleyball and we're gold."

"What do you think, Mae?" Marcy asked.

I just stared at the floor.

"Let's let Mae focus on more important matters," Ferris gently told them, then turned to me. "Honey, we're here at the ward."

"Right. Thanks for driving." I nodded, unbuckled my seatbelt and left the car, wandering towards the hospital's doors.

"Poor girl," I heard Marcy mutter, before leaning out to shut the car door. I'm not sure when they drove away or what they did after. I hoped Greg was right, and they'd get home free and clear. It seemed like such a waste, all the risks we had taken and now here we were, worse off than ever before.

My aunt's medical state would deteriorate.

The doctors were impotent without the help of Dr. Winter's potion. And he was helpless without the missing Valdeez ingredient. Why hadn't the Damocles trusted I would come through on my bargain? Why did they send Petregaard and the others out to the forest? If it wasn't for them, we would have been in and out and everything would be rosy. Now, I didn't know how to save my aunt's life. It was a mistake we would pay for dearly on both sides.

The sterile halls of the hospital fell in and out of focus as I made my way back to Aunt Abeline's room. All around me, buzzers sounded, machines whirred, and procedure beds rolled by with purpose. Everyone was moving. The doctors and nurses were saving the world, one patient at a time. While I could hear the cacophony of sounds and the busy hubbub, nothing made it all the way in to my brain. Every detail felt blurry. It was like being back in a Damocles bubble. I reached out and touched the things in my path. Ledges. Corners. Machines and paperwork. But I didn't feel a thing. The tactile feel of my fingers was spent. All I wanted to do was sit in the bed next to my aunt.

Even in my shock, my feet led me back to Aunt Abeline's room. I didn't realize at first that as I walked, I'd been crying. Now I dragged the dampness across the apples of my cheeks and tucked the tears into my hair. It wouldn't be any good for my aunt for me to go in already weeping. I gathered myself together before I opened the door. I stifled the emotion. When I felt more put together, I quietly slipped in. The shades in the room were drawn, but cracks of light were starting to sneak in across the tiled floor. The empty silence here felt different. More like a peaceful patter. Machines continually thumped and purred in repetitive, mechanical sighs. Something was breathing for Aunt Abeline. She was full of tubes and wires. And she wasn't the only one who'd closed their eyes. There, curled up on his side, squished in one of the hospital's small straight-backed chairs was Beck. My parabond.

He hugged an over-sized stuffed hamster to his chest.

Clearly, he'd stayed here all night, at the side of my aunt, ready to give news of any details or change. In the bed lay Aunt Abeline. Eyes closed, the covers tucked up to her chin. I could see the remnants of one of Dr. Winter's applied medical salves. There were tubes in her mouth and others in her arms, and from every direction, wires hooked up to her chest. She looked peaceful, controlled and small.

Like my Mom when I was six.

The tears pushed up again.

Oh god.

Everything I felt was so familiar. So reminiscent of the worst time in my life.

I had thought we would return victorious, but here it was, replaying around me all again. My mom, frail, lying quiet in the bed. Her body so small the child version of me could cuddle right into the crook of her arm. I stayed for days in that bed. I didn't know how to save Sierra back then. All Aunt Abeline and I could do was sit by her side and hope for the best. She fought for two weeks, until her organs collapsed.

How do you tell a six year old her mother has left? It was the hardest goodbye of my life.

And now, it was happening again.

I couldn't say goodbye to my aunt, too.

"I'm so sorry. I got you into this," I told her. I wept over her body and hugged her small limbs. Her arms were limp. It was like she was absent. Already, I missed that incredible brain. What I wouldn't give to hear some word play. Some stupid pun. Some clever saying. Anything really. An embarrassing story? I longed for it all. At least, I took comfort, she wasn't in pain. "It's not fair," I whispered.

Everything was my fault.

I thought I had the sadness contained, but my sobs climbed my throat and burst into the room. They heaved from deep inside. I tried to hold them in. But the waves grew stronger still. I sputtered and coughed several gasping wails. I shoved my face into the blankets to dry my tears. To stifle the cries.

Beck absently stirred in his chair.

I sucked back my breath and straightened, wiping the remaining tears from my eyes. He opened his eyelids slowly, but seeing me there, he gave me a sad smile. Quickly, I smoothed out my red, ruddy skin. I pulled myself back together.

"Hey, parabond," he murmured, coming around.

"Hi," I forced a smile. My fingers scraped across my cheek, blending out the last minute tears I denied.

"It's gonna be okay," he roused.

I shook my head. "We didn't get it. Petregaard was

there and two others. They ambushed us. The forest started to burn. Too many witches. Too much magic. We got it, but the Valdeez branch burned. It scorched in the fighting. All we have now is char."

Beck nodded.

I figured I knew what he was thinking. '*I told you we should have gone to the High Council elders,*' but at least he had the grace not to say it.

I gestured to the hamster toy in his arms. "I thought that was for my aunt."

He looked down sheepishly at the toy in his grasp. His forearm muscle flexed. "It is. She loaned it to me." He tucked it back beside her hip. I reached across and picked it up. The stuffed toy wore a t-shirt and a tough little expression on its face. The pout he said reminded him of me.

"It's cute."

"Yeah, it is," he smiled.

I tucked it back in my Aunt's arms, ignoring the by-proxy compliment. "Thanks for thinking of her," I said, feeling stilted and weird. I guess that's what you did when someone was in hospital. Sent a card with kind words. Suddenly, I realized in Abeline's room there were actually quite a few plants and cards, even some bouquets of flowers. Amongst it all was a brand new Scrabble board. My fingers touched the new box, covered in slick plastic and dressed up with a bow.

Beck nodded. "The gifts have been coming all night."

On top of the board game was a card. I opened it and read.

Just in case the old one got lost in the shuffle.
I'll have my first victory soon enough.
Get well,
Bonnie Maine.

I suffered a small smile. The gift and the sentiment were so perfect. Aunt Abeline would love it. If only she were awake to see.

Beck put his hands on my shoulders. "Mae, I think it's time. We need to talk to the elders."

"Beck-" I was so tired. I didn't want to fight him.

"Before you say anything, there's more to show you," he told me.

I looked around.

"Not here. At your house." He tried to sweep me into his arms, but I resisted.

"I don't want to go back there," I admitted. "I don't wanna leave my aunt. I just got here."

"She'll be alright, at least for a little while. Little Georgia will take the next shift." He nodded at the hamster.

"That's what you named her?"

"Uh huh." We both looked at the hamster's tough little face. When I still didn't seem certain, he gave me a smile he reserved for the more special things in our world. "You can trust me. It'll be worth it. I promise."

That smile warmed me to my core.

"Little Georgia Hamster," I murmured. "What a strange name for a toy."

He shrugged. "My gift, I'm naming it. When Abeline wakes up, she can change it if she wants."

"*When.*" I nodded.

That's what he said.

Beck's full belief in Aunt Abeline's recovery made everything seem brighter.

He simply nodded. "Come on." He tucked me under his wing. "We'll be right back, Auntie A," he told her unconscious body. "We're on a nickname basis," he told me. I lovingly touched her blanketed foot, but, I let Beck lead me away.

NINETEEN

WHO ARE ALL THESE PEOPLE?

BECK TOOK me out to an old black pick-up truck in the hospital parking lot. He popped open the lock with a fob. "Dad brought it around," he explained, in answer to my surprise.

Together, we climbed inside and drove in silence to my family's lake house.

Or what was left of it.

Beck easily weaved through the early morning traffic. In the small town of Plumpkin, rush hour was in swing. There must have been at least six cars on the road. We drove up to my lane. Two days out from the initial earthquake, the emergency vehicles had moved on, but the vegetation around the roadway was still tinged with damage. The nature had yet to recover. There were tire tracks and footprints up and down the whole road. The mess on the street led right to our yard.

Labelling it our *gaping hole* would had been more on the mark.

I didn't want to be there.

Why did Beck bring me?

Even if Aunt Abeline survived, what was left on these grounds?

Broken toys and smashed mementos?

Rampant destruction?

A lifetime... no, several lifetimes of memories destroyed?

And for what?

So the Damocles witches could prove a point to my coven?

I was so tired of being caught in the trap. Stuck in the middle of a fight that was not my battle. I was a lowly first-year student. I should have been head down up to my ear lobes in school.

I expected the plot of land to be dense and silent.

I was not at all prepared for the reality when we arrived.

The landsite positively hummed with joy and action. There were people working everywhere. Busy in teams. Moving belongings. Piles of ordered chaos were being developed all over the grounds. Volunteers broke down the destruction into smaller, more manageable chunks. All around, helpers were making sense of my broken home. Bit by bit, they were putting things back together. There was a stack of mangled lumber. Another of twisted metal pipes. A group of furniture selections. A pile of household belongings. And other heaps that had started to grow. Aunt Abeline's and my world was being sorted and guided. A salvage operation in mid-action. The community all around had come out to lend support.

Beck raised an eyebrow in my direction as he put the car in park. "What do you think?"

"Who are all these people?"

"Josie organized it. Since she couldn't help you on your mission. Those are some neighbors, I think." He pointed. People I recognized from our laneway saw me in the truck and waved. They tossed armfuls of lumber on the pile and turned back for another batch. "That's Jim and Ping Jiu." He pointed out Josie's parents. "That's Ferris' little sister. Oh, and over there, that's my Dad." An older version of Beck in overalls tapped a hammer at a dangling window frame, trying to carefully remove the glass. Next, Beck pointed past him. "And that's Dad's favorite customer, Carl. He's pretty swell." He looked around. "His wife Nancy's around somewhere. I don't know, it's a whole collection of help. People who wanted to do something. When the town heard about a freak earthquake, some people sent flowers. Others wanted to take action. Josie put out the call and people came running to help."

For a moment, I took in the scene.

Finally, he opened his door. "Come on."

We got out into the crowd and moved through the group like I was some sort of glad-handing celebrity. Only, it didn't feel like at the High Council. These were people who knew me, who knew my aunt, who were friends of my family, or family of my friends. They lived in the community. They helped without credit. No one pretended to be tight with me for a boost to their social status or to impress their local friends. Instead, they offered condolences, and asked after the health of my aunt. Everyone listened. Then, they went back to their work again.

The house was still torn to pieces, but the group effort to clean up was making an impact.

"Come on," Beck said. "I'll introduce you."

I followed him, shyly. It seemed like a big step to meet Beck's Dad, but he started with Josie's parents.

"Mr. and Mrs. Jiu, this is Mae Kingsley," he connected us. Her two parents offered warm smiles.

"Oh, Mae. So nice to meet you. Josie says such wonderful things about you,"

"She does?" I was surprised.

"In her way," her Mom admitted.

"We can interpret a whole host of grunts and frowns," Mr. Jiu winked.

Beck and I smiled.

"We're so sorry about this earthquake. It's a such a blow and shock. How's Abeline?" Mrs. Jiu wondered.

"The doctors are doing everything they can," I admitted.

"We'll keep her in our thoughts," she nodded, without forcing me to spill gory details.

"Thank you so much for - everything."

"You know, anything you need. We'll be here."

Mrs. Jiu put a comforting hand on my arm. They nodded and passed on, not wanting to hog my time.

"Dad," Beck moved us forward.

Obedient, I followed.

"This is Mae, Mae this is my Dad, Nancy, and Carl."

"Hi," I shook their hands shyly.

"Beckham Sr." His dad told me, pulling a work glove off. His hands reminded me of his son's, rough and large. "Mae, we're so sorry to hear about your aunt."

"Terrible tragedy, this freak accident." Carl nodded.

"Hope you don't mind we're all here to help out," Nancy leaned forward. Her perfume tickled my nose. "Figured you have enough on your plate," she told me.

"Thank you, but you didn't have to," I started. "I wouldn't want to put you out."

"Not to worry, these three would help anybody, not just one of my friends." Beck told me.

They nodded.

"Anything you need, you just ask," Nancy nodded. The men agreed, then went back to their work. Beck kept me walking.

"Hi Mr. and Mrs. Schur." This time, I recognized the couple from down the street.

"Oh Mae, how are you doing?" The matriarch wondered.

"Aunt Abeline and I got out," I shrugged. Not sure what else to say.

"You gave us all quite a shock," the woman nodded.

"This is my friend, Beck," I introduced Beck. He hadn't left my side.

"It's nice to meet you. Mae, we'll keep you in our prayers."

I didn't believe in prayer, or heaven, or miracles, but it didn't seem like the thing to correct. They were, after all, being extremely generous, with their thoughts and their actions. "Thank you so much," seemed more in line with the day.

"You must be Mae. I'm Kinsey, which sounds just like your last name without the 'g' and the '*lei*'," a younger, strawberry blonde girl marched my way, interrupting.

"Nice to meet you," the Schur's nodded to Beck and I and slipped away.

The spunky girl hadn't introduced her family name, but she didn't have to, the likeness between the sisters was impressive. I checked in with Beck but he just grinned.

"Ferris' little sister. I've heard so much," I praised.

"All good things, I know." The younger girl was so assured, only twelve or thirteen at most, but clearly used to being boss of her world. "This is my boyfriend, Brandon, with an '*o*' not an '*a*'. He's a lie-guard," she stage whispered.

"You're not supposed to say that," the young boy complained. His voice lisped because of the straightening retainer in his teeth. She frowned in his direction, so the boy wilted. He kicked at the ground and didn't make eye contact again.

"Mae's cool," Kinsey shrugged. "Aren't you, Mae?"

"Actually, Brandon's right. That's not really something that's said," I told her, gently.

"All adults are alike," she rolled her eyes and strolled away. Brandon meekly followed, dragging behind him the remains of what was once a ceiling beam. Beck and I stifled two smiles.

We were adults?

Was the world ready for a younger, tougher, more ballsy Ferris? Who could say.

"Well, look who it is."

"Oh my god, Mae!"

I recognized the next two voices immediately.

Peter Stine and Peter Clatt.

The Peters from my graphic design class at Plumpkin High. How long had it been since I'd seen them? It felt like forever. I spun around in shock.

"Hey girl!" My Peter cheered. Peter Stine and I had been matched in my very first get-to-know-you exercise on my first day of school here in town, and in my mind, he'd been 'my' Peter since that day, but both guys were totally great.

"Peters!"

The boys were carrying a heavy armoire that had once been in my aunt's bedroom. My Peter immediately dropped his end. The piece slipped to the ground with a thud, but I didn't care. He held out his arms and I rushed in.

"Hi!" I hugged the boy tight.

"Oh sure, leave me to do all the work," the other Peter complained.

"Just put it down," I waved the other Peter off. He set it down. "Hi," I hugged him as well. A little stiffer with affection, the other Peter politely patted my back. "Beck, it's Peter and Peter!"

"I see that," Beck nodded, distracted by a gesture from his father, his eyes moving between us and them. "I'll be back in a sec." He offered the two boys a small wave and left, but I didn't budge. I focused on the handsome couple. They were such a pleasant sight for my brain.

"What are you doing here?"

"We heard about the 'quake!" my Peter said.

"Such a freak accident," his boyfriend added.

"We just wanted to help. First Kate, and now this, you've had a tough road into town, hasn't she, Pete?"

But the other Peter didn't reply. He was busy watching Beck walk across the yard to chat with his father and friend. "Okay, spill," the other Peter raised an eyebrow as soon as he was gone. "What was *that*!"

"What?" I also turned.

Carl saw us all staring in their direction, as Beck chatted with his dad. He gave a friendly wave. We all waved back.

"Are you with that man?"

"Who, Carl?" I asked, knowing full well that was not who he meant.

"No, not *Carl*," the other Peter frowned. "Beck Templeton."

"Josie's Beck," my Peter said. I looked between them.

"Well?" They waited.

"I mean, we came here together, in his truck" I shrugged. Again, purposefully not answering.

"Where's Josie?" My Peter asked, leaning in like it was a secret.

"She's here. I think. Beck said she organized this."

"She did," the boys nodded. "She's the one who told us." But that wasn't detail enough to explain. Was I with Beck or not? They cocked their heads. Expectant. Waiting. It was actually pretty fun to watch them squirm.

"Actually, I haven't seen her..." I admitted, playfully looking around, but the Peters couldn't hold out any more.

"Girl, put your eyes back in your head and tell us the deal," the other Peter said.

I caved. "They broke up."

"And you moved right in? Well done," the other Peter approved.

I frowned. I'd forgotten this little quirk about the guys. An acute interest in who I was dating. Even when there was zero dating going on.

"I didn't *move in*. We're just friends."

This was the exact kind of thing I had warned Beck about. Immediate assumptions. All tawdry and quick. Of course, no one ever said this kind of crap to the *guy*.

Just more proof I was correct. We were smart to keep this under wraps.

Whatever *this* was.

"You're friends," the other Peter frowned.

"Like you were friends with Spade?" My Peter grinned.

The boys exchanged a knowing look.

"Actually..." I playfully raised an eyebrow. It was painfully old news now, so it couldn't hurt to throw the guys a bone. "Spade and I kinda dated a bit." I shrugged. "It crashed and burned."

"What!" My Peter's jaw dropped open.

"That's what I'm talking about! Details, Mae. All the details. Immediately, spill."

"It wasn't... it was short lived." I admitted. "He just wanted to have sex, basically."

"Uh, yeah." The other Peter rolled his eyes. "Mae, that's what all guys want."

I laughed. "No. It was more complicated than that. He wanted to control me and my friends."

"And your friends?" My Peter frowned.

"It's a long story. Put it this way, he wasn't boyfriend material."

"But he was fun for a few nights, right?" The other Peter prodded.

I made a playful face. *A good girl never tells.*

The boys ate it up. "Mae!"

"I bet *he's* pretty fun, too," my Peter looked wistfully back over to Beck.

"Um, I'm standing right here," the other Peter joked.

"I saw you. Did you see him?" He mooned.

"Did you see those hands?" The other Peter joined in.

I couldn't help but blush. "I wouldn't know," I said, but not quick enough. They both saw my flush. "Enough about me," I fought off their knowing stares. "How are you? And you?"

"Ugh, so dull and boring." The other Peter rolled his eyes.

My Peter laughed. "I was going to say happy as a clam."

"Well, we are, but that's also boring."

"I'd take boring any day," I admitted. "Just a boring, clammy life."

"Yeah," the other Peter nodded. A darkness came into his voice, as if only suddenly he remembered where we were and why we were gathered.

"Sorry about all this," My Peter added.

Reality set back in.

We looked around. It had been so nice to see the boys, just talk like friends, giggle and laugh and grin, but there was a lot more on my plate. As this shattered lake house could reflect. My eye caught a glimmer of light refracting from the sun. Something shiny on the ground.

The bumblebee trophy from my youthful spelling contest.

The one that until earlier this week, had sat

forgotten in our kitchen cupboard. Now, it was stuck in the brush. I stepped away from the boys to retrieve it. Sadly, I grinned at the fake gold-plated bug. "I won this for participating in a spelling contest. Lost the first round. Participant," I read the label. "Aunt Abeline kept it for the last decade. She's been carting it around. A tiny memory." I looked at the stupid plastic statue fondly. "All this stuff... it's like I lost the whole world."

My Peter put a hand on my shoulder. "You'll put it back together, again."

I looked up, surprised at the sentiment's deep comfort. "Thanks," I said, wildly grateful for these boys.

Suddenly, Beck cut in. "'Scuse me guys, do you think I could borrow her?"

"We're just here for free labor," the other Peter nodded, giving Beck a once over grin.

"I'll keep that safe," My Peter took the little bee trophy from my hands. He tucked it into the armoire for safe-keeping and winked at me. "We'll see you in a bit."

"Thanks guys," I nodded. I watched them depart.

"Make sure you're carrying your weight," the other Peter complained to his partner, falling away from Beck and my conversation. "My end is definitely heavier."

"No, it's not. I'm just in better shape."

"I do curls."

"Try some biceps."

"I don't like them, they're hard."

"They get easier as you try." They muttered and sputtered as they lifted and marched off.

"So what do you think?" Beck asked.

I took in the scene more clearly now. The surprise had worn off. I could see small acts of work happening all around. The land was covered in grunts of effort and cheerful chatter as people pitched in to help. And not just my close friends. A whole crew of strangers and acquaintances had volunteered to come out and put my family's feet back on the ground. They'd loaned their time and sweat equity in service of myself and my aunt. The outpouring of kindness and generosity was overwhelming.

"This is-" I put a hand on Beck's arm, trying to thank him, but adequate words were not coming. "It's really something." I tried and failed to express all the things that I felt.

"I thought you might like it," he grinned. His sweet smile connected deeply with my heart.

All my life, I would have described myself as an outsider. After Mom died, my social circle grew claustrophobically small. Just Aunt Abeline and me, against the world. But now, in the small town of Plumpkin, we'd grown a thousand social ties. While society could be random and cruel, it could also be magical and kind. And Beck was generous and caring every chance that he got. My hand slid up his bicep.

Suddenly, arms full, Josie trudged out of the hole in the kitchen. She looked up and saw us. "You're here," she noted.

"Hi, oh my gosh." Embarrassed to be touching her ex-boyfriend while she did my manual labour, I quickly dropped my hand and went to help lighten her load.

"Don't worry, I'm good," she tossed the pile of wood scraps to the side. "Hope you don't mind, we organized a little salvage before the rain kicks in, or whatever." She shrugged. Magical mudslide, enchanted forest fire, a hurricane windstorm, who could say what would come next.

I nodded.

She wiped her brow. "The Beans offered their barn for storage. We've already loaded a couple trucks. Whatever we can grab, we will. We won't get it all, but a lot of the furniture's already recovered." She rattled off information, then softened. "How's your aunt?"

"Still unconscious," I admitted.

The girl just nodded. Didn't try to say everything would be fine. We sat in the bad news together. I appreciated her silence. I appreciated everything she had done.

"Thank you... for organizing."

She shrugged. "I told you I'd help how I could."

"Who are the Beans?" Beck asked.

"Oh, I'll introduce you." Josie nodded. She led the way to a woman by the vans. The lady looked vaguely familiar, but I wasn't sure where I'd seen her before. Something about her facial structure seemed reminiscent of someone else.

"Mae, Beck, meet Dahlia," Josie introduced.

"Dahlia Bean." The woman offered a firm hand-shake. "I'm Ferris' mother."

My eyes widened. Of course. Ferris was imprinted directly from Dahlia's bones, although, on the older woman, time had begun to run its course. She was beautiful, but also weathered, and I suspected the red hair color on her short bob was distinctly bottle-poured. Other than that, she was the distinct original of her carbon copy children, first Ferris, then the smaller, strawberry-blonder Kinsey.

"Hi," I shook her hand warmly. "So nice to meet you. I hear that you've loaned us the use of your barn. Thank you."

"Oh, that was nothing. It was mostly sitting empty." She glanced furtively at the others, "but Mae, I've been waiting to speak to you."

Josie and Beck shared a glance. "I'll go... help the others," Josie told us.

"I'll help," Beck nodded. They both left us alone.

"Ferris is an incredible girl," I gushed to her mother.

"Yes. She's really grown." Dahlia nodded. "The coven has tested her. I can see it's testing you as well."

This wasn't the coven, I almost told her, but that information would be outside the knowledge bounds. We weren't allowed to speak of coven business. Even with a fellow witch's parents. Of course, I had a strange feeling she already knew more than she let on. Mrs. Bean seemed to know a lot about what was happening.

To stay safe, I offered a vague nod.

"Since all this began, have you slept?"

"Not much," I admitted.

She dropped her voice. "Mae, I'm a dreamcast, still a pretty good one. So this might sound strange, but please hear me out. I'll say my piece. Do with it what you will. There's someone who can help you. Someone..." she hesitated, then just dove in. "Scrabble-related? Does that mean something to you? A Scrabble gift? A gift for word play? When you get back to the castle, you will need to seek them out."

My memory flashed back to the hospital gift from Lady Blue Moon, but I didn't offer Mrs. Bean the thought. My time in the forests had made me wary. I knew full well, a lie-guard could take on any form that they wanted. What if this woman was really a Damocles member? Or one of Petregaard's friends? Trying to trick me into revealing more?

"What was Ferris like as a child?" I tried to ask super casually. I failed.

Dahlia looked surprised, then smiled. "If you need me to prove my identity, you can just ask."

"I need you to prove your identity."

"Smart girl," she approved. She thought for a moment. "Her boyfriend's name is Ethan Grady. And they grew up right next door."

I stayed silent. That wouldn't cut it.

Mrs. Bean tried again. "During her admission season, she and Ethan were kidnapped and she was forced to strip, I believe, by the sister of your boyfriend."

"He's not my boyfriend," I automatically defended, then laughed at myself. "And that is definitely not the point of that story."

Ferris' naked kidnapping story. It was one I'd heard before.

Mrs. Bean was the real deal.

"I can't believe she told you," I laughed.

Dahlia shook her head. "She didn't. I saw it." She vaguely gestured to her mind. "Dreamcast mothers are the worst." She chuckled.

I leaned forward. "Please, tell me everything you can."

"It's not much. Things come in waves. Kind of like mysteries," she told me. I nodded. That's how the casting worked in my head as well. "The Scrabble woman, she'll be like a white knight in battle. Help you get the real answers. You should go to her. Get much closer."

"Alright, I will. Anything else?"

"Two things," Dahlia leaned in. "One, you need to make use of your own special power."

"I'll sleep when my aunt's well again."

"That's not good enough." She frowned.

"What's two?" I asked.

She put a hand on my shoulder. "You're not going to like it," she told me.

I nodded. I could take it.

"Are you ready? Turn around."

TWENTY

NOT EVERYONE IN DAMOCLES AGREED

AS WE SPOKE, Dahlia turned my shoulder for me to look out into the forest. At just that moment, two Damocles coven members came out of a hole in the ground.

The tunnel out of my family's secret bunker.

"You!" I shouted. "Get away from there!" I ran right for them. Put myself in their path. Mrs. Bean just let me go.

The blonde-haired woman stopped in her tracks. Her partner stood beside her. I didn't recognize either of them. They each held boxes full of stuff from the hole.

"That's not yours. That's my family's!" I tried to grab the belongings back. The women let me take them. In fact, they quickly complied. They were older, maybe in their late fifties. There were plenty of wrinkles around their startlingly blue eyes.

"We know, Mae."

"We're sorry."

"We're just here to help how we can."

I yanked the stuff away. The boxes jostled, private items falling everywhere on the forest floor. "Help?" I shouted. "You destroyed it! My home! My whole world!" I shouted. "*You* did this! You and your friends!"

Beck and Josie came running. I was making a big enough scene to disturb the whole forest, but the women were totally passive.

"What's going on?" Josie looked between us, surprised.

I fumed.

"They shouldn't be here," Beck acknowledged.

The two women bowed their heads.

Josie looked between us and the red-wearing women. "Get out," she said immediately, without question taking our side.

"Not everyone in Damocles believed this was right," the older of the two admitted.

"We're so sorry for your loss," the other nodded.

"I'm not *losing* my aunt. Abeline's gonna be fine!" I said. "She would be already if it wasn't for your damn coven! I had the Valdeez in my hand and it burnt to dust because you fought to be right!"

"You *had* the leaves?" The women were shocked. Josie raised an eyebrow.

"Petregaard and the others destroyed them!" I spat on the ground. "Now we're fucked."

The ugly word hung in the air. I never swore, but in the moment it felt right.

"Just leave us alone," Beck ordered.

"Let us help," the older woman implored.

"I don't need you moving boxes," I snapped.

She nodded. "You're right. I understand." She checked in with her partner. "Why don't you come with us, see our full coven for yourself."

"Not on your life," Beck immediately answered.

"Why?" I asked.

"I think it will help you learn some answers," she said.

"I don't need answers. What I need is my aunt."

"Well, maybe we can help with that as well," the other woman added. "Dr. Winters has said he'll help you."

"You can take me to the doctor?" I asked.

"Yes," the women nodded.

I considered this. I hadn't seen him since that initial consult.

"No," Beck frowned. "Mae, you can't go among their group."

"If I talk to Dr. Winters, he can work with Aunt Abeline's condition. He can give her more time. We need it. Desperately. You said so yourself, I should ask for more help."

"But not from *them*. They're the other side."

"We're on the same side," the woman told him.

"You have got to be kidding!" Beck laughed in her

face. He raked a hand through his hair. "Josie, help me out?"

His ex-girlfriend looked between us, only barely putting pieces together, although I'd bet she'd figured out more things than she let on. "I think that Mae should make the decision," she told him. Her eyes went straight to me.

"This is dumb." He rolled his eyes. "I won't let you do this alone."

"Good. Come along." I agreed, my eyes still on the women. "You can drive."

TWENTY-ONE
A LOOMING OMEN OF LOSS

BECK FOLLOWED the two witches in their beat up car. Neither he nor I had much to say on the drive over. It was pretty clear we had stopped seeing eye-to-eye. While we both wanted to save Abeline as quickly and safely as possible, when it came to choosing how to do that, Beck was impotent. The choice was all mine. The women drove out of town, over to the next city limits. Oshanga Township was larger than all of the northern towns combined. It was also a little rough and beaten around the edges, more industrial than places closer to home. Although the textile industry had been dying out, there was a time when the surrounding streets had been filled with warehouses and stores. Most now sat empty. Their fabric and apparel quotas being lost overseas. With the end of the Multifiber Arrangement of the 1970s, garments and fabrics were made cheaper in distant countries. And the tattered remains of a lost workforce studded the land. The communities nearby were better off, like Plumpkin and Alderton. Over time, they'd pivoted to embrace their identities as darling, bespoke, little farming towns. But Oshanga didn't. It simply tapered off. The women pulled off the two-lane highway into an abandoned parking lot.

"What is this?" Beck wondered as he followed their turn. We both stared out the windows. Ahead was a decrepit old shopping plaza. An indoor mall. The kind that was popular before Internet shopping took hold. It was now years past its usefulness. We could both see it had sat broken and depleting, for a long, long time.

The women motioned for us to follow, getting out of their car. They walked towards a rickety entrance, stepping through the broken glass of the mall's weathered doors. They slid a plywood slab out of a way, opening a hole to the interior world.

"Over there," I pointed.

"You're going in there?" Beck asked.

"*We're* going," I nodded.

He frowned, but still, he put the car in park. There were other cars strewn about the lot. Enough, I realized, for their whole coven to be inside. Cleverly, they weren't all parked beside the entrance. Instead, they parked sporadically all over the slab so as not to attract attention, although I doubted many onlookers ever checked on the abandoned mall.

We got out of his truck.

"It's a temporary location," the younger of the two women told me as we approached them. "Natalia thought it best to give some breathing room to your High Council."

And yet I knew full well, if I were to call a member of my coven I would hear firsthand how other Damocles members were presently standing on the castle lawn. I said nothing.

Beck and I followed the women's path across the cracked, derelict pavement. Dandelions thrust forth from their crumbly, jagged home. The weight of years of cars and zero upkeep had pulverized the asphalt to dust. The women waited for our arrival then together, we ducked under the door.

Inside the mall, it was dark and smelled musty. Immediately our eyes adjusted to the dim light.

"Our coven has been traveling a great distance." The first woman explained. "Luckily, there are abandoned buildings like this in most, if not every, town."

We walked through pools of sunlight on faded linoleum tiles. The shadow patterns made by skylights overhead had bleached into their surface. Some of the windows were smashed, but most had stayed intact. The mall, a once powerful cultural symbol of the collective where people gathered, consumed, and conversed, was now a looming omen of loss. The owners and shoppers and products were all gone. Any item of value was stripped to its core. At its heyday, there must have been thousands of plants and green spaces grown in the captured sunlight of skylights and cared for by fastidious caretakers. Now, lone dead trees stood in the concrete boxes in the halls. With no natural access to water, the plants were now dry. Their leaves were all brown, though they did not fall to the ground. It was eerily quiet.

"I don't like this at all," Beck murmured.

I nodded. We didn't have to like it to get answers, to find a way to buy Abeline more time.

In several spots, the ceiling had collapsed, letting rain and the elements pool together. Vandals had come through, roaming the empty structure, taking and destroying to their personal delight. But, although the graffiti remained – some careless, some real art – even those vagrant artists were long disappeared.

Quickly the women walked on.

As the hallway came to its natural conclusion in a wider atrium, suddenly the abandoned structure took on a different feel.

"We've stayed here, to minimize intrusion," the woman noted.

Here was the one-time food court and the central hub of the building. I was surprised. It was now lively and lived in once more. Unlike the hallways leading up to this communal avenue, the space around the food court was well-used. The coven had enlivened the space with seating areas and individual stores made up like homes. People moved through the various areas, working and chatting together, bubbling and inter-acting like they were in their own little town. The atrium was full of blonde-haired, blue-eyed witches. Everyone but us was dressed head-to-toe in red clothes.

"Whoa." In spite of ourselves, Beck and I were impressed.

As we got closer, I could see that in the shops around the atrium the witches had made use of lie-guard illusions, making up their spaces in ways that spanned from enjoyable to opulent in the midst of forgotten squalor of the actual mall. Looking nothing like the rundown remnants of the hallways, their visuals in the stores around the food court had taken over completely.

But our approach stirred up the room. The chatter grew silent, and several of the lie-guard illusions disappeared. The Damocles coven stood at attention, ready to defend what was theirs. Several hands, I saw, grew primed. They were balled in fists ready to be harnessed, or to create illusions, or whatever needed to be done should Beck or I begin a war.

Beck also clenched his fingers, but I shook my head and touched his palm. We weren't there to battle. There was no point in picking a fight that he and I could never win.

"They've come to see the doctor," the older woman said to the others. Several members just stood and stared. Beck and I waited, outsiders without an invitation. But soon, Natalia appeared. She eyed us, warily.

"She had the plant. A shadow team followed and destroyed it," the woman said to her leader. Both women kept their eyes on me. "One of ours."

"Who?" Natalia asked.

"Petregaard," the woman told her.

"And a vine harness, and some lie-guard," I listed them off on my hand. "I had it! Why didn't you tell them that I'd return?" I didn't mean to raise my voice.

She shook her head, "how would I know that we could trust you?"

"Because of my *aunt*."

"All the more reason to think only of yourself," she shrugged. "Come." She walked us through her whole coven, taking us back to her chamber. As we silently passed the rows of witches, conversation restarted among them. If Natalia was in our stead, the threat wasn't quite as real. But every eye stayed trained in our direction. Natalia didn't even flinch at all the unwanted attention. She ended our tour at the makeshift infirmary. She waved me and Beck both inside. Dr. Winters looked up from his store front. "If Damocles members followed you into the forest, they acted on their own accord. I told you, my people are desperate. No longer content just to wait and hope."

"But if they'd just let me bring it home, like we talked about, you would have had your precious Valdeez plant." I scowled.

"It's possible," she conceded. "I suppose we'll never know."

That answer was infuriating. "I don't think you get it. Even if you never meant to harm her, the blood of my aunt is now on your heads."

"Soon there will be more blood than that," she agreed.

I looked to Beck, my eyes flashing in anger. How to make this woman understand?

"Ahem." The doctor cleared his throat.

Beck just shrugged. *You wanted to see them*, his look seemed to note.

"They've come to see you," Natalia passed us off to his keeping. "The countdown continues to march," she warned and then left.

Dr. Winters went behind her and closed the infirmary's doors. It was clear he wanted to keep the discussion private. That suited our purposes as well. He nodded. "I know you are worried about your aunt. I gave my word. I'll keep her alive as long as I can, but, you should know, the bigger picture looms forward. She might sound harsh, but Natalia wasn't speaking lightly. She never does. If you don't return with the Valdeez within the remaining two-day timeline, the Damocles coven will enact all their threats. Though they don't want to, they will take your High Council by force. I fear that some of your coven will be destroyed and most of mine will not go home." He saw the fear in our eyes. "That's not a threat. I took an oath. I'll save all I can. But my people will not go home empty-handed. Not anymore."

"You wanted to come to this guy?" Beck scoffed in my ear. "Bet the elders don't seem so bad."

I brushed him off. "I didn't come for that. I want to hear about my aunt."

Dr. Winters cleared a spot for us to sit down.

"How's she doing?" I asked. Beck and I sat down to hear the news.

"About as well as can be expected," he offered the sort of non-answer that medical school trained all doctors to give. Even witch doctors, it seemed, gave the same non-committal replies. He moved a box off the counter. The containers inside clanged around. A box of small bottles. This was the Damocles dispensary as well. I waited for him to join us. As tactful as he was, I sensed the doctor still had more to tell. Any further news about my aunt could be life-saving, so I planned full well to wait him out. I would give Dr. Winters all the time and space that he needed to get his message across. He checked his chart. The clipboard looked identical to the ones at the hospital. He was keeping exacting notes on my aunt's progress.

"I have her on a high dose of Planoxin which we're supplementing with Dayflis Leaves soaked in Matryll," he read off. When he saw my blank expression, he offered a wry frown. "Not a chemist, I see."

"Dreamcast, harness," I described our roles. For his part, Beck just sat stoic. Sharing coven secrets with their doctor probably wasn't smart, but I figured with doctor-patient confidentiality, it was a reasonable choice. Besides, nothing about this visit was High Council approved. Just one more infraction to add to the pile. Of course, if Natalia and the others had their way, there might not be a coven or coven rules to be followed very soon.

He nodded, bringing his language down to our

level. "We've distributed a painkiller that will alleviate stressors that can inhibit her hormone development. And I applied a chemical load topically to open and strengthen the chest cavity and the ribs. It needs to be changed every four hours. Her torso needs time to rebuild. It's the same technique we're using on patients back home. So far, it's been quite successful. Even long term."

"On your people who need the Valdeez treatment?" I asked.

Beck shifted in his chair.

"Yes."

"Is she improving? Can she feel pain?"

"As I said, the treatment's fairly stable, however, she's in a vegetative state. Nothing is healing at this natural pace, although I am holding her current injuries in check. As long as my supplies can support it, she's zero sum neutral, but without the Valdeez healing properties, the human body can't revive quick enough to regenerate. Eventually, she'll deteriorate. Slowly at first, then all at once. Mae, I don't have enough drugs to keep her going. It's difficult enough to hide all my work from the town doctors. Obviously, the full extent of my kit is back home. These supplies will run out. We're only two days out," he noted, checking his watch.

"Tell me the ingredients again. Perhaps I can augment the supply from our camp. The High Council has a greenhouse. I can't get the Valdeez, but I can talk to some chemists who-"

Almost blindly, he reached up to his neckline and

dragged a tiny locket across his clavicle bone. The habit was an unconscious comfort. Something he likely did often to help him hand over bad news. "Mae, the maintenance-phase potion contains elements that are local to a place very far away," he told me gently.

"Your home town."

He nodded. "Our coven has travelled a great distance. They've been patient. But they're tired of waiting. Every day that passes, the children have less chance of being fully restored," he admitted.

"Children?" Beck squinted.

"What children?" I frowned. We looked at one another.

For a moment, he caught himself, as if considering whether to reveal this information, but he decided it couldn't hurt. "Our patients. The surviving eight. They are youths." Again, he dragged the locket.

"What happened?" Eight children? That seemed like a lot of people in need of one branch.

"A school bus," he started, then cleared the emotion out of his throat, "an accident." The sentence was broken, but loaded. A far-away look in his eyes took over. I could see on his face, even this small mention brought him back to a place of deep pain. The doctor was heartbroken. For the first time I saw him, not as a medical figurehead, but as a person. A man with a sad, crooked smile. He'd seen a lot of pain and suffering. The dramatic baby-blue eyes didn't shine quite as bright in the makeshift infirmary shell.

What had he seen?

As the doctor at their hospital, he must have been surrounded by a flood of gory, bloody stuff. But a school bus full of children... I could almost hear the strained shouts of triage nurses trying to manage the wounds of several injured kids at once.

Bleeding.

Chaos.

Families weeping.

Even now, the doctor seemed to relive the worst of it in his mind.

"Buses don't usually use the route at Jablonski's Curve," he said. His head shaking. "The grade is too tight. It was some kind of detour they were taking." He shrugged, still trying to make sense of it for himself. "The driver fell off course. The front wheels locked as they cornered. He couldn't recover. The bus and everyone on it rolled six or seven times before it came to rest on the valley floor. It took out the giant trees the whole way down. He died, the driver. Probably instantly. Along with another fourteen others. So, we'll never know what really happened. Little children. The benches had no seatbelts. In a rollover, well..." he trailed off. "They didn't have a hope." He cleared his throat and straightened. "In the end, we stabilized eight."

The number sounded gross and ineffectual, but also massive.

Eight wounded children with desperate families waiting for a magic potion. From a plant that another coven held.

And refused to deliver.

No wonder there was so much anger in their bones.

He looked me dead in the eyes, a determination returning to his voice. "We'll heal those eight," he said. "Or die trying."

I felt his defiant tone.

They had lost so much. They refused to lose more.

"This is my daughter, Lana." His hands went to his neck. He pulled down the locket that he played with so often. He delicately slid around the clasp. "Svetlana Winters," he corrected, giving her full and proper name. He uncoupled the locket and a small seed tumbled out. Beck picked it up, as I looked at the girl. She looked sweet, blonde and blue-eyed as the others, but at her young age, her eyes didn't seem to peer into your soul. Instead, it was like you could see into hers.

Perfect.

So innocent.

"She's beautiful," I murmured. "Is she-"

"One of the eight back home." Stiffly, he nodded. Dr. Winters took the seed back from Beck and slipped it in the locket keep-away space. He clasped it closed.

"What's the seed?"

"It's the seed of a Valdeez plant, if you can believe it." He scoffed at himself. "One of the other family members gave it to me. They wanted my hope to grow. Of all things. Excuse me." As he reattached his necklace and tucked it under his scrubs, his professional demeanor returned. He nodded then walked towards the makeshift doors. The consultation was over. But I wasn't budging.

I looked at Beck. Was he thinking what I was?

"Dr. Winters. Forget hope," I told him. "Let's grow the real thing."

TWENTY-TWO
WORK TOGETHER, OR AT LEAST AS EQUALS

I QUICKLY EXPLAINED how we'd come across the instructions to grow the Valdeez plant, but the seeds that were needed were incredibly rare. He had a seed. That meant all that was required were the other ingredients, the underwater soil and the volcanic sap. The Pokna mountains were in driving distance. With a quick growing spell, we could accomplish the task.

Dr. Winters heard my story, then gathered Natalia's attention. Petregaard and two others also joined under the guise of makeshift guards. I wasn't sure if they'd been invited or just decided it was their business, but for the first time since the earth quake had happened, I didn't care how many Damocles were around me. I just wanted to move fast.

Quickly, I relayed the terms of the Valdeez recipe Josie had found in the textbook to everyone assembled there. "The aerated seed was the biggest trouble. But, you already have that. We don't need to steal or take the Valdeez branch from my coven. We can grow our own," I told them, excitedly. "If you're willing to part with it." I admitted. "I know you said for you it was mostly a metaphor, but from what I know, the seed is very rare."

The other Damocles looked to their doctor.

"I'm more than willing." Dr. Winters took off his necklace and started to give it to me, but Petregaard intercepted it first.

"Not so fast. I don't trust her," he scoffed. "She's only thinking of her coven, her aunt, her local business," he warned.

"We'd already have the branch in our possession if you and your friends hadn't come and destroyed it!" I snapped.

"Mae is offering a real chance here," Beck defended. "There are quick grow potions. I've seen 'em. If you got the plant going, who knows how big it could grow!?"

"Who are you, the dumb girl's boyfriend?" Petregaard snapped.

"Who he is doesn't matter," I rolled my eyes, holding a hand up to Beck's chest to stop him from going further down this road.

My parabond had to bite his tongue against the sniveling Damocles member, but, he managed to respect my wishes and hold back from saying more. This wasn't about him or me, it was only about my aunt.

"Screw them, I can do this. I can get the potion," Petregaard told their leader.

Natalia held up her hand to silence the squabble and gestured. He had no choice but to hand the locket over to her hand. She fingered it gently.

"We need some assurance," she told me. "From you, going forward."

"I can do better," I said. I'd thought of that. I was desperate to get going, but couldn't risk a second ambush to ruin this last-ditch scheme. "This time, we work as partners." I told them. "We work in tandem. There are two missing ingredients, and a very short lead." The timeline for my aunt was running shorter and shorter. Petregaard seemed skeptical, but Natalia and Dr. Winters nodded. "We head to the mountains, split up – two teams, one mission. Each coven gathers one ingredient. Both are brought back to you here. It's your seed, you grow it. Our initial terms still intact."

"I can have a quick grow serum ready," Dr. Winters nodded.

"How far is this place?" Natalia wondered.

I checked with Beck, the only local.

"About a half-day drive from our town."

"I know a guy. I can get the underwater soil," I told them confidently. Beck and I exchanged a glance. He knew exactly who I meant. I had no way of knowing if the coven member would agree to this mission, but I wouldn't let on to that hitch. "Can you acquire the volcanic sap?"

Natalia looked to Petregaard. She, the earth-harness and two other Damocles huddled, whispering their opinions of the plan. Finally, they looked up.

"I know someone too," Petregaard growled, always competing and showy. His frown never let up.

Natalia nodded and handed the locket back to Dr. Winter's hands. "Then you will work together, or at least as equals, and the quick growing potion will be ready upon your return."

The doctor re-clasped the locket around his neck. He tucked it under his red scrubs, now imbued with different value. Petregaard and I both nodded.

"But you should know," the Damocles leader's face darkened. "If you fail, or you don't make the timeline, we will move forward with other plans."

"And your aunt..." Dr. Winters trailed off.

I nodded. "I understand."

TWENTY-THREE

STAY OUT OF MY WAY

"TELL ME AGAIN, why we need the volleyball?" Beck wondered.

"Greg said it helps you sneak in like a charm," I shrugged.

We'd agreed to meet the Damocles pair at the hospital in half an hour, just long enough for me to gather the others. I planned to ask two guys to work together, Rick and Vince. Vince was a water-harness. He could move entire sections of a lake, I'd seen him do it. It flew in the face of every known law of science, but, that was alright, as long as it helped Aunt Abeline out. And Rick had a delicate potion that worked as a salve on hot lava. I'd seen him and Hilde use it to walk across blazing fires and never get burned. Although the Damocles coven were the ones tasked with retrieving the volcanic ingredient, and the mountain was dormant, I figured having a back-up in our pocket couldn't hurt.

If the boys said yes.

After all, I was taking a pretty big risk.

The elders had made it clear at the start of the protests that the first year students were not meant to leave the property, and we were not meant to converse with the Damocles members, and I was breaking all those rules.

When I'd first heard the threat to Aunt Abeline's safety, I'd left without thinking. No one could blame me. It was only natural that I'd go. But now, I was returning and recruiting other friends to become team-mates with the enemy.

No, not teammates.

Co-conspirators...

Was that better? Or worse?

My only chance for approval from the High Council was to ensure they never figured it out.

Beck slowed the truck as we arrived at the castle entrance. He stopped just before the clearing. Things looked even worse that we hoped. Red Damocles robed witches clogged the entrance, and a legion of Ladies and Fellows now stood outside, holding their ground. Instinctively, Beck stopped the truck and flipped into reverse. We couldn't risk returning. Better to get out while we still could.

"We can call them or something," he told me. "Maybe they can get out to the highway."

"No. I'm going in," I put a hand on his arm.

"But the crowd," he looked doubtful. "You'll be stopped for sure."

"I'll get around. If we call, the boys can say no. They will. I would. It's a pretty huge ask to come out, break the contract, work with the enemy. Even if it does help. I need to look them in the eye as I ask. I need them to know *I* know, they'd be risking a lot."

"Mae, if you get caught, there's no way they'll let you back out."

"That's a bridge to cross in time. But, two's too much. Beck, can you-" I fumbled. I hated to ask.

"Go back and sit at the hospital?"

Sheepishly, I nodded.

"I don't get you, Mae. What's your problem? You're always tossing me away." He frowned. "Why won't you let me be there? Not as your boyfriend, fine. At least as a friend. You'd rather take Vince? And Greg? And *Petregaard?* I have real powers. This is a huge, stupid risk. I can do something important to help."

"Keeping Abeline safe *is* important." I told him. "It means everything."

"I could do more."

"Beck, no, you can't." Didn't he understand that? I was asking him for help with the most important factor.

"She's lying unconscious."

"And I put her there! *In that bed!* You don't get it? What do you think this is? A lark? A *game?* This whole thing is my fault. She might never wake again. I asked for her help in the Battle of Four. I brought her to the other coven's attention. If I'd just cut off our family relationship like a normal coven member she'd be safe...

instead, in two days, she'll be dead. Just... you know what, forget it. I'm sorry I asked. Do what you want, Beck. Be a big man."

"Mae-"

"I gotta go." I cut the conversation short and hopped out of the truck. I didn't slam the door, much as I might have wanted to. That would draw too much attention, and the whole point was to slip in and out without being found. Beck watched me with dark eyes as I stomped around the car. But fight or not, there was no time to talk it out further. I would do this with or without his help. I stalked around the woods and looked for a spot to cross into the High Council's lush garden lawn. Although it was crowded with witches at the front fountain, on the back side the path was mostly open. There were two council fellows sitting, chatting on a bench. So I backed out of the forest picking the volleyball up as I came.

"There it is," I said aloud, scooping it up in my hands. "Found it," I added, holding the ball up like a prize when the guys looked my way. Then I marched up to the castle, lightly tossing the equipment in my hands, as if I hadn't a care in the world.

Greg was right, the ruse worked seamlessly.

Within seconds, the fellows had forgotten I was there. But that part was easy, inside the coven walls there were a lot more witches to fool. Quickly, I ducked inside the doors.

As soon as I entered, I could see what felt like half of the High Council attendants milling in the atrium, staging their own observational protests. Everyone wanted to know what the Damocles were up to. You could argue they were being nosy, but there was also nothing else going on. The castle was silent. All the usual lessons and events had been shut down 'til the protest was over. As a safety precaution it made sense, but that also heightened the tensions all around. As I snuck across the atrium floor, I felt pretty good about my passage. Although random students waved, no one thought I looked out of place or questioned where I'd been.

No one 'til Brandi.

Beck's sister and a group of her third year posse saw me coming and crowded in my direction, angling their bodies to position themselves between me and the stairs. There was no way to go around them without being caught in their web. I frowned, but didn't stop walking. My time was so limited, they wouldn't put me off my path.

"Where do you think you're going?" Brandi snapped. She crossed her arms and looked me up and down with a frown reserved for her meanest judgment. "What's with the ball? You don't play."

"Get out of my path," I snarled. I had just told her brother to kick bricks and he was someone I really cared about. I had no issue making it a family affair.

"Make me," she dared.

She must have thought I would never do it, never do anything to hurt her, because when I hurled the ball I was holding right at Brandi's face, her eyes popped out of her head. Instinctively she caught the ball, but that was what I wanted. Her hands were rendered busy. I grabbed her harnessing fingers and wrenched them back, behind her body, before she had time to call on the wind.

"Stay out of my way," I hissed in her ear. "Me, my friends, my family. Back the hell off." Then, I dropped her hand and marched away. Purposefully, I turned my back, never looking over my shoulder. I just kept on walking. She could retaliate if she wanted, but we both knew it would look petty and cheap. Pouncing on a girl with her back turned wouldn't do. Brandi was too aware of the optics to try that tact. I marched straight ahead, head held high. Immediately, it paid off. Instead of a counter attack in my direction, Brandi turned on her friends. She smacked the ball on the floor.

"What the hell was that? Why didn't you help me?"

"It all happened so fast," her bravest friend stammered. The others were too shaken to speak. I was free and clear of those girls.

But, I didn't escape the atrium.

Lady Mauve stood waiting on the bottom tread of the stairs.

She'd seen everything.

"My office. Now."

TWENTY-FOUR

ONE MORE LETTER

I FOLLOWED the powerhouse of a woman to her office in silence. Earlier in the day, Lady Mauve had tied her white track suit jacket around her waist, displaying both her sculpted forearms and her sleeves of tattoo ink. For a woman in her fifties, she was a tough little lady. The sleeveless look made her seem even more intimidating than usual, which was already hard to do. With her spikey hair and muscled frame, on a good day, she could cut you to your core. But it wasn't her body you had to worry about. Her words would slice you in half.

She marched quickly through the castle.

I wasn't sure how many rules the instructor was aware I'd just broken, but if the answer was more than zero, our meeting wouldn't go well. I was already short on time. If I was late, Petregaard would be pissed. Or worse, leave without me.

Mauve didn't say a word until we were safely

behind closed doors. Her office was bigger than Lady Blue Moon's and far less crammed with papers. Like Mauve, it was fierce and efficient. She simply motioned me to sit down.

I obeyed but tried to keep my head high.

I didn't want my body language to reveal how I really felt.

I needed all the encouragement I could muster.

"Why did I see you come in from outside?" She asked, right to the point. Lady Mauve sat askance on the desk, her arms crossed in front. She stared down her nose at my face. Her eyes didn't miss anything. From my inert sitting position, her posture towered over my head. Her size didn't fool me. Diminutive or not, I was correct to be afraid.

I cleared my throat. I had prepared for a question like this. "Just retrieving a stray volleyball."

"Oh? Where is it?"

"I... gave it back to Brandi," I said.

"Did you talk with the other coven while you were out there?"

"On the grounds? No. Not at all." I was careful not to mis-speak.

"I feel we've been very explicit," she said, her eyes narrowing. Had she noticed I'd put a qualifier on that denial? She watched me squirm for a moment longer then pressed the intercom on her desk. "Blue Moon, please bring me the first years' paperwork," she said. "Specifically Mae Kingsley's."

"Right away, Mauve."

Lady Mauve released the button.

My heart sunk.

The contracts.

My signature was on it. A legal treaty between me and the coven. Almost every word on that artifact, I had ignored.

"Other than volleyball retrieval, what have you been up to?"

"I've been caring for my sick aunt."

Lady Mauve frowned. "Yes. I heard. Freak accident, that earthquake." She nodded. "An act of god." She looked up to see if I would disagree.

But I didn't sputter.

Why was she playing it like that? Lady Mauve knew the Damocles witches had attacked my house on purpose, Natalia had practically claimed it in front of the whole coven. She clearly understood it was no accident that my aunt had suffered. Lady Mauve was there, at that meeting. I saw her. I ran from her. Why didn't she now admit the truth?

Because then she might have to show a little mercy?

Mauve had a lot of pull in the coven, if she wanted to, she could help me attain the Valdeez branch without going on this mission. But, there was a reason I hadn't asked her. And now, I had all the proof I could need. I was right. The elders were pretending like nothing had happened. They had no interest in helping. There was no way they'd agree to save my aunt.

Only *I* could solve my problems.

If I could manage to get away. But how?

"Here are the papers you asked for - there you are!" Lady Blue Moon walked in with a frown but brightened, mid-delivery, when she saw me. "Are you done with all my data mail?" She asked me. "I've had this girl running all over town," she added to Lady Mauve. Blue Moon's eyes were wild and worried but she managed to push forth a casual smile and flash recognition my way as well.

"Uh, yup. Of course." I caught on quick to whatever Blue Moon was selling.

Dahlia Bean's words echoed, *the Scrabble connection could be my knight in shining armor.* Lady Blue Moon was looking at me now, wordlessly nodding.

"I'm all finished," I agreed.

"Great, I've got two more, that is, unless you still need my delivery girl?" Lady Blue Moon asked Mauve with all the innocence as she could muster.

"Your delivery girl..."

Lady Blue Moon and I both waited her out.

"I thought you said you were looking after your aunt?" Lady Mauve frowned.

"Well, that's why I picked her. I thought, you know, she would be the perfect person, as right now the first year's aren't allowed to leave the castle without permission, what with the protests, and of course, poor Mae needs an escape route to visit her dear Aunt. The darling woman's quite ill. In fact, she's in hospital," Lady Blue Moon said while physically extracting me from the interrogation chair. She pulled me up by my arm and I stood. Slipped behind her. "Such a terrible, natural disaster. I was so worried when I heard." She rolled forward. "But Abeline's a strong bird. Strong mind. She'll wake up soon." She told me, sincerely.

"Thanks," I nodded. "I think so too."

"Yes," Lady Mauve had no choice but to soften. "All the best to your aunt."

"Thank you."

"Well, if that's it, we'll let you get back to it." Lady Blue Moon continued to hustle me out the door, and she'd almost succeeded, when -

"Stop."

Lady Mauve's tone made us halt.

In the doorway, one step from freedom, we froze.

Totally busted.

With slow deliberation, Lady Mauve came around her desk.

Her eyes narrowed, showing deep suspicions. She stared us each down. Blue Moon and I did our best not to flinch. Then, she thrust an enveloped in my hands, the recipient's name turned down. "Here," she said. "One more letter for your route."

TWENTY-FIVE
A FOUNTAIN OF YOUTH

LADY BLUE MOON and I scurried away from Mauve's office just as fast as our legs would carry us, until we found safety in the elevator and headed off her floor.

"Why'd you do that?" I demanded as the doors were closing.

"Um, I think you mean thank you?" She giggled, her fear eking out of her body in strange, silly ways.

"Thank you, but you can't do that. You can't risk your neck like that!"

Lady Blue Moon let out a big gust of air to dispel some of the pent up energy she'd held in her chest. "I can't believe that it worked. Ferris told me her Mom had a dream that you'd be coming and that you might need my rescue. I'm just glad I could think quickly. I'm terrible at improv." She leaned against the mirrored wall, exhausted. "I 'bout near peed my pants!"

"You saved me."

"I saved your bacon," she giggled again. "What comes next?"

"We're growing a Valdeez plant," I confided. "Maybe."

"A Valdeez plant?" Lady Blue Moon sputtered. "Mae, the Damocles coven only just attacked a High Council emissary and left them unconscious, stealing the Valdeez branch. You wouldn't know anything about that, would you? No. Wait. Good lord, don't tell me." She shuddered.

"I heard... they were unsuccessful in their mission," I admitted. "We should leave it at that."

"Leave me right out of it."

"Believe me, you've done more than your share."

"You really think you can grow it?" She looked surprised.

I shrugged.

She went on. "The muddle of one small leaf can heal an army of ancient battle wounds. The combination of homeopathic elements, anti-inflammatory agents and antimicrobial superpowers with an incredibly high bioavailability to the blood system makes it rumored to be pretty cool. Or so say the spell books. I've never seen it work in my lifetime," she admitted. "The plant is so rare, with the added chaser of modern medicine... it would basically be like a fountain of youth."

"Or a healing potion," I figured.

"Yeah. True." She nodded. "Is that what you hope with Abeline?"

I nodded. "That's what the doctors say."

"Do I want to know what doctor?"

"No, you don't."

We both grinned.

So it was real. Blue Moon had read the same thing. The plant really could save my aunt *and* heal their sick kids back at home. If we could grow the plant, there'd be enough for everyone and more.

The vision of Aunt Abeline stuck in my head, so sick and frail in that bed.

Here I was about to team up with the boy who had put her there. Petregaard could think of no one other than himself.

Did he really not know she was home when he struck with his earthquake?

Or did he hope, if she was hurt badly enough, that the Battle of Four champion would jump into action and show them the path?

I wouldn't put it past him. But, I put it out of my mind. That kind of negative thinking didn't help where I was. Or what I had to do next. We were on the same side now.

I would do whatever needed to be done.

"You know," I chuckled sadly, looking at the elevator arm as it slowly rose, almost to the top. "We've lived in eleven different houses, always moving from one place to the next, seeing the best a city had to offer, drinking it in, having our fill. Then, on we went to a new discovery. I've never really thought of a place as mine. We found them, we sold them, sometimes we rented fully furnished apartments. We rarely took ownership of stuff. Even at the lake house. That was my grandparent's cabin. A house full of their things. And it was nice to be surrounded by their belongings, reminded of their memories, but none of that stuff was ever mine. There is only one thing. Aunt Abeline. She's mine. And I'm hers... she's the only family I've ever known. She's the one thing in the world-" the words choked up in my throat. "I will fight to hold on."

"I know." Lady Blue Moon offered a sad smile, then let me think in the silence.

A million memories fought for attention.

Going to museums. Listening to records. A thousand words laid on the Scrabble board. Silent reading. Boisterous cooking. Finding surprising trails. Basking in nature. Shopping kitschy stores. So much word play. Always looking for new and more. Stories... words... adventure.

"Why did we settle in Plumpkin?" I wondered.

"I think the answer's pretty clear." Lady Blue Moon said. "She did it for you, Mae. So you could grow. To have the opportunity she never had, to follow the path of your mom. To enroll in the High Council. So far, it's been a bit of a bumpy road, but-"

Ding. The elevator opened.

We both looked at the empty hallway.

"I'll hold that thought," Lady Blue Moon told me. "See you in a few minutes?"

I nodded. It was time to get down to business.

"I'll be right back."

TWENTY-SIX

WE'RE NOT FRIENDS

"THERE YOU ARE, VINCE." I had checked his room, the washroom, and finally found him hanging out, watching a movie in the common space down the hall.

"Here I am," he nodded, tossing a fresh piece of popcorn in his mouth. He barely looked up. He had a confident swagger about him that was always telling the world to chill out. Lucky for me, he also had the skills and smarts to back that bravado up.

"I hope you don't mind if I don't turn on the lights while we talk," I warned.

"That's super weird, but whatever," he shrugged. He also had a knack for saying the things usually left unspoken. He clicked pause on the film.

"What's with the dark and whispers?" Hilde sat up from her hidden spot on a bench in a separate row.

"Hilde," I looked up surprised at the girl, as she

spun round on her couch. "I didn't know you were here," I admitted.

"We're watching a movie." She nodded.

"In separate rows," Vince noted shoving in more popcorn. Just in case their locations weren't abundantly clear. They were not watching said movie *together*. There was no Greg and Marcy style hanky-panky going on.

"Can you believe Vince has to have a couch all to himself?" Hilde giggled. "He has a bum knee. He has to stretch out."

I looked at the older boy. He shrugged.

"Must be all that scootering," I said.

Vince grinned, tossed a kernel and caught it in his mouth.

"Scooters are so cool," Hilde mooned, the puppy love dripping all over her face.

Vince chomped down on the high praise and winked my way. I felt a jealous twinge. This seemed like such a carefree and low stakes way to spend an evening. How I wished I too could just have a normal day. But time was marching on. I checked the hallway once more to make sure I hadn't been followed. But it was clear.

"Hill, do you think you could give Vince and I a few minutes?"

"In the dark? Mae, you're so weird," she said, but just shrugged. Weird was okay. "Don't start it again without me," she told him nodding at the movie. The actor's face was frozen in a strange mangled way.

"Wouldn't dream of it," Vince nodded.

We both watched her go.

"Seems I've acquired quite a little stalker," he noted when she was safely out of the room.

"She means well." I nodded.

He frowned. Crunched another popcorn kernel. "Mae, what do you want?"

I took a quick breath. Time for the pitch. "I'm not sure if you know this, but my Aunt Abeline was recently hurt."

"In the earthquake. Everybody knows." Vince was unmoved.

"Right. Well, it was caused by the Damocles coven."

He nodded. Also common knowledge.

"They say they didn't know she was there."

This caught his attention.

They say.

When had I and the other coven been conversing?

This was against Council rules.

I barreled ahead. "She was crushed because she was hiding in a secret bunker. Below ground. When the earthquake came..."

"Is she alright?"

"No." I fought off the lump coming to my throat. I pushed out the edge in my voice. "Sorry. No, Vince. She's in grave condition, and the Damocles said for her to have any chance of survival I need a Valdeez plant. They need it too. It's a long story. If we can get one, then my aunt will be saved. And as a bonus they'll leave us alone at the High Council."

"They were already supposed to leave," he muttered.

I just shrugged. I was aware of that fact.

"The Council has the plant. In the greenhouse. It's very protected. Lock and key. I've seen it, out with Rick," Vince told me.

"I was gonna ask him next," I admitted.

"In the dark?" Vince snarked.

I lowered my head.

"They won't give it to you," he said.

"I know." I admitted. "Officially, I haven't asked them. But-" we both knew the truth. The High Council wasn't built to help a lowly first year, like me.

"So, cut to the chase," he said, an eyebrow raised. "Why tell me? I don't have the branch."

I glanced back over my shoulder. The doorway was still clear. Admitting the next part was as good as confessing my plan. Could I trust Vince? I didn't have much of a choice.

"I'm gonna grow a new plant," I started slowly.

"What do you *need*?" His patience ran thin. "We're not friends."

I couldn't put it off any longer. "I'm taking Blue Moon's station wagon and headed to the Pokna Mountains."

His eyebrow raised. "That's a pretty big road trip. In that old, clunky car?"

"With the black racing stripe, exactly."

"A station wagon racer." Vince smirked. "I bet when she bought it, it was already on the car."

I just shrugged. He was floating off topic, but I knew the next part would push him totally off-road. I dropped my voice. "I'm working with the Damocles coven."

His eyebrow shot up again.

"It's an unholy partnership. They'll get the volcano sap, while I gather the proper soil. Both are necessary for the Valdeez to grow."

Here was the catch.

"It's sea-faring fertilizer. In heavy run-off waters. A lake or lagoon, I don't really know. Something big. Some body of water. I'm here 'cuz *you* can open a hole."

"In the body of water."

"In the water," I nodded. "It could save my aunt's life."

I watched his suspicious face tilt up in thought.

"You can get us out of the castle?"

"I can get you out," I nodded.

Vince flicked off the television and shrugged. "Alright. I wasn't doing anything better with my night. But you break it to the mini stalker. And don't you invite her along."

Little Hilde. I wasn't planning on it. Having a cute little shadow must have been growing old. I didn't want to be the bearer of bad news, but I'd do it. I'd tell her we were leaving and she couldn't come.

Luckily, when we exited the common area, she wasn't waiting outside.

"Well, what do you know?" Vince was surprised she had vacated the area. "Guess my charm does have bounds. See you in a few."

"Alright. See you soon," I nodded. He and I would meet in the lobby. He strolled off to get ready and I went straight to Rick's dorm room. I knocked and waited. Rick opened his doorway and stood in the frame.

"Good evening, Mae." He was congenial, but his large torso blocked me from seeing into the room.

"Hi, Rick. Can I come in for a minute?"

"To what does this pertain?" His manner was gracious, almost perfect, but I wished he'd just let me inside. I glanced around the hallway, thankful we were alone.

For now.

"I'm not sure if you heard, but my aunt was recently hurt in an earthquake," I started.

"I did hear." He nodded.

From who? I wondered. Rick wasn't one to engage in gossip. He seemed above such trivial things. I was surprised the information had made it to him. More proof, everyone in the clan really did know all my business.

"She needs a Valdeez branch," I admitted. "I'm trying to grow it. Vince and I are going to get some ingredients from the Pokna Mountain range."

"And you wanted me to create some spells? To carry with you?"

"Actually, I wanted you to come. *And* create some spells."

"Yes. You may come in." He stood out of the way.

I nodded and stepped into his bedroom. It was strange to be in his personal space. He was so stoic in the group, I didn't feel like I knew him very well. There was a afghan with a beautiful hand-embroidered pattern of an abstract mountain range. It had definitely not come with the place. I tried not to stare at his secrets.

"What spells do you need?" He asked. His posture stayed rod straight. He steepled his hands, ready to listen.

"There's a volcano. I know you had a hot burn salve," I said.

He nodded. "Maybe an explosive," he added to the list, mostly talking to himself. "Perhaps a truth serum, in case you need it. A glue could come in handy, and a sleeping potion for yourself."

"I don't need that," I interrupted. "I'm barely sleeping."

"The range is quite far. You can recharge while Vince drives."

"I'm too amped up to sleep," I shrugged.

"You're a dream cast."

"I know, but-"

"You must access your powers." He said. "I insist."

It wasn't a request. "If you want my help, you must take the whole thing. Including the sleeping aid."

"So you'll come?"

"No. I signed a contract," he warned me.

I signed the same one. So did Beck. So did Vince. Greg and Marcy, Ferris... we'd all broken that same contract, but pointing that out wouldn't win me any points.

"I cannot go. I said I'd help."

So I tried another way. "I think I can get you out. No, not think. I know I can. No one would be any wiser."

"I will be wiser," he corrected. "A man is as good as his word."

My face fell.

"But my offer remains. Take or leave it."

"I'll take it," I nodded. "Oh, and can you add a quick-growing potion?"

Rick nodded. "Give me ten minutes." He said, walking me to his doorway. I had kinda hoped to watch him prepare them, but I wasn't in any position to ask for a cherry on top. I followed his exit, but stopped in the doorframe.

"Rick?"

He raised an eyebrow.

"Thanks."

He nodded. "Return in ten." And he shut me back out in the hall.

I looked at my watch. There wasn't much time, but there was one person I wanted to call. I quickly locked myself in my own bedroom and called the person I wanted to talk to more than anyone else.

Beck.

I could have claimed I was looking for an update, but I already knew how sick Aunt Abeline was. Today was the same as yesterday's prognosis.

Still unconscious.

Covered in Dr. Winter's spells.

Temporarily stopped from deterioration.

Growing worse by the minute, without the Valdeez plant.

Our only hope was to get the medicine that she needed. There was no need to check on her now. What I was really doing, was touching base with Beck. I don't know what I was looking for exactly.

Sympathy?

Comfort?

After our fight, would he even be willing to offer those things?

The disagreement was ugly.

Still, I wanted to hear his sweet voice. That he would reject me was a chance I was willing to take. I pressed his contact name and the phone dialed his number.

"Hey," he picked up on the second ring. His voice was stiff. No 'parabond,' I noted. The way he always greeted me, *Hey parabond,* all sweet and intimate. Not this time.

He was still angry.

"Hey, parabond," I answered. I tried to grease the wheel.

He just grunted.

"I made it back in. The volleyball worked, although in the end, I kind of used it as a weapon," I admitted.

He waited in silence. Didn't ask for any more information. Didn't put himself up on my hook. I dropped it. Now wasn't the time to explain how I'd assaulted his sister.

"I wish you were here," I offered. "To wrap your strong arms around me." Saying it out loud, I could almost feel that heat and energy. I could sense he felt it too. I belonged in those arms.

He sighed. "I wish I were too. But a stubborn girl who I'm absolutely-not-dating didn't want me to come in."

"I guess I was wrong about that."

"You're wrong about a lot of things," he pouted.

I let that go, an accusation I didn't need to unwrap. "How's Aunt Abeline?"

"No change," he admitted. Then cleared his throat. "Actually, Mae," he sighed. "She might be getting worse. Dr. Winters isn't telling me anything, but since we've come back, he's doubled the frequency of bandages and leaf wraps. The change comes about once every two hours."

"Huh."

That wasn't good. For a moment, we sat in the dark news together.

"Little Georgia's by her side." Finally, that sweet

voice came around. He knew I needed it. We needed each other.

I forced a small smile at the thought of the toy hamster.

But I didn't add on. For a moment, the darkness held.

"Any luck with the team?" He asked.

Though he couldn't see me, I nodded.

"Both Vince and Rick," I said.

That admittance was a bit of a stretch, since only one of them was coming, but thinking I had a strong trio to help me in the forest might help Beck feel a little better about his place by my aunt. And it wasn't a total lie. Rick was on board. He was making me things to take for my task.

The conversation petered again.

"Beck, I'm sorry I..."

"No, I should have been more understanding..."

We both apologized at once. A warm wash flooded over me.

"Thank you for being there."

"Thank you for asking," he replied.

Suddenly, on his end, several machines starting beeping at once. The hospital room came alive with blaring alarms and warning signs.

"What's going on?"

"Hold on," Beck said, although his voice was barely audible. The words got lost in the mad hospital room chaos. New voices flooded in.

"Code Blue, second floor, corridor three, room 212."

"Intubated!"

"We'll push another epi."

"The numbers are plummeting."

"Young man, we need you to step outside. Young man?"

"What's happening-" I could hear Beck as he tried to get some answers. "Where's Dr. Winters? Dr. Barth?"

"Sir, we need you to step outside."

"Sir."

"Beck, what's happening?" I asked.

The voices and machines became more muted as he stepped out of Aunt Abeline's hospital room. He let them work without him. His voice came back to the phone.

"Beck?"

"I don't know, Mae. She's crashing. She's... they're working on her now."

TWENTY-SEVEN

YOU'VE DONE THE IMPOSSIBLE BEFORE

I WANTED to stay on the phone to hear details of her full recovery, but when the chaos was over, the nurse only reported that they had gotten her back to a stable position. There was nothing more to do or say. As promised, in the given ten minutes, Rick had created all the potions I required, so Beck and I said farewell. Going on this mission was the best thing for Aunt Abeline. We both knew I'd return as quick as I could.

Rick gave me a fire proof sludge, a sleeping potion, a quick-grow serum, a smoke bomb, two explosives, a truth serum, and some vicious snap-ribbon plants that would skin the bark off a branch or chop a finger clean off. I quickly filled my pockets with the spells.

Always proper, he walked me to the elevator where Vince was waiting. The boys shared a congenial nod. I could see they'd grown friendly. As friendly as Rick or Vince chose to be with anybody.

"God speed recovery for your aunt." The strong

boy offered a firm handshake. I shook it. This was as far outside the rules as Rick would tread. I appreciated the effort. Vince and Rick shook hands too.

"Thanks, again." I told him, then we were off. Vince and I quickly took the stairs to the lady and fellow offices.

"Did you tell Hilde we were going?" He asked.

I shook him off. "She isn't around. Must have gone to bed."

He shrugged. "Ain't life grand."

"Try not to hurt her," I warned.

"What, like you with Beck?"

I glanced over, side-eyed, but Vince just shrugged. He was deflecting Hilde's puppy attraction, not making a valid point. It was best not to engage. We arrived at the office hallway quickly and reconvened with Lady Blue Moon.

"I think this is a bad idea," she warned me.

"True, but it's the only one I've got." I told her.

"It's fine. Just an underwater relay and a dormant, old volcano." Vince shrugged. "What's the harm in that?"

"We're delivery people," I reminded her. "Delivering packages for the archives and running errands."

"Right, of course." She handed a box into each of our arms. "Just be careful." She warned us. "Both of you," she looked at the snide boy.

"I can handle myself."

"Blue Moon, it's time," I pushed us forward.

"Alright, delivery team," Lady Blue Moon pointedly announced as we marched through the atrium crowd. "You know where to take these. You've delivered packages for me before." She made a big show. I wished she'd just chill out. "They're making a delivery," she told another batch of ladies and fellows who had not asked and clearly didn't care what we were doing. "Just a couple of delivery students," she loudly proclaimed. "You be careful out there... on your... deliveries."

I gave her a stiff grin. "We will." For a second, I paused.

"We gotta go," Vince said. I nodded.

"If anything should happen..." I trailed off. "Do your best for Abeline."

Lady Blue Moon nodded. "You've pulled off the impossible before." She handed over the car keys. We shared a tough smile. "Oh, and hey, don't forget to deliver this." She passed me the postage-stamped envelope from Lady Mauve.

I tapped it twice in my hands. We both nodded. "See you soon."

Vince was already at the car. It was easy to spot in the lot. He'd tossed the packages inside.

"It was unlocked?"

"What was your first clue?"

"Do I get that attitude the whole ride?"

"Package deal," he grinned, but his tone lightened from a surly inflection to a smile.

"Are you're okay to drive?" I checked. "Rick wants me to sleep." I showed him the sleeping potion.

"I'll be fine." He frowned. "Keys? Dude was right. I didn't want to say it, but you're starting to look like the walking dead."

"Nice."

"Truth hurts."

I tossed my packages inside as well, and handed over the fob. We both climbed in and he pulled out of the drive, leaving the castle in the rear view.

"We've got to pick up the rest of the group," I told him.

"And then?"

"And then I'll drink the potion and have a nap." This satisfied him.

Vince drove straight to the hospital. There, Petregaard and another coven member climbed in the back. Their red clothes stuck out like a bright, throbbing thumb.

"I'm Mae, this is Vince," I introduced us to the new Damocles member. "That's Petregaard," I introduced the one I knew to Vince.

"You're late." Petregaard answered. He didn't bother to make introductions.

"Well, we're here now," Vince countered. "What's your name, buddy?" We looked to the other Damocles guy.

"You don't need to know his name, just get us there," Petregaard muttered.

"Awesome, I was just saying I really wanted to take an extra-long road trip with a couple of dickheads,"

Vince snapped, putting the car in drive. Petregaard and the other Damocles member didn't answer back.

I checked in with Vince. "Still want me to sleep it out?"

He nodded.

True to my word, I opened Rick's sleeping potion and took a large swig.

"It probably won't even work," I told him. "I'm so wired out of my mind."

But before I could even finish the sentence, I was out.

TWENTY-EIGHT

IN AND OUT AND ROUND THE FOREST

IN MY DREAM, a haunting chorus of children began singing.

In and out and round the forest.
Round the forest, round the forest.
In and out and round the forest.
Tick, tick, boom.

The little voices floated in through a window into the room where I was standing. Wafting gauze sheets gently blew in the breeze. I walked through them, moving towards the voices as they sang.

Sweet and pure.

I shifted the thin sheets out of my path, the route looking the same in every direction. My only guide through the haze was their virtuous voices. Over and over the chorus sang.

In and out and round the forest.
Through the fabric, they came into view.
Round the forest, round the forest.

As I moved a final curtain aside, they appeared more clearly. There were eight of them, hand in hand, softly singing as they moved. I watched as them skip and lightly dance to their tune.

In and out and round the forest.

There was no choreography to their moves. Instead, they threaded in and out of each other's arms, smoothly up and over. Over, under. Their paths moved playfully and quickly. A life-size, never-ending snake of human appendages, twisting and tying into knots.

Tick, tick, boom.

They collapsed in time with the tune.

Several children giggled. But the song was never over. They rose, held hands again and restarted the same performance.

In and out and round the forest.

This time, the eight separated and went in opposite directions in smaller groups of four. Both ribbons of hand-holding children folding back and over each other.

Round the forest,
Tying in knots.
Round the forest.
Twisting and forming. Singing the children's tune.
In and out and round the forest.
Tick, tick...

TWENTY-NINE
WHO ARE YOU?

BOOM!

The whole car jerked and tossed its passengers from side to side. I awoke with a start, sitting straight up in the chair.

"Rise and shine," Vince griped as he re-established control of the car, now driving much slower on the gravel side road. He had turned off the county highway onto the less-travelled laneway far too fast, but course corrected fairly quickly. Both the Damocles boys in the back and I were roused in the bumpy transition.

"Easy," the nameless boy complained.

"Whatever dude. It's like a frickin' time machine in here," Vince complained. "Everybody snarfs while I do hours of work."

We sat up, wiping the drool from our mouths and looking around. I checked the clock in the dash. Vince was right. I'd been sleeping for hours.

"Are we almost there?" I asked.

I tried to catch my bearings. It didn't look like we were much of anywhere at all. Plant life had overtaken the smaller road we were on. It wasn't two lanes, more like one and a half. I looked back at the Damocles guys. They were taking the scene in as well.

"According to GPS," he nodded, then dropped his voice for my ears alone. "Did you dream?"

I nodded. "I usually write it all down." There was no pen or paper around.

"Lock it up tight," he said. He tapped his forehead and raised an eyebrow.

I frowned. I'd do my best.

Suddenly, a strange snore echoed out through the car.

"What was that?" Petregaard snapped.

I turned around. "I don't know."

Vince checked things out in the rearview. It had definitely come from the trunk.

The boys in the back bench spun around and looked over the seating., Along with Lady Blue Moon's fake packages, and Lady Mauve's real letter there was a bunched up blanket. They yanked the fabric off the floor of the car.

"What the hell?!" Petregaard snapped.

The nameless' boy's jaw dropped. "Who are you?"

"Uh hi," a familiar little voice sputtered. "Are we there yet?"

"Hilde!" I gasped.

Vince was so surprised, the car swerved and lurched.

She sat up in the cargo space. "Hi." She said to the boys in the back. "I'm Hilde Dove," she properly greeted them, rubbing her eyes. "Hi, Vince!" She waved up to the front. Having fully regained his senses, he gave her a thin-lipped frown and a two-fingered salute from the front.

"What are you doing here?" I asked, incredulously.

She looked embarrassed. "I wanted to come on the trip."

"You tricked us," Petregaard raged towards me. "Two and two was even. Now another witch? What's your game, Mae? I *knew* you couldn't be trusted."

"Me?!" I snapped. "I didn't even know she was there!"

"It's your car!" He huffed.

"Actually it's another coven member's car, but we should have checked the trunk," Vince glared in my direction.

"Not you too!" I sputtered. How was Hilde's deception my fault?

"I knew, I just knew. Didn't I say it?" Petregaard fumed.

"You did say it," his friend rolled his eyes.

"What'd you say?" Hilde wondered.

"Your coven's full of liars." The earth-harness snapped.

"Now hold up-" I interrupted, but Vince spoke even louder.

"Mae didn't know she was coming. Hilde kind of - follows me."

"She's his stalker," I shouted, my anger still apparent.

"I am not a stalker," Hilde pouted, but since she'd snuck into the back seat to follow Vince across the countryside, she didn't have much of a position. "I just didn't think you'd let me come."

"For good reason." Vince frowned. "How'd you even know where to hide?"

"There was only one wagon with a racing stripe." She shrugged.

Vince's mouth dropped open. Fair enough.

"This is unacceptable!" Petregaard wasn't done.

"It's fine." The other Damocles member tried to calm everyone. "She's a dumb kid."

"You're a dumb kid," Hilde combatted.

The Damocles member chuckled. "She's what we've been fighting for," the boy reminded his partner.

Petregaard stiffened. "Fine. Whatever. The girl stays."

"Well, it's not like you could chuck her out of the car," Vince laughed. He turned his attention back to the road and suddenly we bounced over a rock. The car lurched twice. While our belts held us in, Hilde tossed around in the trunk.

"Watch it!" Our four voices rang out in tandem. Even Hilde's.

"It was a rock! The road is gravel." He shouted right back. "Great. Four back seat drivers."

"Hilde, you can't stay back there. It's not safe. Put on a seatbelt." I frowned, unhappy to be her keeper. If

Rick had worried about how I'd keep Vince intact in this situation, he'd be downright angry to know I was now caring for Hilde as well. The girl was his precious parabond. "Come up a row."

Obediently, Hilde climbed over the bench in between the two Damocles coven members. Luckily she was still fairly small and everyone fit comfortably. Her normal clothes were a refreshing sight between all the red items they wore.

"I'm Hilde." Since she was now sitting beside them, she offered the Damocles boys an official handshake.

"Petregaard," the earth-harness softened. No surprise there. Everyone softened around Hilde.

She turned to the other guy.

"Niall." He shook as well

"Nice to meet you, Niall," I added from the front, since this was the first we'd heard his name. He gave a stiff nod to both Vince and I. I guess after several hours of driving he'd decided we weren't so bad after all. I turned around in my chair. "Much farther?" I asked, looking ahead. We'd been traveling on the side road for quite a distance, or so it felt.

"You think I've been here?" Vince scoffed.

"No."

"The GPS is done. This road's uncharted. When it stops at a lagoon, I guess we're there."

"How much farther?" Petregaard repeated.

I turned back to face him. "We're not sure."

Hilde let out a big sigh, stretching out and smacking her lips.

"You know, it's strange," she said, yawning. "I dreamt it was dark and stormy, but here the sunlight's streaming in through the trees. I'm a dreamcast," she told the fellas. "We were having a picnic, on this cool beach full of pebbles, and I really wanted my mom to be there."

Mom.

Something about the way she said it made us all realize how young and sweet she really was.

"That sounds like a nice dream," I told her.

"It's a good day to save the world," Niall smiled. "Don't you think?"

"Perfect," she grinned at her new friend.

To save the world... to save my aunt....

For a while, we bumped along in silence, until as Vince said, the lake appeared and the road ended. He slowed. We'd reached our destination. He made a three point turn, extended into something more like an eight-pointer, because the lane was so narrow and there was no handy parking area. He reversed the car so the station wagon faced the direction of the exit. Then, he turned off the ignition.

Vince smirked, tugging the parking break up. "On foot from this point."

We all looked outdoors. The forest here was ancient. The trees stood tall and thin, their branches spreading out to the skies well above our heads. And Hilde's observation was correct, it was a beautiful fall day. Perfect for hiking, but a bit cool for swimming. Luckily with Vince here, we wouldn't get wet. The sunlight streamed in. Quickly, we poured out of the car. Staring up and out around us. Our limbs were stiff. We stretched our legs and arms and looked around.

"So cool," Hilde noted.

"Lodgepole pine," Vince agreed.

"I see the lake," I pointed.

"The volcano's much farther," Petregaard complained.

"It's the end of the road," Vince shrugged. Literally. He'd driven all the way he could on the gravel. The route extending from here was only a walking path. A car would not fit. Or maybe barely. Plus, Vince had already turned around. There was no way he was driving any further up the hill.

"It's fine. We can walk," Niall responded. "We split up, get our stuff, and reconvene?"

I nodded.

Petregaard just scowled.

"Oh!" I dug into my pants pockets. I pulled out several of Rick's packages and picked out the perfect one. "I have a burn salve that works on lava. Makes it so your feet can walk on something hot." I offered it forward, stuffing the others away for later.

"The volcano's dormant," Petregaard scoffed. He didn't reach out to take the package.

"I know, but it's a back-up, just in case. You never know." I raised it again.

"We don't want your poison."

"It's not poison, its-"

"Don't waste your breath on this guy," Vince said.

Petregaard crossed his arms and puffed out his chest. Now that there weren't car seats between them, the testosterone between the two boys had plenty of room to expand. Vince didn't back down.

"We'll be okay," Niall translated, diffusing the situation. "Thanks anyway."

I shrugged. "Fine. Do it your way." I tossed the salve in the car and slammed the door.

Vince and Petregaard continued to glare. But neither pushed the conflict forward.

We looked up to the distant mountain.

"I'm thinking maybe two hours round trip?" Niall suggested.

I looked out. Seemed about right. I checked with Vince and nodded.

"We'll be here," he said.

"See you kid," Niall told Hilde.

"Bye," she waved. "Bye Petregaard."

They both nodded. The Damocles witches set off on the greenery-filled route. It had at some point been a dirt roadway, maybe, but that must've been ages ago. In the years since, it had devolved into an overgrown path. And it wasn't an easy hike. We could all see that their track would quickly start ascending up and up the mountain soon. We had clearly picked the easier task.

"Good luck." I offered.

"Just do your part," Petregaard told us over his shoulder. "Don't screw it up."

We watched them both go.

"Nice fellow," Vince mocked as they left.

I laughed. "He kind of reminds me of you!"

"I knew I liked him," Vince teased. "Let's go."

"What are we looking for?" Hilde wondered.

"Uh uh." I frowned. "*You* are going to wait by the car."

Hilde's jaw dropped open. "What? No!"

"We can't just leave her," Vince disagreed.

"Why not? We're in the middle of nowhere! Where else could she go? You'd rather take her with us?"

"I'd rather she be tucked away safe and sound at High Council, but someone didn't tell her she couldn't come."

"Guys-" Hilde tried interrupting.

"This is on me?" I scoffed.

"Well, it's on someone."

"You have got to be kidding. The girl stole away in the trunk."

"Guys-"

"And now she's your problem."

"My problem! You mean *our* problem."

"No, *your* problem. This is your thing. I'm just along for the ride. A ride I drove."

"Cuz you told me to sleep!"

"And did you have any visions?"

I looked away, embarrassed. "Children singing and playing. It wasn't really a thing."

"Great. So, I did all the work all for nothing."

"Not for nothing. Your driving's the thing that got us here."

"Mae-mae, Vince-y, stop! Stop fighting! Please." Hilde raised her voice. Vince and I frowned at each other, then turned our frowns on her. "I'll be a big help on the mission. I swear! Don't leave me at the car. I don't want to be alone."

"Fine." I gave in. I had no choice. "Just... be careful."

"Can do. Come on!" Hilde ran ahead. For the young girl, all the tension was immediately forgotten. Vince and I frowned at each other but followed her down. We couldn't leave her alone. Wouldn't want her to get into *more* trouble. We picked our way through the trees and headed towards the water, until the ground opened up to a rocky shore.

"Slow down," I instructed.

"It's big..." she said.

Real big, we realized.

More than five acres in size. Maybe ten? I shuddered.

"I hope the soil's not in the middle," Vince groaned. In the distance, we saw the Pokna Mountains and the rocky hillside of the dormant volcano.

I pointed to show Hilde. "That's where they've gone."

"They seem like nice guys," she nodded.

"Til you get to know them," I frowned.

"H, they're Damocles members," Vince told her.

"They were Damocles?!" She was shocked.

Vince and I looked at each other. How had she not known? "Didn't you see their red clothes?"

"But.. they... seemed so normal."

"Sometimes bad guys do," he said.

I checked my instructions in the picture Josie had sent on my phone. "This is the place."

"It looks like all of cottage country," Vince frowned. "What makes this lake so special?"

I looked around. "Well, to start, there don't seem to be any properties, so no development."

"Who'd want to live all the way out here?" Vince groaned.

"I think it's pretty." Hilde shrugged. "But, it's missing a sandy bottom. I love having sand squish between my toes."

She was right. The entire beach was made of pebbles, rocks and stone.

I scrolled through the details for more information.

"The whole lake is a runoff from the mountains. That's what makes it special. We're looking for the soil under the cucumber coffee tree. Dense with algae. And we're supposed to keep it moist."

"Ugh." Vince frowned. "Just say wet."

"What's wrong with saying moist?" Hilde wondered.

Vince visibly shuddered.

Hilde and I raised an eyebrow and giggled. A rare Vince soft spot.

"We'll use the sachet to keep it *moist*," I said, watching Vince wince.

Hilde giggled. "*Moist,*" she repeated.

Vince stopped in his tracks. "Do you want my help or not?"

"Sorry, we're sorry." We hung our heads in shame.

I snuck the young girl a private grin. She beamed with pleasure.

"Let's get this over with."

"Lead the way," I said.

He stood on the shore, looked out across the water and lowered his right arm to his side. He balled his hand into a fist and kept his gaze looking out. Ahead in the current, the water stirred, then grew more disturbed. It started to churn. The waves grew bigger and bubbled higher, until suddenly, the body of water unnaturally split. It was like the liquid became solid earth and Vince had dug out a hole.

Around the void he created, the walls of water held firm.

His magic defied the laws of physics.

The unearthed bottom of the lagoon glistened. Slime and sludge covered the stones. They were slick now where liquid had been before. Vince held the walls of the lake in the energy generated from his palm. If I hadn't seen him do it before I never would have believed it was possible. But it was. The void held strong. Frisky, daring fish jumped through the divide and landed in the opposite pools. Soon, his witch-made, water-free space was large enough for us to traverse.

"We're good," he solidified his task, registering only the smallest of strain.

"Come on," I led them out into the sludge. All three of us trudged into the lagoon. "Watch yourself on the rocks. They're slippery," I warned Hilde. The girl nodded. Nervous at first.

Vince controlled the water-free pocket around us in the palm of his hand. As we moved forward, more of the waters opened. The drop off on the watery floor of the lagoon was quite steep and soon the clear path he was holding was well over twenty feet tall.

"This lake is large," Vince murmured.

"What does the cucumber coffee tree look like?" Hilde asked. Her initial fear had dissipated and she was starting to poke and prod around.

"I've actually never seen one before, but the book said red foliage on dark purple stems. Everything down here seems kind of murky and gray." I worried, but Hilde shrugged it off.

"That just means it'll stand out!" She ran ahead.

"You okay?" I checked in with Vince. His frown was growing more pronounced.

"I'm fine. You just gather your dirt."

"Over here!" Hilde shouted.

I hurried up to the girl. She was right, the plant she'd discovered was indeed purple and red. "Nicely done! The book said to dig below it." I dropped to my knees and grabbed a sharp stone. I removed a quick layer of smooth rocks and then scratched at the algae surface below. In three or four pulls, I'd exposed the soil. "Jackpot."

We scraped a large sample into the waiting leather sachet.

"Keep it moist," Hilde giggled, looking over her shoulder to her friend.

"You wanna swim back, shortie?" He threatened, but that was just bravado.

We all knew he wasn't so cruel to the girl.

Still, Hilde bit her tongue and didn't poke him further. I loaded the small bag to the brim and when it was full, I sealed it up.

"Here, you can carry it," I told the young girl.

Suddenly, a dark shade loomed over our heads. Inside the void, everything darkened. Then, just as quickly as it had appeared, the shadow moved on and the sunlight filled the surroundings again.

"Storm clouds," Hilde noted. "Told you." Our mission over, her curiosity took over. She explored all the facets of the underwater scene, touching everything she could, leaving no stone unturned.

Vince and I looked up to the sky. Still bright blue. It wasn't a cloud that had blocked the light. The shadow moved too quickly. Then and gone. Suddenly, the darkness overtook our small pocket again. The void felt dim and cold.

"What is that?" I asked.

"Something large enough to block out the sun," Vince noted.

The shadow was intense, but short. In moments, it moved on again.

"I think we should go," I said, getting up from the ground.

Dread filled the marrow of my bones.

I couldn't see any actual danger, but I could sense it.

Something was wrong.

"Have you got enough soil?" Vince checked. I could tell he felt it, too. But neither of us wanted to worry the girl.

I nodded. "We should go," I repeated.

"Okay, kiddo," he teased Hilde, who was lost in her own wide-eyed observations. Seeing everything that was normally hidden underwater filled her with a sense of joy. He tried to keep it light, but I heard the edge in his voice. "We got what we came for. Time to go."

"Well that wasn't hard." Hilde grinned. "Race you to the car!" She ran forward.

The shadow set in overtop of us once more.

The hair on my neck stood on end.

Something was definitely coming.

The whole lake around us had gone black.

"Hilde, stop!" I shouted, my scream scaring the girl.

She crashed to a halt. "What?"

In the place she would have run to if I hadn't stopped her, a giant tentacle smashed into our void. It slammed into the ground.

"Holy business," Vince murmured.

"*Ahhhhhh!*" Hilde screamed.

"Come to me," I instructed. I held out my arms and Hilde raced to my hands. I wrapped her in my safety. Her breath was hard and scared. "I got you," I told her. "What do we do?" I asked Vince. Both of us were frozen.

Slowly, the tentacle retracted. It was so large, I instantly feared the animal that arm was attached to was huge.

"I'm not sure," he said. "Get out of the water."

Suddenly, before he could flinch, another tentacle burst through our water void, smacking into him. Direct hit. The impact was so hard, it tossed the strong boy clear across the ground. He skittered on the rocks.

"Vince!" I tried to yell, but the rushing water drowned me out. From all sides, the void collapsed. His harness released on impact and the walls of our magical void came crashing down, filling back up with waiting water.

It happened fast and hard.

The physics of water took over.

All the science lessons in school were correct. The pressure was immense.

Giant waves took control. They swooped up my legs, tossing and turning me in an undercurrent. I tried to hold on, but Hilde's hand snapped from mine. I had no idea where the little girl was swept. As I fought to regain my bearings in the undertow, I caught sight of something else.

The giant beast's eyes.

It was some underwater monster, the likes of which I had never seen. A squid, or an octopus, or something, but worse, with what seemed like a dozen undulating arms, squiggly, long, and bold. As I tossed and turned in the tumultuous waves, I could sense I was swirling into a trap.

No.

Swim, damn it.

Pffft.

I released a large batch of bubbles and watched the route they took. It was an old water safety trick I'd learned in my childhood; if you were disoriented underwater, to see which way was up, release your breath. In deep enough water, the darkness could come from all sides, a person might not know which way to swim, but their bubbles would always know which way lead to the surface. The buoyancy would always win out. All you had to do was watch. I tried to follow the tiny air pockets' trajectory, kicking my legs and pumping my arms. My heavy clothes and water-logged shoes both dragged me down.

A tentacle swung down on my left, nearly hitting me, but I swerved just in time. The momentum of the limb swirled the waters, but I worked hard to maintain my course. I kicked my legs with force, intent on resurfacing. The lack of oxygen burned in my lungs. Only five more strokes 'til I'd surface.

Hilde.

My chest ached.

Where was the girl? Was she safe?

Had Vince made it to the shore?

My throat tightened more and more as I suddenly burst forth from the depths. On the surface, I gulped for air. I sucked and coughed, sputtering, flailing, unable to dispel all the water I'd accidentally taken inside. I spun around, searching the shoreline, as two of the beast's great tentacles raised up into the sky. They were the only things that broke the surface. I didn't see the heads or splashes of Vince or Hilde anywhere.

Where were the other two?

Trapped underwater?

Gripped in the behemoth's grasp?

No.

I wouldn't believe it.

"Over here!" I swatted the water surface and shouted. If I could draw the sea creature's attention, they'd be free to escape to shore. "Hey!" I screamed. "I'm over here. Come get it!"

The tentacles smashed down, but I dove towards shore. The great momentum of the suction-cupped arms dredged the flow below, it created a tide that pulled me back down. But I was a strong swimmer. I kicked up again, desperate for fresh breath. But the water wouldn't let up. It spun me in circles. The undertow dragged me downwards, washing me across the stony floor. I felt the rocks scrape my skin as I bounced out of control.

The lake bottom was jagged.

Unforgiving.

But, then, as I swirled back up again, suddenly, I wasn't still floundering. The water disappeared. With a rapid descent, my body dropped on the stones.

The liquid drained out of the hole.

In shock, I coughed and sputtered, prostrate on the ground.

I sucked air into my lungs.

Vince had regained control of the void. He was soaked and wild-eyed like I was, but thankfully, he had the water back under control. He was watching the depths for dark shadows, for a clue the monster was coming back for more. I picked myself up off the rocky ground.

"Vince!" I spit.

"You alright?" He asked, his eyes never leaving our surroundings.

"I'm okay. Where's Hilde?" I asked. But then I saw her small, limp body. She too had been smashed on the stones on the floor, but Hilde wasn't moving. "Hey!" I ran towards her.

"We gotta go." Vince warned. "It's coming back."

"I know. I'll get Hilde!" I ran forward.

Vince nodded curtly. There was no way we'd leave without her.

"Wake up," I called racing over the stones. "Hilde! Come on!" My screams must have awakened her senses.

The young girl propped herself up on one arm. "What's going on?" she asked, bewildered.

"Can you stand? We gotta go." I closed the distance between us. But we were moving too slow.

"Mae..." Vince said. "Mae!"

I looked up as well. Behind the girl, the growing shadow loomed.

"Hilde, now!" I shouted, but she had turned and saw what I saw.

The return of the impending sea creature locked Hilde's feet to the ground.

She was frozen in terror.

"I want my Mommmm!"

Mom.

A childhood plea.

The children's voices in my dream returned to me.

That's right.

I swiped the hair out of my face to see more clearly. But the image was a memory in my brain. There were children singing. Weaving. Holding hands. Going up and down.

In and out and round the forest.

"Take my hand!" I shouted.

I ran right for her.

Right for the monster.

Never once breaking stride.

Our hands locked in place and I dragged her on her feet just as the next tentacle smashed down, obliterating the space where Hilde's tiny body had been.

"What are you doing? Wrong way!" Vince yelled.

But I didn't turn my back on the creature. Instead, Hilde and I acted out the instructions of the song.

In and out, around the forest. Under the great sea creature's body we ducked and wove. Over and under between the legs. Back and forth like the children that I'd seen. We wove again and then, I remembered, the dream kids split.

"Go that way!" I shouted.

We split apart and Hilde followed my directions, continuing the pattern. I did the same. The tentacles tracked our movements until they wrapped themselves up, tangling into knots. Hilde and I ducked through one last hole, pinching the tentacle tight. The beast let out a horrible howl.

"Hilde, now! Run for the beach!" I yelled.

The creature fell over, its underwater impact shaking the very ground on which we ran. There was a great shudder, as it came loose from its own knots.

"Come on!" Vince shouted, holding his free, non-harnessing hand out to receive us.

The monster was down, but not defeated.

Hilde ran forward. Four paces ahead of me.

Vince grabbed her hand.

I chased, right behind.

Together, we raced out of the lagoon.

Vince closed the water void as we retreated, but before we could hit the beach, the dark shadows began to loom.

"We're gonna make it!" Hilde cheered.

Twenty feet from shore.

Bam!

A tentacle swerved through the opening. I shoved

Hilde to safety, but took the brunt of the stroke in my side.

"Mae," Vince stopped on his heels.

"Get her out of here," I told him, getting to my feet once more. "Go! Move, Hilde!"

Bam!

Another tentacle hit me from the other direction. This one was so hard I was knocked right out of Vince's void. The water crashed over me. But I couldn't slosh or flail. A slippery arm wrapped around my hips, pulling me by the waist. The suction was strong. A wash of bubbles released from my mouth. But this time, it wasn't to guide my orientation. I hadn't grabbed a good breath before going under again.

I needed more oxygen.

Through the water fractals, I could see Hilde and Vince had made it safe to the shore. At least they were free.

I punched and shoved on the sea creature's elastic skin, but the buoyancy of the water made my strength practically null. Weirdly, I became well aware of the fact that most underwater predators didn't actually bite or slice like a bear would. They would wait out their prey 'til they drowned. Then they could feast as long as they wanted on the remains. This ugly creature didn't have to fight me to win. It could just hold me down. Wait until my air all ran out.

I could drown in water only six or seven feet deep.

My eyes adjusted.

Although everything was slightly hazy underwater,

I could see the creature more clearly now. It was built like a squid, but had a mouthful of teeth like a snap ribbon plant. A hole of jagged edges waiting to greet my limbs. I watched with disgust as its jaws contracted and expanded.

This wasn't an animal that occurred in nature.

At least not one that I'd ever seen before.

I wondered if it had been created by someone or something specifically in these waters. A misguided attempt to guard the precious soils of the Valdeez plants? I wouldn't have put it past some chemist witch to cross pollinate vicious plants and animals.

With a monster like this out in nature, someone should update the encyclopedia listing's risks. Once I was free, I'd get right on that, I thought with a wry smile.

I was going delirious without air.

Whether it had evolved or was created, the squid-monster was winning this war.

It had been ages now since I'd sucked back a breath.

The world grew more and more blurry.

On the shore, Vince might have been casting random air pockets in an attempt to help catch me or find me, but we both knew he wasn't strong enough to drain the whole pond. I would drown before his scat-tershot harnessing found me.

In last ditch effort to show where I was, I pushed out a final gasp of bubbles, all the oxygen I could muster shooting out in a whirl. I blew the air out in hopes the bubbles might pop on the surface and give a hint to my coven about where I was in the lagoon.

My head swirled.

The tentacle started to pull me closer. The animal sensed I didn't have much fight left in me. It dragged me lower, downwards in direction. Or was that up? I could no longer tell. Its mouth gnashed closed and then open in preparation for its next meal.

In and out and round the forest.

The children sang their tune.

Round the forest.

The young voices gave way to one sweet, older woman's song.

Round the forest.

It was a voice I hadn't heard in years.

Mom.

My mom.

Like Hilde, in a moment of panic, my thoughts went to my mother.

Come on Mae, the voice seemed to encourage.

I wriggled, desperate fighting the creature. My fists pounded away on the slimy surface.

In and out and round the forest.

Tick, tick, boom.

I'm coming, Mom.

In and out and round the forest.

If there were a heaven or hell, we'd be united again soon.

Round the forest.

Which spot was reserved for witches? I wondered.

Round the forest.

The insistent song grew louder in my mind. The monster wasn't yet victorious.

Ahhhh!

I let out an underwater scream, but it didn't help anything.

In and out and round the forest.

I had nothing left to give but the clothes on my back. And my pants...

Tick, tick... boom.

Rick's chemicals.

They were in my pants!

I reached around the slimy arm to the cargo pocket of my pants. All of the packages he'd so diligently made for me were thrust there together. The explosives, the truth serum, the smoke bomb, even the snap ribbons. The only chemical I wasn't carrying was that lava potion I had offered to the Damocles coven.

I needed an explosive.

But which bag was which?

With such low visibility, it was impossible to know. Would they even work, underwater?

There was only one way to find out.

I didn't have the capacity left to think.

In and out and round the corner

I took every package that I had and shoved them all into the beast's gnashing teeth. The monster sucked them back, its bite raking across my arms as it did. Red blood swarmed the water. My blood. But still, I shoved them in.

Take that! In my mind I shouted. *Eat it!*

Then braced for impact. I covered my face with my hands.

Tick, tick...

I tried to duck and cover.

I waited.

But nothing happened.

The explosives didn't go off.

No.

My body went into shock.

I started shaking, convulsing, uncontrollably.

I couldn't hold it together for even another moment.

Mom. I'm coming.

Aunt Abeline. I'm so sorry.

The world went watery and soft.

Beck. I want to tell you, I-

Tick, tick... BOOM!

THIRTY

WHAT NOW?

ALL AT ONCE, the chemicals from Rick's packets must have opened inside the sea monster's throat. The explosion ripped the beast from inside out with such force it hurled me out of its arms and shot me into the sky and through the air. I landed with a thud in only a foot of water, near the rocky beach.

Blood, guts, and innards exploded in every direction, the sonic boom rocked the entire shore. I hit the stones hard, sputtering and coughing, vomiting lungfulls of water. Luckily, the liquid where I landed was deep enough to soften the blow. A little. All around me, waves smashed on the beach, the disturbance and impact of the animal's destruction was so large it pummeled the shores.

But I survived.

I picked myself up and stumbled. Everything felt woozy. The waves tossed to and fro. They crashed onto my back. I moved towards the beach but was too shook up to walk straight.

In the distance, I could see Vince and Hilde hugging.

They stared out at the rollicking lagoon as the remains of tentacles and other body parts washed up on the shore. I knew why they searched the waters. They were looking for my body. I climbed to my feet and stumbled across the shore. I tried to call out, but couldn't catch my breath in my throat.

"She's really gone," Vince mumbled.

"What do we do now?" Hilde cried, wet tears on her face.

Vince stood behind her, hands on her shoulders. They looked like long-suffering drowned rats, but also stoic.

Respectful and calm.

A deep sadness between them.

Neither took their eye off the horizon, watching the chaos of destruction unfold. "I'm not sure," he admitted. The water violently churned before them.

I stumbled closer, but they were so lost in the carnage in front of them, neither heard me approach. "I'm here," I said, the words only a whisper. I joined them and looked over their shoulders at the visible chunks of the monster that had almost defeated me. "I didn't want to destroy it." I murmured. "I'm sorry. It was the only escape option that I had."

"Holy business," Vince gaped.

Surprised, both he and Hilde abruptly turned.

"Oh my god! Mae! You're alive!" Hilde lunged into my arms. The sudden impact of her tiny frame caught me off guard.

"When the thing dragged you back under, we thought we'd lost you. Then the whole lake went up in a crazy boom! Squid guts came flying. Blood and stuff, everywhere. I can't believe you made it out good!"

"Are you alright?" Vince had the presence of mind to check.

"I've still got the soil!" Hilde proudly pronounced. She showed me the sachet. "You're tough as nails, Mae. Tough as nails!"

Vince hadn't stopped staring. Through his concern, I realized how beaten and bedraggled I must actually look.

"I'm good, I'm alright." I told him. We'd come this far. I wouldn't let my aunt down. "Only trouble is," I sighed. "I fed the rest of the sleeping potion to the beast."

Above us, the mountain side started to rumble.

"Uh, guys?" Hilde looked up.

We nodded. Our eyes lifted to the dormant volcano.

"I don't think that's the only trouble..." Vince quietly said.

THIRTY-ONE
THAT'S NOT A HILL, THAT'S A
VOLCANO

THE SHUDDER WAS SO loud it shook the trees.

"What was that?" Hilde wondered.

"An echo of the explosion?" I suggested.

We stared around, looking for more clues, sights or sounds. For a moment, all was silent, then, the air sliced open with a large-scale cracking sound. It came from the mountain.

"Look over there!" Vince pointed.

Both Hilde and I stared.

Our eyes rose past the rough waters of the lake, still rocking and roiling from the violent explosion. Past the lagoon and the forest. Up, above the tops of the lodge-pole pines. Up to the Pokna mountains. To the dormant volcano.

"That's where Petregaard and Niall went," Hilde said.

We could see what looked like small pebbles falling off the side of the hill. The rumbling around us grew stronger. From this distance, I realized, those pebbles must have actually been boulders. Smashing and rolling down the mountain. Obliterating everything they hit. The side of the volcano was groaning.

"That is not good," Vince muttered.

Crack!

We braced in the quake of a booming thunder.

"Oh my god!" Hilde pointed.

A giant shelf of stone split itself from the side of the hill like a glacier calving in half. It ripped off the mountain and crashed to the earth below, picking up debris and forest trees while it fell.

"The explosion made the hillside fail," Vince realized.

"That's not a hill," I warned. "That's a dormant volcano."

"Holy business." With hushed astonishment, he pointed again.

In the wake of the mountain's new gaping gash, a gray cloud started to bloom. It mushroomed out, colliding with the dust from below, thickening together, and rapidly building in size and speed. Towards us, it billowed. Doubling and doubling over. Obliterating the sight of the sky above and the earth below in its stead.

"We should go," I warned them, but instead we stared, struck in awe. I had never seen something build so fast. So magnificent. It seemed to rub out the sun and the sky in a great gray plume.

The cloud sucked everything up in its path, growing exponentially as it moved.

Suddenly, the danger set in.

It would swallow us too.

"We need to go now!" I realized. "Move!"

We spun on our heels and raced for the car. Feet flying over small stones and roots in our way. The gray cloud set in from above, heating the air as it came.

"It's so hot!" Hilde cried.

"Cover your nose and mouth with your clothes," I instructed, and we held our wet shirts up to our faces as we ran. The cloud was almost on top of us. More and more pressurized air pushed its way down. As the gases compounded, the temperature sky-rocketed. We were soaked in humidity. Sweat was pouring out of our pores.

"Get in! Get in!" I shouted.

"Watch the metal door!" Vince warned.

The help came a moment too late, as I jumped back from the touch of the handle.

"Don't touch!" I warned. Little Hilde obeyed.

Along with the heat, the cloud seemed to absorb all the sound.

We had to scream just to be heard.

I could barely see Vince anymore, on the other side of the car.

I cupped my grip with a bunch of leaves to soften the heat on the handle and cranked it open. Hilde jumped in with me beside. We both squished into the front seat as I slammed shut the door. Vince made it in the driver's side. In the car, we could see and breath once more, but the heat was oppressively warm.

"We gotta go," Vince said.

"Get us out of here." I spun to look all around. It was no use. We were socked in on all sides.

"Move!" Hilde whimpered as well. She couldn't cry.

None of us could.

The hot air had dried out our tears.

"Come on." Vince cranked on the engine but the car refused to start. "Move it!"

"We're gonna die," Hilde cried. "It's getting so hot. It's even hotter now."

"We'll be fine," I assured her, not sure if I was properly hiding the fact that I was scared out of my mind.

"We need to get out of this cloud," Vince said, cranking the motor again and again. The engine refused to kick in. "It's basically steam."

I looked back where we had come from.

The air was only growing hotter.

"Come on, come on!" Vince cranked the key. The engine turned and sputtered.

Hilde stared out the windows around us. "Oh my god!"

"Hey," I calmed her down. "We're alright. That isn't helping."

Obediently, she lowered her chaos to a whimper, her eyes never leaving the steam. She had no choice. It was all we could see.

"The engine's too hot," Vince feared.

"What do we do?" I asked.

He didn't answer.

"Vince!"

"I don't know!"

"Give it all you got-" I instructed.

"I've been giving it!" He cranked the key and revved the engine. The machine coughed but didn't kick in.

"I know!" Hilde lunged her small body forward. Her fingers dashed to the console, cranking the fan dials, setting the air conditioner to full blast. Cool air blew into the cab.

Vince and I looked at each other, over top of her forehead. A child's stupid innocence. That would never help. But, suddenly, the vehicle revved to life.

"Holy crap. It worked!"

"Yes!" Vince cheered and threw the car into drive.

"Go! Go! Go!" Hilde shouted.

"Wait!" I said. "In reverse!"

"What?" Vince and Hilde were shocked.

"Petregaard and Niall!" I looked from one to the other. "They're still out there. We have to go back."

"Into the hot?" Hilde seemed surprised. "Do you think they survived?"

"Yes!" I exclaimed. "Maybe... I don't know," I realized.

"That's just a small path. On the best day in prime conditions I wouldn't drive it."

"Vince, we have to. They're probably running for

their lives."

"Unless they're already dead," he said.

Hilde let out a small gasp.

"Vince."

"Mae, I can't see anything."

Hilde reached forward on the dashboard and flipped a new switch. A single wiper blade swished down across the window. For a second, we could see half a foot before the steam cloud socked in again.

"We have to try." I said. "At least a bit. I wouldn't leave you," I reasoned. "Would you leave me?"

"Fine." He rocked the car in reverse and we started driving back up the small trail.

The progress was slow but it was possible.

The little wiper blade dragged over and back in its path.

"This is stupid," Vince muttered.

It seemed like forever, but carefully we moved back, inching deeper into the steam cloud. But, there were no Damocles witches to be found. I was about to tell Vince he was right, it was a lost cause, when something moving caught Hilde's eye.

"There they are!" She shouted.

Up the hill, we saw the two boys blindly racing down. They had wrapped their faces in their t-shirts. They were escaping as fast as they could.

"Honk your horn!" I instructed. "So they know where we are."

Vince did, in case they couldn't see us. The Damocles guys quickly followed the sound. With the honks,

Vince guided them to our vehicle. The boys flanked the car and Hilde and I leaned out from the front row to open the back doors as they raced to meet us. They jumped into the back bench and re-slammed the car doors. We could feel heat emanating from their bodies as they arrived.

"Get us out of here!" Petregaard shouted.

"Without a doubt," Vince agreed.

He cranked the car into drive. Going forward, he turned the front windshield wipers on full blast. Back and forth they cleared the window for only microseconds at a time. But still, he drove as fast as he could.

The boys unwrapped themselves in agony. Their skin was red and blistered and raw. The steam had stripped them of all their derma-elasticity and any water content. As we passed our initial parking spot, Niall realized it and frowned.

"You came back for us," he acknowledged, his lips barely moving. "You came back up the path."

"We weren't sure if you would make it," Hilde admitted. "Or if you were alive."

"I just wish we could have come sooner," I surmised, looking at the tender skin of the destructed bodies. Their painful frowns. Neither boy flinched.

Moving at all seemed to be hell.

The steam had caused deep burns.

Left untreated, I worried the boys would surely die.

Neither moved an inch, staying collapsed on the bench just where they were.

"Mae, where's Rick's burn juice?" Hilde wondered.

"Oh, the salve!" I dug it out of the front seat where it had been discarded as useless in the hours before. "You think it will heal the steam wounds as well as fire walk?"

She'd seen her partner make it before. Perhaps he'd told her all its powers.

"It's worth a try." She shrugged. That was true. No reason not to.

"Would that be alright?" I asked the guys.

Niall barely nodded. Petregaard, I thought, might have gone into shock. It wasn't much consent, but I think they would have agreed to anything to help.

"Here." I scooped a small amount onto my fingertips and gently touched it to Petregaard's face.

"Ahh!" He hissed in pain, but almost immediately, the redness and swelling started to go down. Hilde took some to help Niall.

"Keep it thin," I instructed. "We have a lot of skin to cover."

Hilde nodded.

Bit by gentle bit, we covered their faces, chests and arms with the salve.

In the front, Vince continued to drive through the wild as the Damocles boys recovered from the steam. When their front sides had healed, Hilde handed the rest of the sachet back and they helped each other apply the jelly-like substance to their backs and legs as well.

The burn salve took their skin from a fire engine red to a more manageable blush. The tears and cracks in their skin closed as well. The potion brought them back to life.

"Thanks," Niall heaved a huge sigh. They didn't recover every inch perfectly, but the honeypot of salve covered more than enough of their legs and arms. In under ten minutes, they were almost fully human once again. As human as any witch could be.

"We can make more at home," I offered seeing the tub was now coming up empty. But, I caught myself. My home wasn't their home. "Or... Dr. Winters can, I'm sure." I recovered. The High Council was only a refuge for the witches in the front seat, not the two in the back.

"Thank you for your rescue," Petregaard said, quietly. "And the second rescue with the salve."

"You're welcome," I told him. I smiled, that was the first time I'd ever heard him speak to me nicely.

All it took was me saving his life.

Twice.

"I-." I squinted.

The rear window's wiper made its pathetic route back and forth, but low as the visibility was, something caught my eye. I concentrated. Something in the back view was changing behind us.

Hilde saw it too. "Uh, guys? What was that?"

The boys also turned around.

Petregaard leaned back and smeared the condensation off window from the inside, trying to get a clearer view, but the gray fog around us was too thick to wipe off.

Still, even in the haze, we'd definitely seen something.

There was something happening in the forest outside.

Something coming.

Something red, like the Damocles wardrobe.

"Did either of you drop your T-shirt?" I wondered, although we'd already driven far from the spot where they'd jumped in the car. Still, both boys were still shirtless on the back bench. They checked for their stuff. No, their soaked T-shirts were both there, heaped in the pile.

The back wiper streaked again.

"Vince-" I said.

"What?"

"What is it?" The others wondered.

"Oh my god..." I realized.

"What?!" Vince was too busy squinting to avoid the trees up ahead to take the chance to look back.

"Holy business," Hilde agreed, using Vince's catch phrase, seeing what I saw.

"Get us out of here," I warned.

"Don't you think that I'm trying?!"

"What? What's going on?" Niall asked. Both he and Petregaard insistently wiped at the window. More and more red came into view.

"Well, try harder!" I told him. "The volcano's not dormant anymore!"

THIRTY-TWO

IT'S GONNA EAT US ALIVE

VINCE SMASHED ON THE GAS, lurching us forward. In the rear view, twice as fast, the magma ate everything in its path. The rollicking red river of fire was headed straight for us. Coming in hot.

"Holy crap, holy crap." All I could do was mutter, watching the chaos unfold.

"Oh no," Niall murmured.

"Punch it!" Hilde squealed.

"It's gonna eat us alive," Petregaard feared.

Vince pressed the gas pedal as hard as he could, but it was impossible to tear out on the gravel road. The car was beat up and the road was rough, with almost zero visibility. He could only see the jogs, the twists, and the turns in the laneway when we were already on top of the bends. Several times, at the last second, Vince had to wrench the wheel. More than once, we bottomed out. I glanced ahead. It was like driving thru pea soup, if the pot you were cooking it in was still on the stove top, and the element was cranked up to full blast. We were lucky the wipers hadn't melted clean off.

Behind us, the river of fire built stronger.

Each new tree or shrub the lava touched burst into a blaze, but the items only had a moment to flash, then the river of molten lava swallowed them hole. Vince cranked the wind-shield wipers to maximum power, but he could barely cut a ribbon through the steady shower of ash.

"The road's acting like a funnel," I warned. "The lava's speeding up, not slowing down."

"Feeding on its own energy," Vince agreed.

"It's like a glowing avalanche of stifling beauty," Hilde murmured, staring behind us, her body lodged half in the front seat, half in the back.

Her words were so poetic they seemed almost out of character, maybe they were, as the visual had her in a light trance. But her description was dead on. We all felt it. The flow of lava was angry and ravenous, but there was a magical grace and dexterity to its power.

Constantly changing.

Burping and hissing and swallowing its own self.

It exploded over and over in greedy, destructive gulps.

And we were mesmerized.

But, the destruction was coming.

"Maybe I can help," Petregaard realized. He balled up his hand. His face grimaced. Clearly his harnessing palm wasn't fully healed. But he concentrated and suddenly, a crevice appeared in the rear view. It ripped across the road, opening the earth. The lava flowed forward, right to the edge, then tumbled over, its hot river sucked deep underground. The distance between us and the eddy in the fire river grew.

"You did it!" Hilde cheered.

Petregaard sat back, feeling proud.

But the lava wouldn't go down without a fight.

At its underground waterfall point, the liquid burped and smarted.

Sparks burst up into the sky.

Spatters of small embers at first, then bigger projectiles, shot straight into the air.

"Holy crap," I said.

More lava blasted into the sky.

A fireball smashed down on the hood of the car.

"What was that?!" Vince shouted.

"It's-" I didn't know how to describe it.

"The lava is shooting at us!" Hilde wailed.

Another blast of hot lava shot into the air. This time, I understood.

"Swerve right!" I shouted.

Vince did as he was told and the lava bomb missed to our left. But there was no time to celebrate the victory. The river of fire had filled up the entire crevice Petregaard had made and once again, the fire was coming on strong.

The lava overtook a large rock.

Another flurry of fiery projectiles shot up in the air.

"On your right!" Niall shouted.

Vince swerved.

The fireballs missed us.

"Hooray!" Hilde cheered.

"When it swallows something large, it seems to cause an explosion to shoot up- on the left!" I shouted.

Vince veered around another lava bomb as it smashed the ground. To avoid the collision, we flew into the trench on the side of the road.

"Hold on!" Vince told us. The car leapt and lurched as he pulled us out of the ditch and back onto flat ground. Our bodies bounced with the car shocks. The turbulence was so bumpy Hilde and I flailed.

"The lava is coming," Niall warned.

"We've got to slow it down!" I told the others.

"I think Vince should speed up!" Hilde complained.

"Believe me kid, I'm trying," he said over his white-knuckled grip on the wheel.

"Can you perform another round of magic?" I asked Petregaard.

"Maybe one," he admitted. With so much stress on his body, his powers had grown dim. "But we've already seen it was overtaken by the lava. It's no use just to build another hole."

"On its own. That's true," I said. "But together, maybe it will be strong enough to work. Vince, if you and I switch spots, you can water, and Hilde can wind harness.

"Mae, I'm not very good. My primary's a dream-cast," the girl warned.

"We'll take whatever we can get," I told her, trying to calm her nerves.

She nodded. "What about Niall?" She half-asked me, half-asked him.

"I'm also a dreamcast." He shrugged. "I can't harness a thing."

"Well, you can clean the back window!" I instructed. "Give the others a good view. Alright? Ready?" I asked Vince. There was no time to stop the car. We'd have to switch spots while the wagon was still on the move.

"I'm ready," he agreed.

"Hilde, back seat," I told her.

The girl scampered over.

"Vince, put down your seat.

Vince pulled the lever, dropping the seat back into Niall's lap. Then he transitioned the gas pedal from his right to his left foot, abandoning the brake altogether, ready to go.

"We do it all together," I told the others of the harnessing.

Petregaard and Hilde both nodded.

Behind us, the lava was coming. Time to move.

"I'm sliding back," I told Vince, pulling my own lever, knocking the passenger seat back too, so there'd be enough room to climb through. Vince held the car steady, both hands on the steering column. It was now or never. I decided to move.

I hopped over, in behind him. "Got it." I put my first hand on the wheel. Suddenly, I was steering, while his foot on the gas surged us forward, only inches from destruction in the fiery river of doom.

Vince straddled the gear box.

I fit in beside him. "I'm ready," I told him, my toes keen and prone. "I can take it."

"Whatever you do, don't get us killed." He said.

"Gee, thanks for the conviction and assertion."

Despite the chaos, Vince grinned. "Those are ten-dollar words."

I grimaced, gripping the wheel with determination. "I do what I can."

"Letting go in three... two..."

"One!"

He released the gas pedal and I punched it forward. We all lurched in the change. Accidentally, I put far more pressure on the pedal than required, but I gripped the wheel, eased my foot off and careened us back under control.

Success!

We'd switched drivers.

I yanked the driver seat lever to pull the chair back to full mast.

There was no time to lose, the lava was over-taking us.

"Now!" Niall shouted. "Harness. Harness!"

At once, Petregaard, Hilde and Vince tried to bend the universe to their hands.

The car dropped deathly silent as they used their empathic skills to manipulate their worlds. The earth opened up. From nowhere, water gushed forward. And straight ahead, a large wind blew in as well.

"It's not enough," Niall feared.

Although all three crashed their energies behind us, the lava was still gaining ground.

"I can't do it!" Petregaard shouted. His earth-harness started to fold.

"Switch with me!" Hilde shouted.

But there was no way for her to help expel extra energy. It was up to the Damocles boy to carry the load.

"Oh my god." His agony filled the cab. But still, Petregaard cut a huge hole in the ground. The earth opened up. Vince blasted the lava with water and Hilde blew the heat back.

"Do it!" Vince commanded himself as much as anybody.

"It's working!" Niall cheered.

"I think it's working!" Hilde squealed.

I checked the rearview mirror. The trio of elemental harnesses' rapid cooling built up a black, solid wall in the lava where the hole, the blast of water, and the wind hit the same goal. The lava hardened on contact. Cooled right off. Made itself into a substantial wall of black, crusty ash.

Hilde gave the boys a hug. "We did it!"

"We're almost out of the forest," I told them, facing forward.

"It's alright! The elements are working," Hilde told me, dropping her hand.

"Hilde, concentrate," Vince chastised. Forcing more water down.

Argh!

Petregaard collapsed against the car bench. "I can't do anymore."

"We don't have to, we're home free!" Hilde told him.

"No, we're not." Niall's voice sent a chill through my spine.

My eyes flashed to the rearview mirror.

A tiny sliver of hot orange dribbled over the wall of black rock.

"What was that?"

Hilde flew to the back of the back seat to have a better look. "It's just a little bit of fire." She reported.

Then came a few more dribbles.

"That's alright," she nodded.

"Harness!" We all told her. But it was too late.

Whoosh!

Suddenly, a giant waterfall of lava shot over the side of the wall and in seconds it overflowed over our structure, eating it whole. The scalding liquid came flooding towards us.

The new wave came on angry, even stronger than before.

Argh!

Vince collapsed like Petregaard had.

Hilde, who had finally remembered her powers, couldn't hold it alone.

The lava soared over the road.

The new flow was moving at twice our car's speed.

Closing the distance between us.

Fast.

"Hold on," I threw caution to the wind and pressed the gas down as far as it would go. The car veered wildly over the bumpy surface. I gripped the wheel and steered with determination. I had only split seconds to make driving decisions. The rest of the passengers held on.

"We're not gonna make it," Niall realized.

"Mae," Hilde worried.

"Almost there. I see the main road." I held a steady course.

"We're not gonna make it," Vince echoed.

The cushion of room between our wheels and the river of fire was rapidly closing.

"Mae-" Vince warned.

"I can see it." I told him.

"The fire-" Niall stuttered. But he didn't offer more.

I saw what he saw. The rearview mirror was now a full wall of fire.

"Almost there." I held on.

The flames licked our bumper.

Our back wheels spun and faltered.

"Whoa!" Hilde fell over.

"Get away from the walls," Vince warned.

"We're going under," Niall said aloud the thing we all feared most.

"No, we're not!" I shouted, pushing the car to its limits once more.

We're getting out, I told myself, hunched as close to the wheel as I could.

There it was.

The roadway exit.

The lava melted down our bumper.

We were so close.

So close to safety.

I jerked the wheel as we shot out of the forest road. I wrenched the car's tires to the right, blasting in a new direction, away from the lava flow. As we made the final sharp turn, I couldn't hold onto my control.

We spun out of the trees onto the wide rural highway, our wheels veering and swerving beneath us as we blasted from the forest, and escaped the lava's flow.

The molten embers and the river of fire behind us didn't understand the concept of a roadway, only the physics of flooding, so within seconds we found freedom, outside the monstrous flow.

I slowed, but drove forward.

In shock for a moment.

When we were a safe distance away, I slowed us to a stop.

"Don't stop it," Vince warned.

I nodded and left the engine running.

For a moment, we all watched the magnificent fire river as it overtook the road. It spread across both laneways, then slowly widened its course. We were safe.

"Whoa." Hilde murmured.

Careful with the touch of the doors, we got out of the cab. We looked at the remains of the car. It reminded me of a melted candle. The trunk and bumper and even the exhaust pipe had all liquified into metal sludge.

"That was close," Hilde told us.

"Too close," I agreed.

"Definitely too close," Petregaard nodded.

Niall just shook his head.

Vince crossed his arms and let out a low whistle. "Now I get it."

"Get what?" I asked.

"Why, at the chance for a once-in-a-lifetime adventure, Rick said no thanks."

THIRTY-THREE
FAILSAFE

WE WATCHED the majestic lava tide flood out onto the four-lane country highway. No longer directly in its path, we could pause to marvel. First, it continued forward, unrelenting in its march as it had been following us down the dirt road. But before the lava reached the middle line of the highway, it had already begun to slow its path. Here on the main roadway, there was so much space for the lava to move into, the fires widened out, following the least resistant path, growing longer and spreading thin. Although it could have eaten through all the forest in front of it, the lava spread across the asphalt instead. It filled out the manmade divide already cut into nature, saving the trees on either side of the road. Soon, it was like a giant, fiery pond in the middle of the highway. The incessant demand for fresh real estate to devour eventually slowed. Instead, the hot lava built and pooled in its own puddle. The way it consumed itself over and over was unlike any destruction we had seen before.

Mystified, we watched it unfold.

The group was quiet.

We were safe, up on the laneway, our car still running, although all its passengers were out on the road. Vince was smart not to shut the car off, worried that if we stopped it, it might never start again. But on the main drag, there was no traffic to fear, the road was little used even on a good day. Today, future drivers would have bigger problems. Nothing could get by the lava, so there would be zero congestion on the road. We were all by ourselves in the middle of a molten hot highway. And for a few moments in the quiet, we enjoyed the natural, violent determination of the lava's endless flow.

But soon enough, the march of time beat its drum in our ears once more.

"We have to get back," I told the others. Aunt Abeline's condition still worsened by the minute. One by one, they nodded, peeling their eyes from the fiery road. We were all exhausted from our escape, but there were still big problems at home. We had a long journey in front of us. It was time to go.

Everyone loaded back into the car, reclaiming the same seats we'd taken when we started our journey several hours ago.

"Oh, good. I'll drive," Vince snarked, but the rest of us just shrugged.

As we drove away from the mountains, Hilde

settled in between the guys, who, their skin fully recovered, had both returned to their full red garb.

"Can I see our soil?" I asked Hilde. "How's it look?"

"Oh sure." The younger girl pulled the sachet out of her pocket. She pulled the string to open it. "Looking good. Still *moist*." She grinned. She paid special attention to the keyword she knew Vince hated. She raised an eyebrow, waiting.

"I will turn this car around," he warned. "You want to go back into the lava?"

"No," she giggled. Happy to hear what she was looking for. "I'll be good."

Hilde handed me the small pouch. I fingered the dirt. It was true. Even after our steam attack and our brief brush with fire, the soggy soil still looked pretty good. It was indeed moist.

"Did you guys get the sap?" I asked them.

The guys exchanged a glance.

Niall nodded, but he didn't look happy.

Petregaard was trying to get a signal with his phone.

"We got it." Niall reached into his pocket and handed their package over.

"You got it..." I tentatively opened the pocket. There in the small bag was a thimble-sized amount of amber colored nectar. They'd managed to acquire quite a bit. "So, we did it? We did it. Holy crap," I realized. "We did it!" I looked up, in shock. "We got all the ingredients. Vince! Look!" I tried to show him.

"Mae, I'm kinda busy driving." He frowned, but I could tell that he was pleased as well. A grin crept out on his lips. It was so nice to see him smile.

I laughed like an idiot. "We did it!"

"Yes!" Hilde cheered.

"We did it!" I spun back to the boys. "Even with a sea monster and an erupting volcano, we did it!"

I expected them to be happy.

To cheer.

At least grin.

But the Damocles boys looked miserable.

The smile slipped off my face. Something was definitely weird. "We got what we needed, what *you* needed," I told them. "You should be celebrating! We can grow a new Valdeez plant. Dr. Winters has the seed. We take these back, add a quick growing spell and-"

Niall checked with Petregaard. The other boy gave a small shake. His cell phone wouldn't connect. The device sat limp in his hand. Niall frowned.

"What's wrong?"

The boys looked helplessly at each other, over the top of Hilde's head.

"Why aren't you happy?" I asked. "We just accomplished everything that we wanted."

"Vince is never happy," Hilde explained. "If you're wondering about his face."

But Vince wasn't causing a pit to grow in my stomach.

"Mae," Niall started. They exchanged another glance.

"What?" I sunk down in my chair. "What aren't you telling us?"

They hesitated. "When we came on the mission, we didn't know if it was a trick, if we should trust you, or what. So our coven put in a failsafe." Niall shrugged.

"A failsafe," I repeated.

"What's a failsafe?" Hilde wondered.

"Like a back-up plan in case they failed the mission," Vince told her in the rearview mirror.

"If we weren't successful, or in case of any funny business, our leaders didn't want to wait," Niall explained.

"*Or* if the mission went sideways," Petregaard added. "Like Niall and I were betrayed."

"We would never betray you," Hilde frowned. "We would save you. We *did* save you. We came back to rescue you."

"To save the sap we collected," Petregaard tried to spin it.

"If you didn't have the goo, you think you'd still be in the forest?" Vince snapped.

"Mae attacked me once," the Damocles boy defended.

"Because you set up an ambush!" I sputtered.

"To take what was rightfully ours!"

"I was getting it for you!"

"Well I didn't know that! I didn't trust you!" He roared.

"Do you trust me now?"

relationship with Beck from our friends. My whole life was full of secrets.

Vince drove as fast as he could.

Hilde frowned. "So we've discovered the cure, but no one knows it."

Niall shrugged. Yes. "And now our coven has no choice but to destroy your castle."

Petregaard looked out the window. "And anyone who gets in their way."

THIRTY-FOUR

WE NEED MORE TIME

WE HAD SUCCEEDED in our mission. But it didn't matter.

I still didn't have a Valdeez plant to heal my aunt.

Not yet, anyway.

And now, we had failed to stop the battle between our covens. The doomed witch fight might already be raging. We had no clue what we were driving home to find.

"Maybe we'll get there before they do any damage, you never know." Vince said, his usual cynical tone stripped out of his voice. He offered me a gentle, hopeful smile.

That scared me even more.

If we were so lost he'd decided to handle me gently, it was only because he thought I couldn't take anymore.

Maybe he was right.

Maybe I couldn't.

My whole face felt like it was about to crumble into tears.

I thought I was hiding it well. Guess not.

There was nothing to do now but drive. None of our phones worked. We'd arrive at the castle as soon as we could. Until then, we were helpless. As the time passed, Hilde and the guys in the back seat yawned and stretched out. The adrenaline wore off and left us cold. We were exhausted to our bones. Soon, Vince and I heard the gentle rhythmic breathing of the three of them dozing in the back.

"You should sleep too," he told me, gently.

"Stop being so nice, Vince. You're creeping me out."

"Fine. Don't be dumb. Take a damn nap. You're a freakin' dreamcast."

"Much better." I nodded, but I just stared out the window. My head was throbbing.

We were out of time.

Down to the wire.

Aunt Abeline was on her last day.

The Damocles coven had given up. Their only remaining option was to smash and grab and steal the plant. Loot it out of the greenhouse plot. But Cornelius would be ready for that. There's no way he'd leave it unguarded now. He'd probably put it in a vault. Little did he know, they'd burn the whole castle down before they gave up on the task.

That's what I'd do for my aunt.

Or maybe he did know. That's why he was ready.

He wanted this over as soon as possible. The whole thing made him appear weak, I thought. A confrontation played well to his credit. It was an opportunity for Cornelius to show real strength, to cast them out, once and for all. No matter how many witches it injured. And the Damocles were serving the moment up. Right on a silver platter.

Round and round my crazy thoughts went.

Images of revolution. The Damocles coven charging the castle walls. My aunt's lifeless body on a bed. Beck's worried face. Hilde's gentle snores. The cries of all my friends as they rushed to protect their coven. The Damocles mothers and fathers trying to bring their children back to life.

Everyone suffering.

Each one in agony.

The whole thing replayed again and again. I stared off into the middle-distance. But I could not free my thoughts.

Now that we were out of the hot zone, Vince turned down the blasting air conditioner fan. The loud roar of the small motors receded. If only I could also dial down my thoughts. As the car warmed back up to room temperature, things started feeling more cozy in the cab. Unbeknownst to me, my eyes drifted closed.

In my dream, I took a letter to the mail box. Big and red on the side of the road. I walked there, my head still aching. The envelope in my hand. It was a task that needed to be done. I opened the lip, dragged the handle down. The whole metal mouth of the box opened wide. The metal flap came down. But as I tried to slip the sealed white square into its jaws, a gust of wind blew it out of my hands. The letter dropped far down on the pavement. I picked it up, and went back to the box.

This time, when I opened the mouth of the mailbox, the container was full of rocks. I clanged it shut and tried again.

The third time, it re-opened, unblocked.

I went to drop in the envelope, but Vince went zipping by on his scooter. He clipped my hand. I recoiled in shock.

"Sorry!" He blew on past. "Not sorry!"

"What was that?" I shot up, fully awake. Vince was rustling in the glove box. He'd accidentally bumped my arm.

"Sorry, Mae. It's my phone."

I flattened myself in the chair. Once I'd moved to the side, he could snatch it easily out of the console in the car.

"I thought you said it didn't work" I groused, rubbing my eyes.

"It just started to ring," he shrugged.

I shot wide awake in recognition. "Wait a minute, it works! Who's calling?"

He rolled his eyes, as if to say, if he knew he would have told me by now. He clicked a button to answer. "Hello?"

I stared wide-eyed and waited but Vince frowned.

"Beck," he said, "is that you?" He pressed the

button for the speaker phone feature.

"Where's....and Mae's voicemail." Beck's voice crackled. The connection was poor.

"Beck, I'm right here." I reached for the phone. "You're cutting in and out."

Vince listened too, but concentrated back on the driving. The three in the back seat continued to snore.

"Mae-?"

"It's me. I'm here. Why are you calling Vince?"

"I tried yo- a thousand times. It just goes straight to voicema-"

The static on the phone grew louder.

"I know, I'm sorry. My phone doesn't work. We thought none of them did. I can barely hear you now."

"Tell him you'll call him back," Vince suggested.

"No way. What if it doesn't work again?"

All our phones had been through the ringer. The technology wasn't made to battle extreme heat and water submersion. But, I didn't bother to explain all that to Beck. If he was calling, he had news.

"Beck, what's going on?"

"They had to - Abelin -"

Although I couldn't piece the details together, his tone stopped me cold.

"It's not good - and - Win - says - out of supplies."

"Beck, you're cutting in and out." Vince and I exchanged a worried look.

Win was Dr. Winters. He said they were out of supplies?

"She went through - fast - than -'d hoped -

completely out. Abeline's - are - shutt- down."

"No!" I thought I caught the gist. "Beck, we've got the cure! Or we will! When we get there. You can tell him! Tell Dr. Winters that. He can tell his whole coven. They don't need to attack. We've got the pieces for the plant. You can get the message across!"

"I - They're not - hospital - left the site - the whole town. Sloane sai-" The connection was getting worse. The Damocles weren't at the hospital anymore? "Ready for a figh-." Beck continued. Vince and I leaned forward, trying make sense of his words.. "I - try to - breach the castle walls."

"Beck," my voice implored. "We need more time."

He stayed silent. That wasn't something he could offer. For a moment, I lowered the phone in despair.

"You were sleeping. What was your dream about? Did it have any answers?" Vince asked, glancing over, trying to help.

"Damn it! I don't even remember. Why didn't I write it down?!" But of course I couldn't have, even if I'd thought of it the second I'd awakened. We had no pen or paper as we barreled towards our home. "Arghh!" I slapped the dashboard with my palm.

"Hmrph?" Hilde woke in the backseat. The impact jarred the others awake as well.

"Sorry," I looked back at the three of them. "Sorry. I shouldn't have yelled."

"It's oka-, we'll -ough this," Beck's tattered voice tried to call me. He didn't realize I was talking to the others in the car.

"Beck," I murmured, my attention snapping right back to him. I dropped my volume. "Is she in pain?"

There was a silence for a moment. "No." He said.

This time, it wasn't the fault of a bad connection.

Beck had paused.

Was that true? Was Aunt Abeline free of suffering? Or was this just another guy being nice to a girl who couldn't handle what was really going on?

"By the time we get home to you, find Dr. Winters, grow this plant, and stop the fighting, Aunt Abeline could be gone." I sat back in my seat.

"She'll be here." Beck assured me. The phone crackled. "She'll hold on."

I bit my bottom lip, trying to hold in the emotion that was building.

"Beck, you've got to bring her to us. To the High Council. If that's where Dr. Winters can be found. Can you get her safely out of the hospital and over to the castle?"

"I'll do - best," he agreed. The phone cut out once more, but I could still picture his hand raking through his hair, a worried expression on his face as he promised to do all that he could.

"You have to tell everyone. If you get there first. Keep her safe, but spread the word. We have the plant. The ingredients. We got them. We can grow the Valdeez branch. They don't need to fight anymore. We're on our way. We're coming. Tell everyone. We've got it. We've got the answer. We-"

The phone died in my hands.

VINCE ROCKETED the beat up station wagon across the country roads, back to the castle. A heavy silence fell over the car. We all knew what was ahead, but the question was, could we get there in time: for the children, for my aunt, for the Damocles clan, for the High Council coven? To save both of our covens and our loved ones back home.

Would anyone listen to us when we arrived?

"Hold on," he told us, veering off the two-lane highway onto the High Council's familiar gravel road. I'd been over and back on this drive to the castle many times since I'd joined the coven, but this time, Vince didn't brake for any curves. He barreled ahead. Clouds of dust plumed in the air. Hilde and I held on with white knuckles. The boys bounced around in their seats. But none of us told him to slow down. He'd proven his driving skills back at the volcano. If he could steer us safely through ash, lava, and smog, he could get us down this gravel path.

Without a single back-seat driver.

"There's Beck!" Hilde leaned over the gear shift to gape out the front window, pointing ahead. He was parked just before the widening entrance to the castle yard. The same place he and I had stopped and fought only a day before.

Was that just yesterday?

It felt like a lifetime.

"He's in an ambulance!" She squealed. He stood in front of the cab, watching our approach.

"Should I stop?" Vince asked, coming up way too fast.

I shook him off. "Go through. We need the seed to grow the plant."

He nodded, and we raced by. I spun back to try to catch a view of my parabond. There he was, with Carl, his father's client in the driver's seat. Why had he brought Carl along? They watched us pass, then Beck hopped back in the ambulance and followed us into the Council yard.

As soon as we made the turn I could see why they'd stopped.

The dark scene we were entering wasn't anything like the castle we'd known.

"Oh my god," Hilde whimpered.

The others said nothing. Everyone stared out at the new world. There were crowds of people on the asphalt and gardens, spells flying, items harnessing, and sparks and fires blazing across the bedraggled Council grounds. Chaos and violence spilt out across the lawn.

Coven ladies and fellows desperately tried to put out the fires, while others stood active, protecting their home. We could see in all directions, witches were in hand-to-hand combat, blasting each other with various weapons that came from their minds or their spells. Harnesses spun the atmosphere into an inhospitable rage. Lie-guards used illusions to defend and attack. There were signs of chemistry-warfare. A thickness hung in the air.

Like the very atmosphere was choking.

The energy field around the building walls was well past the point of extirpation. Sparks shot out with each cast spell.

Everyone looked damaged.

Exhausted.

The battle had raged on for far too long.

We were late.

Fires burned in all directions. Flames licked the vegetation, incinerating whatever they touched, even as storm clouds let torrential rain pour down. The bottom floor windows in the castle had all been blown out.

Vince slowed our car to a crawl.

Damocles witches continued to try to storm the building.

Fellows and ladies valiantly held them off.

A lightning bolt crashed just inches from our car.

Vince wrenched the wheel to swerve away. Luckily it just missed the hood.

"Whoa." Petregaard said. "That was close."

"Too close," Hilde murmured.

"We're too late," Niall spoke the thing unsaid.

How many witches were hurt? Beaten? Wounded? With so much happening on all sides, all in tandem, it was impossible to gauge.

Since the first floor entry was so aptly guarded, the Damocles witches had begun to create their own ladders and climb the trellises to scale higher up the castle walls. But the ladies and fellows also fought back on the upper levels, tossing them over, hurling the enemy witches back down to the ground.

The sky above the castle raged with thunder. Rain came streaming down. The deluge pummeled both covens. Heavy clouds loomed. Everyone was soaked to the skin. Thunder rumbled both near and far, and man-made lightening scorched through the sky. Murders of crows and other birds swooped in large circles. Death spirals of feathers over the masses of witches on the grassy fields. Some swooped low to attack. Several bombed into the building itself. White track suit jackets were torn and tread in the mud, their colorful pipings now indistinguishable from muddy puddles. Tatters of red linens littered the gardens as well.

Plus, there was more red.

Blood.

And fire.

No coven held an advantage. Although the battles raged on, clearly the Damocles hadn't retrieved what they'd hoped. The ladies and fellows were gritty, strained, and dirty. Even the students of the coven were no longer held back. I could see my friends sprinkled here and there throughout the grounds. Greg and Marcy were putting out fires. Sloane was applying some sort of salve on an injured witch. Tej and Rick were on an upper balcony, knocking down Damocles ladders. Other second years tended wounds off to the side.

Everyone suffered.

Beaten.

Battered.

Discouraged.

Vince drove as close as he could to the castle before pulling up to a stop. Carl and Beck in the ambulance pulled in behind.

"You're up," I told the Damocles guys, but they were already climbing out of the car. We had given Petregaard both Valdeez ingredients. He raced out to find Dr. Winters in the crowd. He alone carried the seed. He would need to plant it with our sap and soil in order for the Valdeez to sprout.

Niall went hunting for Natalia.

How they would find two individuals in this chaos, I didn't know.

Hilde, Vince and I sat in the car.

We were breaking the rules even delivering the Damocles pair to the castle. The contract we'd signed said we couldn't even speak to the other coven. We couldn't be seen acting together, as partners. So, we waited impatient in the car. Impotent. Scared.

Watching the paths of the boys.

Petregaard found the doctor fairly quickly, after an animated discussion he seemed to be on board. Heads low, the two ran back to the ambulance's side. It offered some shelter from the fighting and also the raging storms. I was about to get out to join them, when suddenly, from nowhere, a wolf jumped onto the hood of our car.

"Oh my god!" Hilde ducked down. Scared, Vince and I sat back.

"What the hell is that?" He asked.

"Someone's animal harness," I guessed. How much control that witch still had over this carnivore was anyone's guess. "It's alright," I assured the young girl in the back seat. "It can't get inside."

The beast growled through the glass. Baring great teeth. Dripping saliva. Vince and I didn't budge in our seats.

It shook it's head and sparks and ashes rained down on the car.

"Enough with the fire," Vince muttered.

Rawr-rawr-rawr!

The beast snapped and pawed at our window. But luckily, I was right. It couldn't get in through the glass.

The creature let out a fierce howl towards the heavens then leapt off the car and scampered into the forest.

But, the animal left a trail of fire on the hood.

Vince leapt out to see where it had gone.

"Stay here," I told Hilde.

Scared, she nodded.

I got out as well. I used my soggy clothes and the rain to beat out the fire. As I worked on the car, Beck ran over from the ambulance.

"You're alright!" He shouted. He wrapped me in his arms.

"I'm okay," I agreed, burying myself in his grasp. His embrace blanketed me, I felt warm and safe inside. "How's Aunt Abeline?" I searched his eyes.

"She's a tough gal. Mae, she's here. She's holding on."

"I wanna see her," I said. Beck took my hand and started to lead the way to the ambulance. I didn't object. I wanted him to take care of me. To hold me. I wished he could hide me inside of caress of his palm. Where I'd be safe and comforted forever.

Still, the rain poured down.

Hilde watched us go, but didn't venture out to join us.

Better that way.

She was safe in the car.

At the bumper, we saw Petregaard and the doctor working on growing the Valdeez plant. Vince had joined them. The Damocles boy looked up as I approached.

"How's it coming?" I asked. I had to shout over the fighting and the rain. Two other witches had their hands in the pot as well, chemists, I realized. They were sprinkling various potions into the ground.

"Doin' our best," Petregaard shouted back.

"Keep it moist!" I reminded Vince, grinning in spite of everything.

On top of hating that language, in this witch-made weather it would have been impossible to keep the dirt dry. I had only been out of the car for a moment, but already Beck and I were soaked to the bone.

Up ahead of the car, in the midst of the field, Niall had given up the search. He hadn't found Natalia. So he was trying to get everyone's attention instead.

"Listen to me!" He shouted. He ran forward, flailing his arms. The erratic actions caught my eye.

"What's he doing?" I turned. "No, Niall, don't."

"Listen! We've got it!" He shouted, flailing back and forth.

Running quite aggressively.

Charging towards the castle.

Calling attention to himself.

"Niall, stop!" I shouted. But he couldn't hear me. "Niall!"

From nowhere, a giant lightning bolt scorched the sky and hit the boy square on the back. Immediately, he collapsed to the ground.

"Oh my god." I spun away in horror and shock.

Niall's clothing smoldered. His fingers twitched with electricity. His hair smoked, but he didn't get up.

"A weather harness," Beck looked into the crowd for the clenched palm that caused it. But it didn't matter who had called the lightening down. The damage was already done.

"Niall!" Hilde's scream filled the air. She burst from the car.

All around him, little fires had started to thrive. We could see steam vapor rising from his clothes.

"Hilde stop!" I warned her. "Everyone'll know you're together!" I tried to catch her.

"I don't care!" She screamed. "Secrets suck!" The girl was too quick to be caught.

"Hilde!"

She raced straight for him.

Straight towards the castle walls.

A second witch running.

Rushing right into battle.

It looked like an attack on the other coven.

From the opposite side of the field, there was a great blast sonic blast. Hilde didn't have a chance to react. The energy field swiped her from the side. Direct hit! The young girl collapsed in the grass. Her little body fell mere feet from Niall's side.

"Oh my god!" I raced towards her.

"Mae, come back!" Beck tried to grab me, but I ran to the younger girl.

As I heard another blast emitting from somewhere over my shoulder, I dove to the ground. I couldn't see it, but I could hear the energy burst coming, some sort of audible shockwave intended to knock me down.

I hit the turf, muddy but unharmed.

When it passed, I picked myself up and scrambled

across the field, this time being sure to stay low. I made it to the side of the young girl.

Little Hilde was limp on the grass. I crouched low over her body. Put my ear to her lips. She was breathing but still unconscious. Beck raced to join us as well.

"Stay down," I implored him.

He dropped to my level.

"Is she alright?"

We continued to check for vitals. Her heart beat was regular. Her little body was just in shock.

"Hilde," I tried to rouse her. "Check on him," I pointed to Niall. Beck was about to, when Vince also arrived.

"Is she alright?" Vince joined us, looking Hilde over.

I turned to face him, rage in my eyes. "*Nothing about this is alright!*"

This caught both Beck, Vince, and even myself off guard, but of course I was right. A ten year old had just been attacked at her home. For caring about the welfare of her friend. Who happened to wear different colored clothes.

Both boys nodded.

"I know, Mae," Vince said. "I know."

I smeared the tears from my eyes. "She's okay. She will be. Let's check on Niall."

We crept over to check on the Damocles boy. As we cradled his head, he coughed.

"Did we do it?" He moaned. His body trembled as

he coughed harder, his limbic system processing the terrible shock, still barely able to move.

"Not yet," I told him. I turned to look back at Dr. Winters. The doctor was staring at me as well. Slowly he shook his head. I didn't know the details, but it was clear what that meant.

The seed hadn't worked.

The plant wouldn't grow.

We were helpless and hopeless again.

"What do we do now?" Beck asked.

I sat back on my heels.

All the secrets.

All the lies.

All for nothing.

Secrets suck! Hilde had shouted.

So true, I thought. For all the half-truths and misconceptions, we were right back where we started. Aunt Abeline needed the plant. The Damocles needed the plant. *I needed the plant.* And Cornelius refused to help us.

Hundreds of witches were paying for that choice.

His agenda.

But it wasn't just up to him anymore.

Hilde knew what was important in her life and she didn't care who knew it. Damn the consequences. Same with Marcy. And Greg. Beck had been begging me to be honest for weeks. Aunt Abeline should have known what might have been coming for her but I kept it from her. I'd both kept and been left out of so many secrets, things were hidden so much of my life, but what was the point. Were any of us really better off?

It was time to put it all in the open.

I don't know why I waited this long.

I should have been as brave as Hilde from the start.

"Pick her up." I instructed Beck. "Vince, get Niall if you can." The boys nodded. I stood up and marched back to the station wagon. I climbed up on the hood.

"Hey!" I shouted into the field, but no one listened.

"Give up!" A Damocles witch shouted.

"Get out of our home!" Ladies and fellows returned.

"You lost the Battle." Someone else shouted.

"We'll win the war!" Someone cried back.

There were voices everywhere. No one was listening. Everyone was mad.

"Please everybody," I held both hands up, but it didn't quiet the crowd.

"Give us the Valdeez!"

"We're not leaving without them."

"Well, you're not staying!"

I turned around.

"Carl, hit the cherries! Full siren!" I shouted. I'm not sure if he heard me, but he was watching. I signaled with my arms spinning, hoping to mimic the lights and sounds of the specialty truck. In the ambulance, he caught on. Carl nodded and flipped the switch.

Behind me, the sirens blasted to life.

Wee-woo! Wee-woo!

Witches all around me looked over. I held up my hands.

Wee-woo! Wee-woo!

Carl turned the siren call off, but the red lights continued to flare. More witches turned in my direction. Petregaard looked up from the defective plant.

"Hey, put a spot light on her," he told his lie-guard friend, the one who'd helped ambush me in the forest.

"But-"

"Just do it!"

The Damocles lie-guard shrugged. He balled his fist, and I was engulfed in a great light. Beck carried Hilde, draped in his arms, Vince propped up Niall. Stoic like centurions as well, they stood at the headlights of the car. We made a striking tableau, shining in white light, intercut with the blood red cyclical glow of the ambulance behind.

"Please." I held up my hands.

"Hey, there she is."

"That's Mae, the champion!"

"Back from the forest." The Damocles members also recognized me. "With Niall and Petty."

"Mae, the sucker," someone else shouted.

"Everybody!" I maintained my demands. Standing here, all eyes on us, Vince, Beck, Hilde, Niall and I were in a wildly vulnerable spot. If the witch who'd created the sonic boom turned their rage in our direction, or the harness with the lightning shots...

But I couldn't worry about that.

Like Hilde, I had to stand up and be counted.

No matter what anyone thought.

"Stop! Call it off," I shouted in both directions. "This won't help anybody. Look what you've done. No one is better off!" I pointed out into the crowd. Whatever harnesses had called on the rains released it now. The sky drizzled, then the faucets turned right off.

The witches took note of each other's bedraggled appearances.

Dr. Winters came forward. He stood by Beck's side and put a hand on his shoulder. Petregaard on the other side performed a similar action as well, solidifying the visual that my plea was represented by both sides.

"Give us the plant!" Someone in red shouted.

"Not gonna happen, *Natalia*." A lady shouted back even though it wasn't their leader who'd cried out.

"We don't need to fight!" I said.

"We have no choice," another woman shouted angrily.

"Yeah!" Others answered in ire.

No.

It wasn't just animosity between them.

There was sadness too. They were a sad, determined lot.

"You will die trying," Someone growled back.

The Damocles witch who started the cry didn't flinch. "So be it," she said.

"No. Enough!" I tried to intercede from my elevated spot in the crowd. "Please stop."

A hundred red angry faces turned in my direction

and stared me down. My coven or the other, it didn't matter. No one wanted to see me there.

"Hear her out!" Dr. Winters shouted.

"Please," Vince echoed as well.

For a moment, the crowd hushed. Sensing that was as much permission as I was going to get, I had to make this count.

"Do you know why you're fighting?" I asked them.

"Send them back to their house!" A witch yelled.

"They want our Valdeez," someone else shouted back.

"Yes. You're right." I nodded. "My aunt is sick." I told them. "There was an earthquake, I... it doesn't matter. The point is, she's very ill. Dying actually. And the Damocles coven has been able to keep her alive. They knew how to do it, because back home they faced an accident as well."

"That wasn't an accident!" Someone shouted. Petregaard shifted, looking at the ground. But I ignored it.

"What brought them to our town was a catastrophe in their community," I barreled forward. "A horrific crash. A bus full of school children. *Children.* Sweet, innocent kids. Just a horrible wrong place, wrong time."

As if on cue, little Hilde woke up. Innocently, she rubbed her eyes.

"You're alright," Beck whispered. "I got you."

"Where's Niall?" She wondered.

"Hey kid," the Damocles boy quietly nodded as well.

Hilde smiled, relieved but also exhausted. Quietly, she cuddled into Beck's arms.

"Back home, eight children are still surviving," I told the others in our High Council. "Still fighting. On life support. But they have deadly, impossible injuries like my aunt. The human body can't survive every wound on its own. But, with the right spell, we can *save* them. We can heal their tiny bodies. We can make them whole. Restore the whole coven. There *is* a cure. But it's something very rare. The Valdeez branch."

A great stir moved through the crowd.

This question was asked and answered.

The Damocles couldn't have the coven's only greenhouse Valdeez branch, no matter how many different ways that they asked.

But that wasn't the Valdeez plant I was after.

"I know." I tried to settle them. "I know they're rare. They're special. Believe me I get it." Some of the coven members looked down at the tattered, lava-melted car on which I stood. "But, it's a cure. A guaranteed salve. It's in our hands. If we have the means to save them, to save my aunt, to save *anyone*, why would we hold back?"

"They can't take them!" someone shouted.

"We will not be held hostage," another witch added.

More witches started to murmur. A din rose up in the crowd. Louder and louder the people's voices grew.

Until no one could be heard above the crowd. I turned, and locked eyes with Carl. He nodded.

Wee-woo! Wee-woo!

The ambulance's sirens clicked on again.

The covens returned their attention to the ambulance. He turned them off. I held up my hands. The groups quieted down. Somewhere from deep in the crowds, Cornelius Child, some of the other elders and Natalia emerged. They worked their way front and center.

"You're right. You're all right!" I exclaimed. "They can't take them by force. We won't let them. We absolutely won't let them." I agreed. But, here was the truth. "But you can *give* them, if you *choose!*" I let the word hang in the air.

Cornelius crossed his arms.

"Look! I know it's a big ask. I know. But when they rescued my aunt, they put her on life support. I made them a deal. If I could get even one branch of Valdeez leaves, then the Damocles coven would do two things. *One*, they would help save my aunt and *two*, they would leave our town for good. So, if you won't give it up for the sake of my sick family, for *their* sick families, think of it like this: the donation of one little plant can give you back your whole world. It's what you want! For things to return to normal. For things to go back to the way they always were."

Cornelius was about to speak, but another coven member beat him to the punch.

"Mae, honey," this time I recognized the voice in

the crowd. "I'm sorry about your aunt. Like, I really am. But how can we trust that they'll go?" Fellow Silverfox asked. "You above all know, they're already supposed to be gone. We won the Battle, fair and square."

"The Battle of Four," in the crowd I heard Nicolette's quiet voice correct to the proper title.

"I know," I nodded. I found him in the crowd and gave him a sad smile. He and I had fought valiantly in that battle together. Against all odds, we had won. But the Damocles witches hadn't stuck to their part of the deal. He was right. That was all true.

"And, Mae, not to be crass you know, but if they'd left when they were supposed to, your aunt would be just fine." He added. "Not on death's door."

"I know." I nodded to that as well. I wanted to give him that moment of truth. But once I acknowledged it, I barreled ahead. "But that doesn't change where we're at." I shrugged. "At a preventable crossroads. In desperate need of the plant. We tried to grow them. We found the recipe. We fought for the ingredients. We thought, if we could just grow a new batch, we could save everyone from... a lot of pain." I looked around at the dark faces and frowns. "But-" I glanced at Dr. Winters.

"It might grow," he said. "But it hasn't yet."

"We can't guarantee we can grow it anew. But if we share what we have, maybe we can propagate from that." I pulled the whole group back on the track.

"Cornelius and the elders refused!" Someone shouted.

"That's right. We did." Cornelius Child nodded, finally giving voice in the crowd. He stared me down.

"I'm not talking to *him*!" I roared. "I'm talking to *you*! Do you have a Valdeez branch?" My eyes searched the crowd. No one met my gaze. A bad sign. But I wasn't beaten yet. "Look, I know. Secrets abound. That's a witch's life. We've all grown up with things that were scary or scarce or... or... silent and like my good friend Niall said, every family has secrets to hide."

The Damocles boy sheepishly nodded.

In the crowd, I saw some other witches nodding as well.

"But there are good and bad secrets. There's a time to hoard and a time to share. We've all got stashes hidden under rocks. Private stuff to help just our own families. I had a secret bunker in my basement." I shrugged. "I bet you've got secrets in yours."

More nodding.

I was on a roll.

"Cornelius will not give us the plant. Even though I know for a *fact* that they have it in the greenhouse." I couldn't keep the anger out of my voice.

"There's more to running a coven than what serves *your* purpose," he told me. He had the nerve to look down his nose.

But I wouldn't be cowed. "He'll let you fight. He'll burn down his home. He'll let their children die. *Chil-*

dren!" I told the whole group. I pointed to Hilde and Beck. She was so tiny in his massive arms.

Cornelius didn't flinch.

Time to bring this pitch to a close.

"Secrets don't always work. Manipulations can destroy. I know firsthand." I trailed off. "There are no tricks. There's no demand. All I can do is ask. We need it. Please. If you have some. If you were saving it. Just in case, for your family. If you can spare it. A twig, a leaf, a branch. Now's your chance. We need your help. Please."

The field stood silent.

There must have been a hundred witches gathered, but you could have heard the cough of a small child. The weight hung in the air.

"Cornelius is right." Brandi decided to do the dirty work for the gathering. She stepped forward, crossed her arms and held her head high. She'd found her way through the mob to a group at the left of my car and now she mimicked Cornelius' righteous pose. "Get off your high horse, Mae. You should have known, we don't negotiate with monsters. Even if they say 'pretty please'."

A Damocles coven woman, the one closest to me, one I'd never met before, stared across the hood of the car at the black-haired girl. Her anger bubbled over. She could contain herself no longer.

"*They aren't monsters,*" she screamed, pounding her fist on the hood of the car, leaving an indent where her hands had been. "*They're children!*" Her anguish gasped from deep inside. Openly, she burst into tears.

The wretchedness was palpable.

Somehow, this high-pitched wail silenced the field in a new way.

The loss became real.

In the distance, we could hear other Damocles mothers and fathers quietly weeping.

"If we give in today, who's to say they won't come back and hold us captive next time they need something?" Silverfox asked.

I shrugged. The answer seemed clear. "We can share what we have now. And if some other awful time they come back because they need something else and they're desperate and we can spare it, we can share with them then too. They aren't *monsters*," I repeated, my voice calm and honest. "They're the parents of sick children. Worried friends and family. Tired, lonely travelers. And in desperate need of help. Just like my aunt," I helplessly waved to the ambulance behind me. Seeing the anguish of the Damocles woman in front of me released a truth I was holding as well. I could *not* lose my aunt. I stared down at Silverfox and admitted the last truth. "I would do anything to save her, Silverfox. *Anything*," the word caught in my throat. "I would rip apart my whole world..."

The threat hit. I dropped my voice.

"And so will they. For the ones that *they* love. So if you have a branch you can spare..."

The impassioned plea hung in the air.

Dozens of witches' faces lowered to their shoes. Again, no one dared to speak.

No one met my eyes. Until-

"I have it. I have a clipping." Fellow Stone said. Grimly, he nodded. "You can have mine."

My jaw dropped open.

The closest Damocles coven-mates turned in surprise. "Do you mean it?"

Fellow Stone frowned. "I'm so sorry about your loss. I didn't know."

"I have some too," another lady stepped forward.

"So do I," a second year student added.

"Me, too."

More and more ladies and fellows nodded. They offered bits and bobs of their secret stashes to help. Suddenly, we realized almost half the coven had pieces of the plant we had thought was so scarce.

All of it hidden, squirreled away from sight.

As the knowledge gained traction across the field, the tension and anger that had crackled between the covens began to slip from sight. More tears were shed. This time, of relief and laughter.

The skies re-opened to sunshine.

The birds, insects and animals of the forests were sent home.

The stalemate was over. Everyone could have what they wanted. The children could be saved. The invading coven could go home.

I slipped down off the car that had served as pulpit

to be met several hugs from the Damocles coven members.

"Thank you so much," several strangers told me, reaching out, touching my hair and arms.

"I didn't do anything, not really," I shook them off. "Thank the High Council coven, they're the ones who will provide." As quickly as they tried to approach me I stepped back, out of the limelight, happy to see two familiar Damocles faces move towards me through the crowd. Natalia and Dr. Winters.

"Mae, I don't know how to thank you," she said.

"We'll save your aunt first," the doctor told me.

"Is there enough?" While I desperately needed it, I didn't want to take from their children back home.

"There's enough," their coven leader firmly nodded. "You can count on that."

"Thank you," I breathed deeply.

"Where is the plant?" We all looked to the first volunteer.

"It'll take a short time to bring it out," Fellow Stone admitted. "It's hidden and safe. That sounds so foolish now." He looked around at his other ladies and fellows and shook his head. But the others nodded as well. We all knew exactly what he meant. Retrieving the precious branches from their secret family stashes would take time.

Dr. Winter's lips formed a deep frown. He didn't say it aloud, but I knew what he was thinking. My aunt didn't have that long to survive.

My face fell.

"Go bring it from the greenhouse."

I spun around.

Lady Mauve stood only two feet behind me. She ordered two fellows. "Stone's stash can replace the coven's plants when it arrives."

The guards looked to Cornelius, but he nodded. They ran off to retrieve it from the safe hiding spot inside.

"This isn't over." He told me, but I'd clearly won this round.

"I see you weren't exactly the mail carrier you purported." Lady Mauve frowned. "Did you at least deliver my letter?" She asked.

"Yes," I murmured. "Of course."

She looked me up and down, clearly deciding whether or not to trust me. I couldn't tell which conclusion she'd reached. The two elders turned and left us alone to wait for the branch. They both knew they couldn't punish me on the day I saved both of the covens. But they were a patient sort. The reprimand could wait.

No doubt I would pay dearly for breaking the rules.

I just hoped none of the others would be dragged down in the mud.

"Let's get your aunt." Dr. Winters said.

"Yes, of course."

We hurried to the rear of the ambulance. The doors were already open, fresh air flowing into the cab, my aunt was tucked into a hospital bed in the truck bay. Beck was sitting nurse by her side. She looked so small, so fragile, almost hidden beneath the blankets. He was holding her hand. Several machines repeatedly conveyed her on-going status. I heard the gentle ebb and flow of the ventilator's rhythm, as it kept a steady flow of oxygen pumping in and out of her chest. A heartbeat monitor let out a slow pattern of blips and flashes on-screen.

"How is she?" I asked, climbing in beside her.

His sad face looked up. "I don't know," Beck admitted.

"Let me have a look," Dr. Winters took over. We both pushed back in the cramped car so he could fit. I reached out for her rough, scaly hand. Nothing felt like my warm and vibrant aunt. But I was here, and I wanted her to know it. Dr. Winters went to work, checking machines, redressing bandages, preparing the mixture for the arrival of the Valdeez branch.

I leaned in. "Aunt Abeline, it's me. I'm back. Don't worry, we did it. We got you the plant. Just what you need. Everything's gonna be fine, now. Okay?" I tried to believe what I was selling. If she could just hold on until the plant made it down from the greenhouse, Dr. Winters could heal her right up. It would arrive any minute. She'd stayed strong for this long. Everything would be fine. I held back the tears in my eyes. "You've been a really good patient," I told her. "With the best nursing care in the world." I smiled gratefully at Beck.

"I don't know," Dr. Winters admitted, muttering almost to himself. "The chest cavity's sagging. The

Matryll leaves application's worn off. Damn it. Where is that branch?"

"It's coming." Beck squeezed my shoulders.

I wiped the tears as they started to build.

To come this far, only to lose in the final moments? The idea was too difficult to bear.

"It's alright," Beck embraced me. "Any minute."

Beep... beep...

"The heartbeat's too slow," the doctor warned us.

"Beck... this isn't happening. I don't want her to go," I whimpered. But Dr. Winters had warned us. Three days was all he could give. The time had all run out. When his supplies were gone, there was nothing he could do to alleviate this truth.

Beep... beep...

Miserably, my eyes flashed out the open door. Where were those guards?

"I can't bear the thought of-" More tears sprung to my eyes. I tried to wipe them away, to maintain my dignity, but I could see I was losing that war. My breath grew thick and heavy. Every second they dallied meant she was closer to the end. Where were those plants?

Tears tumbled over my cheeks. They staged a coup on my lashes.

There were more than I could hold.

"Hey, Mae. Down here. I'm out here," Lady Blue Moon called in from the ambulance bumper. "Wanna play a game of Scrabble?"

"What?" I sputtered, my tears coming on thick. I couldn't swipe them all in one sleeve's length.

"Ask your aunt. Ask Abeline to join us." Lady Blue Moon nodded, encouragingly.

"I'm in!" Ferris piped up, standing only another few feet back as well. "Aunt Abby, you ready to school me?" She asked my unconscious aunt directly, then smirked to the gathered group. "I learned I don't speak good, or play good," she joked, picking up where Blue Moon had started the plan. The women smiled at each other, slung arm-in-arm in half-embrace.

"You'll lose for sure," Lady Blue Moon told her.

"Hell yeah I will," Ferris nodded.

In spite of myself I laughed a little, unable to control all the water works, spittle dropping from my lips.

"Ask her," Lady Blue Moon encouraged.

"Ask your aunt," Ferris told me.

I couldn't hold the smile together, but I didn't want the sadness to win.

Beck squeezed my shoulder. "Go on, ask her."

"Okay..." It seemed kind of silly, but maybe it would help? "Aunt Abeline, Lady Blue-" I caught myself. "Bonnie Maine and Ferris are here to see us. They want to play a little Scrabble. Stay here and play, alright?"

"I'll let you use all the triple word scores..." Lady Blue Moon offered, then reconsidered. "All but one, maybe." She grinned. "Or you could give them all to me. Gotta give me a fighting chance."

Beeeeeeeeep...

The monitor's heart rate flattened.

"No!" I shouted.

Ferris and Lady Blue Moon exchanged worried glances.

Dr. Winters flipped several switches at once. There was no difference. "Mae, I'm sorry," He turned to me. He sadly shook his head.

"No! Aunt Abeline, you can't!" I flung my body over her frame, hugging her limp shape in my arms. "Please."

The long slow drone of the monitor filled the car.

"You can't leave me. You can't. You're my family. The only one I have."

Beck put a warm hand on my shoulder. Ferris and Blue Moon lowered their heads.

Dr. Winters reset the monitor sounds. The droning beep disappeared.

"No," I wept. "She's not gone."

The space grew heavy with sadness.

"We got them!" A guard came running. He burst around the ambulance doors. "Here they are! Here, you can have 'em!

"Give them to me." The doctor grabbed the plant and mushed it into a muddle with the other ingredients he'd already prepared. "Ms. Kingsley, please stand back."

He dosed her with the mixture, forcing it into Aunt Abeline's mouth and washing it down her throat with a saline wash. He forced her to swallow, but nothing happened. Quickly, he prepared defibrillator paddles. He charged them to full capacity.

"Clear," he instructed, but he didn't need to tell us. We were all already backed away in preparation, watching, desperate for any small hope.

Anything at all.

He pumped the paddle once and sent a shockwave through my aunt.

Nothing.

Dr. Winter's shoulders slumped.

"Do it again," I told him.

"Mae, she's gone," he sadly shook his head.

"Do it again!" I shouted.

There was no harm in trying. "Clear," he instructed. He pumped and primed the paddles and sent a second shockwave through my aunt.

We looked to the monitor for a quiver. Any motion. But she still wasn't there.

I slumped against Beck. This time, it really was over.

"You did everything you could," Beck whispered in my ear.

"Mae, I'm so sorry," Dr. Winters told me.

I tried to nod. Tried to let them all off the hook. I understood. They did everything they could.

It wasn't enough.

None of our efforts were enough.

We had tried everything we could think of and failed.

I had failed Aunt Abeline.

All I could do was close my eyes or stare straight ahead.

The tears had all dried.

The tears had held hope.

All hope was gone.

Beep.

The monitor gave off a small blip.

"What was that?" Lady Blue Moon asked from the field.

We all looked up in shock.

Beep... Beep.

The monitor kicked in again.

Beep... Beep.

The pattern was slow at first, but then grew steady.

"Oh my god." I hopped up, wiping the tears away. "Aunt Abeline?" I leaned over her bed.

Dr. Winters checked her vitals. He looked up in joy and shock. "The Valdeez plant is working," he said. "The effect is incredible. I've never seen anything like it."

"So, she's alive?" Beck confirmed.

Dr. Winters dragged his locket across his neck. "She's and getting stronger by the minute."

I held her hand in mine. I looked back at Beck and he sat back, finally able to sigh in relief. Against all the rules of science. Like so many of the special witch powers I'd seen, the spell had worked wonders. Together, we watched her come back to life. A little at first, then more and more drastically. Dr. Winters continued to check for positive signs and seeing one after another, he turned the ventilator off.

"She's breathing on her own." He acknowledged. "It's incredible." He took the tube out from her throat.

"Will she wake up?" I asked.

"I think she might. Soon. Day or two at most. But we need to get her back to full care," he said.

I spun to Beck. "Can we take her back? How'd you get this ambulance anyway?" I asked, suddenly realizing how strange it was to be here in this car on castle grounds.

"It's a lie-guard," Beck admitted. "This is my truck in sheep's clothing. Dad's buddy Carl is in the cab holding things together for us."

I had been so lost over the health of my aunt, I'd even forgotten that Carl was present.

He waved through a window from the front seat. "Shall I take us back?" He asked.

"Please." Beck and I nodded.

Dr. Winters climbed down out of the truck.

"You'll be alright now," he told me. "Abeline will be alright."

"Thank you, I don't know how to repay you."

"And I you," he nodded, stepping back from the car. Over his shoulder, my other Damocles friends nodded as well. Niall and Petregaard and even Natalia. I waved. Ferris and Lady Blue Moon closed the back of the ambulance up then rapped on the doors as we departed. Through the back window I saw other members of our class and coven also watched as we went. We drove back along the bumpy gravel road and transported her straight back to the hospital, without the sirens or cherry lights blasting.

They weren't required.

Aunt Abeline still had a long road of recovery ahead of her, rest and rehabilitation, and everything else, but the whole car ride felt different.

Things had changed.

Aunt Abeline was going to live. And things were right with the world.

THIRTY-SIX

I'D LIKE YOU TO MEET MY BOYFRIEND

"WHERE AM I?" A groggy voice broke into the room. I hopped up from the chair I'd been sharing with Beck and leapt to my aunt's side.

"Aunt Abeline! You're here."

"I'm here. What happened?" She struggled to take it all in.

"There was an accident. A freak earthquake. You were hurt." I told her, softly sweeping the hair off her face. "I thought we'd lost you," I admitted. "But now you're alright. You're in the hospital, recovering. The prognosis is hopeful. Welcome back."

"Oh..." She tried to take it all in. "Thank you," she said. Then she looked down at the hamster she'd been clutching while she slept. "And who's this?"

"That's Georgia the Hamster." I told her.

"She kind of looks like you," Aunt Abeline murmured.

"So I've heard," I grinned. "See, she's got a little t-shirt with some word play. It says '*get wheel soon.*'"

"Clever." Aunt Abeline noticed Beck floating in the background. "And who is that?"

His eyes flashed to me uncertainly. He raked his hand through his hair. "I'm just a friend from Mae's school. I'll let you two reconnect." He offered. He gave us a respectful smile and started to back out of the room, but I caught his hand.

"Aunt Abeline," I pulled him closer, until he was standing shoulder to shoulder beside me. "He's the one who bought Georgia the Hamster for you. I'd like you to meet my boyfriend, Beck."

—-

Before they left town, the Damocles coven healed my family's land, closing up the crevice. The cottage was destroyed, but most of our precious heirlooms were salvaged and stored in the Bean family barn, ready to be returned after we rebuilt our home.

I spent several days in the hospital with my Aunt, rotating turns at losing at Scrabble with Lady Blue Moon and Beck. When she was well enough to leave, we rented her a one bedroom apartment above a store in town.

"It's not forever," I told her. "But I hope it's fine for now."

"As long as we're together," Aunt Abeline told me. "At least in hearts and mind."

But when she was well enough, we both knew, I would head back to my studies at the High Council. I caught up with my classmates just after dinner that night.

"Hi Mae," several students waved as I entered the cafeteria.

I smiled and waved back.

"You eating?" Sloane checked, but Beck and I shook our heads. Aunt Abeline had made Mac n' cheese, my favorite, in celebration of being out of the hospital ward. We gorged. She even added bacon. It was a delicious, cheesy, salty way to welcome her home.

"Mae-mae, how's Aunt Abby's new home?" Marcy wondered. She and the others cleared their plates. Hilde ran over and gave me a hug. I squeezed her back. Together, we all walked to the lobby.

"She's good. She's using a cane for walking," I nodded. "Totally relocated into an apartment in town."

"And you've made it back just in time," Sloane noted.

We all stood at the elevator, waiting to take us back to our floor.

"Classes start again, full schedule tomorrow," Nicolette informed me in a tone that seemed a little huffier than her usual pout.

"Last night of freedom," Greg concurred. He scooped his girlfriend into his arms.

"Babe!" She squealed, loving every minute of attention.

I snuck a little smile at Beck. He wiggled his eyebrows in return.

"It'll be good to get active again," Tej rolled up his sleeves like he was about to perform a new spell. The elevator dinged and we all climbed aboard the box. Sloane, Beck, Vince and I in the back row. Nicolette, and Rick in front. Hilde was about to join, but she had a weird smile on her face and stood back with Marcy and Greg.

"Aren't you coming?" Nicolette asked.

"Now!" Greg told the young girl.

"Race you to the top!" Hilde squealed. She dragged her fingers across every button on the elevator, lighting all the floor request icons. All three cackled with pleasure and raced for the stairwell in the hall.

"Probably good for them to burn off a little energy," Beck joked, as the elevator doors slid shut. He caught my eye and I smiled. My eyes danced down to his lips, then worked their way back up again. He smiled, almost sadly, then stared straight ahead in the box.

Ding.

The doors opened on the second floor.

In the distance, we could hear Greg, Marcy and Hilde having a ball. Their laughter echoed through the halls.

As the doors slid shut again, I inched my hand away from my side and skimmed Beck's leg. Through the cloth of his pants, I let my fingertips graze his thigh.

Our bodies connected. Both he and I stared straight ahead.

Ding.

The doors opened again. It was a long, slow ride. But I didn't mind. The energy built in my hand. I could feel him so close to my side.

"Well, this is just dumb." Sloane frowned. She got off. Rick and Tej followed. One could walk to the fifth floor much quicker than this elevator ride could take you. Vince and Nicolette shifted to spread out in the emptier box. But Beck and I didn't budge.

Behind me, hidden from the other teens' view, Beck's hand came up and slid across my back. He settled his palm into my gentle curves. The touch of his fingertips sent waves of desire crashing over my skin. I felt weak in the knees. I wanted to moan aloud with pleasure, but kept everything controlled. An exciting brush with danger.

Ding.

Fourth floor.

Arms crossed, Nicolette stomped out of the car.

"You guys are on your own," Vince nodded. He too had given up the ride.

We watched them both head to the stairs. The double doors closed achingly slow. Neither of us budged until they were shut.

"What are you tryna' do, get us caught?" When we were alone, Beck laughed.

"Just enjoying the ride," I teased back. "There's a lot we could do in this tiny, metal box."

"Oh yeah?" He raised an eyebrow, intrigued. "Like what?"

"Like... this." I kissed his left cheek. "And... that." I moved slowly around his face, our lips only inches apart. I kissed his right cheek. Slower. Softer than the first.

"Anything else?" Beck murmured.

"Maybe... this?" I kissed his lips softly. But when I leaned back, he followed me forward, not wanting our mouths to part.

"I like that," he agreed.

"The door will open," I whispered, the words dancing across his mouth.

"Let them stare," he replied. Together, we sighed.

Ding.

The doors started to open.

Obediently, we both pulled ourselves apart and straightened up. We acted like nothing had happened between us.

"Haha, beat you!" Greg cheered.

I could see the others were all there as well. Beck and I stepped out of the box.

They laughed. The light-hearted moment now over.

"Uh, guys, hold up just a second." I stopped everyone's natural progression down the hall. "Two things."

"Oh no. Mae wants to hold court... again," Tej joked.

"It'll just take a second," I frowned.

"Say your piece," Sloane overruled her parabond.

"I just wanted to say thanks. Thank you so much

for all your love and support over the earthquake and the missions to find the Valdeez plants and your worries and well wishes for my aunt."

My classmates nodded. Greg bounced Marcy in his wrap-around arms, a little impatient.

"That's one," Marcy grinned. "What's the second?"

I smiled and took Beck's hand. "Ladies and gentle-men, I wanted to introduce you all to my super-hot and sexy boyfriend, Beck." I grinned at him and raised an eyebrow. Pleased, he pulled me in and planted a kiss right on my lips.

"Ugh. Tell us something we don't know," Vince rolled his eyes.

"We waited for that?" Tej complained. "I thought she was gonna tell us about the sea monster explosion."

"Great, another couple." Nicolette groused.

"I think more couples is cute!" Hilde smiled, not so subtly staring at Vince.

"That's the end of my speech," I told them, as Beck and I pulled apart.

"Get a room!" Greg laughed, as we all strolled together.

"I couldn't have said it better myself," I grinned. I unlocked my door and motioned to Beck. He followed me inside. I winked at my friends. "See you tomorrow." I said.

Then I shut them all out.

"That was quite an introduction to us as a couple,"

Beck mused. His hand snaked around my waist, pulling me in. "You know they're all gonna think we're sleeping together."

I tossed a hand aside. "Oh, let them think."

He pulled me in and held me in his arms and looked deep in my eyes. "Hey parabond," he whispered. His voice was thick like honey.

I stared into his eyes. "Hi."

The stillness was electric.

For a moment we just smiled, entranced in the soothing proximity of the other. Then, he moved in and put his lips on mine. Slowly. Gentle at first. My hands grazed his strong forearms as they closed around my waist and pulled me closer to him.

I tucked perfectly into his embrace.

Here, in his arms, I could feel his heart beat next to mine.

I pulled slightly away, my bottom lip grazing across his, but he didn't let me go.

He kissed me again, harder now, more insistently.

I opened my mouth and let his tongue slip between my lips.

The kiss was soft and warm. Waves of desire shuddered through me and his strong hand sensually slid across my shoulders and cupped the back of my head.

"I have something I wanted to show you," I murmured.

"Oh?" Appreciatively, he looked down at my chest.

"Not that," I laughed. "Although I can see how you

got there," I giggled, stepping back. "Come on." I led him further back into my room.

"A guy can dream," he agreed, but he wasn't in any rush. Instead, he sat comfortably on the end of my bed, waiting to see. While I busied myself, he checked out the wall of clippings about my dad. "The search has kinda been on hold," he mused.

I followed his gaze. "Well, that's just it." I dug a slip of paper out of my pocket. "Here." I gave it to him, then sat beside him on the bed. The weight of our two bodies brought our legs together. Thigh to thigh.

"The Konya Thomas Special Collection," he read. "What is it?"

"It's the address from Lady Mauve's letter. Blue Moon's packages were all fake. The boxes she used to claim that Hilde, Vince and I were her delivery minions. The addresses weren't real, the boxes were never sent. Were never supposed to be. But this one... Lady Mauve's letter. I saw it still in Blue Moon's trunk on our ride the other day, back from my aunt's. I popped it in the mail box to avoid any suspicion, but this address is real. I wrote it down. Do you think it exists?"

"The Special Collection?"

I nodded.

"I'm not sure. She might have made up a place, just to see if you were messing with her." He shrugged.

"Yeah. That's possible" I nodded, but I couldn't let it go. "But what if it's true?" I asked. I hopped up and paced. "It would explain why any real answers are so hard to find here in the archives. Because the detailed records aren't in the library at the castle, they're off campus, somewhere else." I pointed at the paper. He reread the address. I didn't need to see it again. It was already burned into my brain.

"Maybe," he hedged again. "We'll check it out together," he offered.

I grinned. That's what I wanted to hear.

"But," he laid the paper on the desk, "we can't do anything more about that tonight." A mischievous smile played on his lips. "It's too late... lucky for us, there are other fun things to do to pass the evening."

"Oh?" I raised an eyebrow, intrigued. "Like what?"

I moved closer, his arms opening for me. I slid in and straddled his thighs, facing his chest. His warmth coursed beneath my legs. I slid my hands into his hair and played with it delicately, a delicious smile spreading between him and I.

"What'd you have in mind?" I asked, teasing, his mouth only inches from mine.

His hands slipped around my hips and in one strong motion, he tugged me closer to his lap. As he plopped me forward, I giggled. Our bodies were completely in line.

"We'll solve the mystery together," he said softly, sweeping a tendril of hair from my eyes. His finger brushed my ear, tucking the wisp back. A shiver of desire ran through me. "But for now... hi, parabond."

"Hi," I told him. Soft and slowly. His lips only

inches from mine. I tried to hold it. To tease him longer, but I just couldn't resist any more. Playfully, I pushed him back on the bed. Beck's strong arms closed around me, and together we got lost in our own little world.

WHAT NOW?

Want to dig into sneak peeks, learn about the next releases and find all the other freebies and literary goodies? Join my newsletter at www.juliecatherineau thor.com.

Xo
Julie

ACKNOWLEDGMENTS

Phew, book four in the High Council series is complete!

This book was a bit of a tough nut to crack. I actually wrote the whole story, put the first draft aside... then several weeks later, picked it back up and wrote it *again*, and boy am I glad I did.

I never knew where I was basing my story geographically (I kind of like to make it up so I don't have to research or be accurate, haha) but it turns out, the world of Plumpkin and the surrounding towns looks a lot like the border between Quebec and Maine. I road-tripped there on vacation this summer, and if you haven't been yet, I highly recommend it! The rolling hills, beautiful farmland, stunning lakes and ponds and the pristine forests are amazing. No dormant volcanos though... There's a bit of creative license in that!

Thank you to my editor, Allana Stuart. You point so many things out that I just didn't see. My writing is so much better after your input.

Thank you to Allana Giesbrecht, and David Guthrie for your support.

Mae's really coming into her own now, exploring her strengths, her weaknesses, and the tenacity of her relationships. Now that she and Beck are officially a public couple, in book five, you'll see that romance really start to soar.

See you there!

Xo
    Julie

GRAB

your free ebook copy

a prequel novella

get yours at
www.juliecatherineauthor.com